JAMES LOVEGROVE

James Lovegrove was born on Christmas Eve in 1965. After spending a year at art college, he read English at Oxford. He abandoned an unpromising career in rock music to become a writer. THE HOPE is James Lovegrove's first novel.

James Lovegrove

THE HOPE

First published in Great Britain in 1990 by Macmillan London Ltd.

Sceptre edition 1991

Sceptre is an imprint of Hodder and Stoughton Paperbacks, a division of Hodder and Stoughton Ltd.

A CIP catalogue record for this book is available from the British Library

ISBN 0-340-55108-9

Printed and bound in Great Britain for Hodder and Stoughton Paperbacks, a division of Hodder and Stoughton Ltd., Mill Road, Dunton Green, Sevenoaks, Kent TN13 2YA. (Editorial Office: 47 Bedford Square, London WC1B 3DP) by Clays Ltd., St Ives plc.

Thanks to Nick Archdale,
Lawrence George, Ray Hearder,
John Kunzler, Philippa Leach
and Mark Nelson-Smith,
all of whom in their own way
criticised and contributed

The *Hope* was five miles long and two miles wide and one mile high.

One night, a Philanthropist had a dream of her and he used the vast sums of money he had earned in his lifetime to make his dream come true. He went with his dream to a Designer and a Builder. It took seven years for the three of them to have the *Hope* built. They shaped her hull in a low sweeping arc to take into account the curvature of the earth. They hinged her in two places with immense joints so that high waves would not break her back. They gave her two gigantic turbines which left a wake of churned grey foam tailing fifteen miles behind her. She had a displacement of one thousand million tons. She cost the equivalent of the gross national product of a small nation. She would carry nearly a million passengers. People scratched their heads and said it was folly, and said it was madness but wasn't it wonderful, and said that the *Hope* was the crowning achievement of the industrial era.

In the end the Philanthropist's dream bankrupted him and he hanged himself the day before the *Hope* was due to be launched. He had seen what he had done and thought it was no good.

They launched her all the same.

There were celebrations and ticker-tape parades and bands and dancers. Thousands of people flocked to the quayside to see the *Hope* off.

To look at her now, you would never have thought she had been a dream, not the sort of dream that men work and die for. Rust lined her sides in streams like orange puke. Several thousand gallons of paint had peeled away to reveal her bare, iron-clad flanks. Smoke belched from her funnels and coated the decks a greasy black. Her turbines shuddered as they

1

turned, and some of the passengers said she did not have much life left in her; she would run out of steam; she would burn out and die; she would never get them to the other side of the unending ocean. Most, of course, were too terrified to contemplate such a thing and laughed at the idea. Nothing to worry about, they said.

Oblivious to them all, the *Hope* sailed on . . .

A
Bath
of
Blood

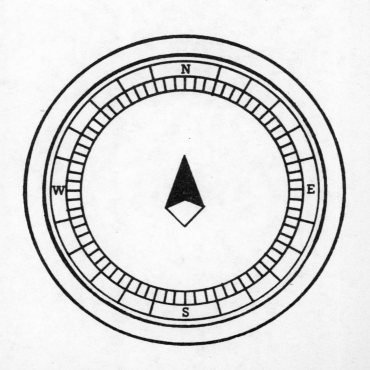

Mary Shitshoes's children were crying again. Adam was beating the table with a spoon, his face red and creased with rage. Mark was squatting naked and silent on the top bunk. Sophie was repeating, 'Mummymummymummy', as if it was the only word she knew, a private mantra. Mary spoke to them as soothingly as possible, ruffling Adam's hair and trying to avoid looking at Mark's swollen belly, but there was a slight waver in her voice which the children picked up on immediately. The more she soothed, the more they cried and the more they cried, the more she soothed.

Their crying evolved into a single note, which rose and fell, a fraying sound speaking of days that stretched back beyond counting without a proper meal, only scraps, a fortuitous fish or something small scrounged and even then it had to be divided equally three ways (and you were too hungry and too greedy to ask what Mary was eating). The cabin began to buzz, its bulkheads and bunks and empty bottles seeming to catch the sound and shiver. Mary was growing distant, Mary was growing outside herself, until in her mind's eye there were her and the three children ranged round the cabin, four corners of a distorted square.

As she watched, she saw herself getting up and plucking one of the bottles off the shelf. Holding it by the neck, she shattered the base against the table and thrust the jagged end at Adam's face before the last shards of glass had reached the floor.

Adam screamed. Mark screamed. Sophie screamed, highest and loudest of all.

Thrust.

A spit of blood.

Thrust.

Curls of Adam's face scraping back. A blood-streaked howl. Pathetic arms flailing at her.

Screams.

Mary came to herself with a shudder. It would never come to that, would it? And yet, how much more could she take?

Adam, with a hurt and wounded expression on his face, was asking when would they get something to eat, Mummy, he was starving, they all were starving, it wasn't just him. His attempts at elder-brother unselfishness were as touching as they were half-hearted. The bags under his eyes made him look much too old.

To avoid the question, Mary examined the backs of her hands and found they were withered and liver-spotted and also much too old. There was no mirror in the cabin. She had not seen her own face for months now, and for that she was glad.

Eventually she said, 'There's nothing. Nothing to eat.' It was no comfort, but how could you explain the way of the *Hope* to an eight-year-old, even an eight-year-old who looked more like eighty?

Adam's rage diminished to a sulk and he sloped off to his bunk below Mark, hunkering down in the shadows and muttering to himself a sort of song, the lyrics of which went, 'Food and fish and fish and I want a dish of food, a dish of fish in my place, a plaice in my place . . . ' He was in a daze, staring at nothing.

Sophie was still humming, 'Mummymummymummy.'

There was a cupboard where the slop-bucket was kept. In better days they had had a proper bathroom, but now there was only this cupboard, popularly known as the Poo Place, and it was used less often than was healthy.

Through the salted panes of the portholes Mary could see it was raining (wasn't it always raining?). She took her red plastic raincoat out of the Poo Place. The smell of shit made her wrinkle up her nose. She had not got used to it and she thought she never would. It threatened to invade the cabin so she shut the cupboard door, but it always clung to her raincoat like an Old Man of the Sea she would have to carry for ever on her back. She slipped her feet into her shoes – her shitshoes – and did up the toggles of her raincoat tight. The children had stopped crying on cue, seeing that she was about to go out and find food and they could keep quiet till she came back, oh yes. Church mice. Ideas of food like inflated balloons filled their heads. *Food*, a thing of happiness that was breathed with life.

It had been this way since *the Man* left, four bitter years during which Mary's dignity and standing had decayed. She had been pretty once, and well respected. She and *the Man* and the three children, as close a family as you could ever want to see, would go out often to enjoy the social life – dinners and parties where the wine flowed, and the fish was always good and fresh, and sometimes there were fruit and sweetmeats. He was handsome and smiled and had a respectable job on one of the upper decks. They lived in a cosy three-room cabin on H deck. Smiles and gaiety and food . . .

To think that way was bad, Mary knew, and at times it seemed as if she had made the whole thing up just for something to tell the children. This did not console her. Nor did the fact that the *Hope* and all she had to offer had been Mary's for the asking, and she had lost it. These days, living meant having to scavenge or to accept handouts from neighbours and even from the very women with whom she had once socialised, shared smiles, swapped stories, broken bread and drunk wine as an equal.

She gathered the dozen-odd bottles off the shelf and dropped them carefully into a plastic carrier-bag. They were the trophies of many hours spent combing the rubbish-tips. If she was lucky, she could exchange them for money for food.

At the door she said goodbye to the children. Three pairs of dull eyes gazed in her direction without contempt or affection. If she brought something back, they might have the strength to offer her one or the other.

She did love the children.

Rain fluttered on to the skin of her cheeks. It drizzled from a distant, dreary slice of grey sky viced between deck upon

7

deck of windows and walls and walkways that rose up high on either side. You could not see the sea from here, this being one of the *Hope's* innermost areas and lowest decks. Only the thrumming of the turbines in the steel underneath your feet and the shroud of smoke across the sky informed you, if you did not know already, that you were on a moving ship the size of a small city. Skeletal walkways were attached to each level and led off in multiple parallels in either direction as far as the eye could see. Gangplanks crossed between them at odd intervals. They looked tentative and fragile. It was only a matter of time before one of them or all of them rusted right through and gave way.

Mary hurried on. The bright red of her raincoat said she did not belong here among the blacks and greys and stained whites of the background.

On her way, she passed a couple of large bundles of cloth piled against one side of the walkway. Bundles of cloth with yellow eyes. The lonely ones. Stoppers.

It was said that, when they could get it, stoppers drank a type of alcohol distilled from the contents of the *Hope's* fuel tanks. But then, there were lots of stories going around.

I'd rather kill myself than sink that low, she thought, fearful that it might just come to that.

A few minutes later, she passed a knot of women huddled in the shelter of a doorway, effectively blocking off the walkway. They had been exchanging their juiciest slices of scandal until one by one they spotted Mary coming towards them and one by one they fell silent. She had to step over and around their feet, through a gauntlet of stares. As soon as she had passed, they started whispering. She heard them pretending loudly to sniff the air. She heard the sibilants of *that name*. She held her head high.

She was going to Bart's. There were two things you noticed about Bart's. The first was the queue of people clutching bags full of personal effects, junk mainly, with no value except of the sentimental kind. Ninety per cent of this stuff Bart rejected out of hand. If he took it all, as he was fond of saying, he would need a shop as big as the whole deck. He would guffaw at this. It pleased him to be popular or to be needed, he wasn't sure which. The second thing you noticed was the shop front – a fair-sized hole torched out of the steel and covered with a sheet of polythene on which had been stuck paper letters reading BART'S MART. Underneath some wag had put 'Where Trash is Art'. It was generally suspected that this wag was in fact none other than Bart himself.

Mary took her place in the queue. If anyone was downwind of her, they were being terribly polite about it. Perhaps they had other things on their minds.

Half an hour later, she was inside the shop. After another quarter of an hour, she was at the counter.

'Mary, Mary, and how are the little ones?' said Bart, peering up at her. Broken since birth, Bart had used crutches all his life. He was a hobbled, bent thing, habitually dressed in a long black coat which flapped around him when he did his crippled insect walk. He had a long beard and straggling hair. He was a shrewd man and a generous man, proof that the two qualities are not wholly incompatible.

'Well. Hungry,' she added. Bart did not like picking up gentle hints. He made a habit of failing to, and it meant you were forced to beg and he hated begging.

'Hungry, poor devils. And what about Mary, eh? What's she eating these days?'

'Not much. But I'm OK. It's the children, Bart.'

'Yes, well, what have you got for me?'

Behind her someone was getting impatient, shifting from foot to foot and coughing.

'Bottles. Lots of them.' She began to lay them out on the counter individually.

'No, no, don't do that!' Bart interrupted. 'No time, no time. I can tell what you've got if you show me the bag, Mary. I have eyes.' He leaned over the counter as far as his crutches might allow and scrutinised the contents of the bag. The person behind Mary ahemmed loudly.

'Yes, yes,' Bart grumbled to himself, 'all very useful, I'm sure, but there's not much call for bottles at the moment. What can I do with them? I can't take them upstairs until I have at least five hundred and I'm nowhere near that yet. Not worth my while.'

'Please, it's all I can find. Surely you need them. You

won't get five hundred if you don't take every one you get.'

'I'll be honest with you, my dear. There's no call for them any more. People aren't interested in re-using things, see?'

'But I need some money for the children. At least let me have credit.'

'No, Mary,' he said, making up his mind, 'I'm afraid I can't help you this afternoon. So sorry.' He assumed an air of implacability that wouldn't take 'Oh, please' for an answer. Mary left the shop as quickly as she could, trying to hide her tears from the people in the queue. Her bottles chimed together in the bag.

She took the gangplank over to the middle area of P deck. The handrails left stripes of dirt on her palms. On either side she could see lines of washing extended across the gap, above and below. The rain was gradually making the whites grey and the greys black. On the other side of the gangplank she followed a route that avoided the most crowded areas until she came to a major companionway. The walls here were choked with growths of graffiti, for the most part illegible with the exception of a slogan lower than the rest, which ran 'Small is beautiful.' There was an official sign on which Mary could make out the words:

RECREATION
SHOPPING
STAIRS TO UPPER DECKS

and in smaller, more discreet letters:

Waste Reception Centre

but she knew anyway where she was headed. She had last checked this particular rubbish-tip a week ago and the pickings had been so slim that it hardly merited a repeat visit, but she was desperate. Who knows, there might have been a windfall – someone dead and their belongings chucked out to make room for a new tenant. Something Bart would be prepared to buy. Once upon a time, in another life, Mary would have been disgusted with the idea of having anything to do with the dead, but now . . . well, her shitshoes were dead man's shoes and she did not mind stepping into them.

As she rounded the next corner, she saw *the Man*.

It was his posture, his gait, those were his clothes. He was hurrying away from her. Had he seen her? She had only glimpsed his back view. Was it really him?

She gave chase. She could forgive him, she could forgive him, if only things could be as they were before and the children could be happy and not hungry. Where was he? She was not going to lose him twice.

There! He had stopped, hunched over to tie up a shoelace. Her shoes clattered to a halt and he glanced round at her.

When she saw that he was a stranger, she found she could say nothing. It was not that words failed her but that there were no words at all, nothing to create the words, just a numb shame. He had not been running away at all. He had not even seen her. Rain plastered wisps of hair to her face. He stared at her staring at him.

'Yes?' he challenged.

'I'm sorry . . . I thought . . . '

Stupid, stupid, stupid woman, thought Mary. *You stupid woman*.

'Can I help you?' he asked. His manner was uncharitable. Mary realised that he had a glass eye. It did not glitter like the real one, was not even the same colour, and this gave him a peculiarly intimidating appearance. His face was unbalanced, off-centre, and this made you assume he possessed a brain to match.

'I thought you were a friend.'

He drew himself up, as if she had given him an invisible signal.

'I could be your friend, you know.' He made a lopsided grin.

'I thought you were someone I know . . . knew—' Mary took a step back. 'It was a mistake. I'm sorry. That's all. A mistake.'

He took the flush in her face for coyness and his grin widened.

*A sharp jab with a finger in his good eye and his light
would go out for ever. Why not? Why not?*

Abruptly Mary felt sick of his sycophantic, odd-eyed face
and her instinct was to get out of there. Her legs agreed
with her instinct and she spun away from him, every second
expecting his hand to grab the hood of her raincoat and
yank her towards that mouth and that eye and that other
eye . . .

In a minute she had made it to the companionway where
the sign hung and then she had no more energy to run, only
to slump against the wall, her body sagging, her raincoat
crumpling around her with the sound of old bones. If anyone
passed by now, they would think she was a stopper.

'Let them,' she mumbled to herself, just like a stopper.

The Man was lost. That was how the story went. One
morning he had set off to go to his job – purser? navigator?
captain? – and he had not returned. It was as simple as that.
The memory of his last peck on her cheek had stayed with her
ever since, as if there was still a translucent oval of his saliva
clinging to her skin. He had become a ghost who haunted
her face as a kiss.

His departure had been followed quickly by her fall. No
one knew where he was, no one cared, and soon no one
would talk to her. She took the hint and found an empty
cabin down on P deck where she hid with the children.
There was plenty of bitterness and guilt to feed on when the
money and the food started running out. For no accountable
reason, it was her fault. That, she supposed, was the way of
the *Hope*.

But she loved the children. That was her way of com-
bating everything the *Hope* threw at her. She loved them
with a primitive, self-wounding love. Once *the Man* had
told her, no doubt as a roundabout kind of compliment,
about mothers of long, long ago (many centuries before
the *Hope*) who cured their sick infants by bathing them
three times in a bath of their own blood. The idea of the
giving of healthy blood to an unhealthy child stuck in Mary's
mind, for she thought that the sharp and rusted misery of
slicing open your own veins was a cure in itself – 'I love

you this much' – giving with no expectation of return. It was being God.

The Waste Reception Centre had once been a hole the size of a swimming-pool, one of many on board, with a collapsible bottom leading down chutes as big as hallways to the recycling plant deep down in the hold, where what was good could be used again and what was bad could be spat out into the unending ocean. At least, that had been the plan. Inevitably, the system had broken down. Re-usable material soon became less and less re-usable (everything finite, everything finding its limit) and the chutes began to pack up, the piles of rubbish and filth swelling until they burst out of their pores. No one on the *Hope* could be bothered to pretend that one day the mess would be cleared up, although janitorial divisions came along every so often to rearrange the dirt and take away a couple of sackfuls for dumping overboard.

There was a joke (like most jokes on the *Hope*, not a very funny one) that went: What comes once a year and isn't a birthday? A janitor.

There was another joke, this one about the Captain, related to the one about the janitor, but more involved and somewhat disrespectful.

Mary's windfall went like this. After a few minutes of investigation, wading ankle deep in boxes, broken bottles, scraps of peel, books without covers, clouds of forlorn flies, turning over the blank faces of jigsaw-pieces to discover the pattern and the picture underneath, she found a small cardboard carton. It was promisingly weighty. The seagulls that strutted over the tip squawked at her in frustration. Mary sat down where she had found the carton, willing herself not to get too excited yet, not yet, but all the same feeling loved and loving and humbled.

She broke a nail as she struggled with the lid of the carton. The staples popped and the flaps of the lid flew up like ugly petals. Inside tin circles gleamed at her. Hunched over, stinking, with a carton in her arms, Mary began to weep and giggle at the same time. There was ham, processed peas, carrots, raspberries . . . Mary did not dare wonder how anyone could have overlooked all this, because to do so placed a gift from God into a disappointingly human frame of reference. Someone had smiled on her, that was all, on vile, filthy, worthless her.

She headed back to the cabin struggling to resist the urge to skip like a schoolgirl. The seat of her raincoat was wet and smeared.

She thought of the children as she ran cradling this true happiness in her arms, and then she thought of *the Man* and the memory did not seem so crowded with shame and pain any longer. No surprise, then, that she had taken that stranger to be *the Man*, because *the Man* had become a distorted memory, an image beneath water, infuriated.

Mary had a charm against his evil eye – the carton. Yet a small voice whispered privately to her that nothing lasts for ever.

Certain areas of the *Hope*, almost inevitably on the lower decks, you simply did not enter unless you belonged there or you were clinically insane or both. Mary's happiness was a white and blinding thing and it made her take a left when she should have taken a right. She ran a few steps before she realised her error. The walls were filthier here and the turbines louder, although there was no apparent reason why this should be. Gangplanks and walkways colluded overhead to shut out most of the sky, although the rain managed to insinuate itself and dribble down the walls in streams like thin, twitching veins. Long chains hung lazily down, measuring with their swinging the *Hope*'s massive lumbering through the waves. They clinked against each other. A nearby service-light buzzed as if a fly was trapped behind its glass.

There were footsteps behind her. The carton felt heavy in her arms, the carrier-bag unnecessarily bulky, its plastic handles cutting into her hand. The turbines growled distantly and the chains clinked and the light buzzed.

'Hey, it's a scarlet woman!'

'Ha ha, that's a goodun!'

'What have you got there, miss? Looks heavy.'

'Carry it for you?'

How many of them were there? Two, three?

'Looks like food, boys. Looks like dinner.'

'With afters thrown in!'

The small voice inside her piped up again, suggesting that she deserved this for being too happy. She wished (and hated herself for wishing) that *the Man* had been here. If *the Man* had been here, he would have seen these creatures off with a punch to the jaw, a stiff uppercut, a blow to the stomach . . . 'Take that, you ruffians!' And perhaps this was the reason he had abandoned her, to leave her splayed and vulnerable to life.

A hand grabbed her shoulder.

'Look at us, woman,' was hissed in her ear, a parody of intimacy. As she obeyed the instruction, a corkscrew seemed to twist and tighten in her belly.

'Ugly bitch, in't she?'

'Smells too.'

The combined ages of all three could not have totalled over forty. They had fashionably severe crewcuts and fashionably bulky epaulettes. One had a sailor's hat. Another, the eldest by about a year and probably the leader, had an earring shaped like an anchor and his earlobe was puffy and red around it. He took his hand off her shoulder.

'You're so young,' she murmured.

'Young! Ha!' scorned the one with the hat.

'Old enough for you, dear,' said the eldest, grinning and nuzzling up to Mary. 'Are you going to let me fuck you?'

'Go on, Popeye!'

'Shall I, lads?' said Popeye, playing up to his fan club.

'Fuck her brains out, mate.'

Something like poison welled up inside Mary from the part of her that was Shitshoes, rubbish-tip scavenger (or Waste Retrieval Expert, if you like), she who was abandoned by *the Man*, and it spat itself out of her mouth: 'You couldn't fuck a porthole.'

She could hardly believe she had said it. Nor could they. Popeye's face registered astonishment and when his mates started to jeer the astonishment turned to livid rage. He leaned forward and struck the side of her face with a half-clenched fist. She should have told him she was used to humiliation. Because his fist had not been fully clenched, it hurt him more than it hurt her. The force, however, sent her crashing against the wall. Droplets of rainwater pattered on her raincoat.

'Hit her again!'

'Shall I?'

'Yeah, hit her again! Go on!'

Mary had dropped neither carton nor bag. She was proud of herself for that. She mumbled, 'You couldn't fuck a porthole,' again. She was not so proud about that.

It had the desired effect. Popeye hit her once more, a couple of grunting punches to her hips which her raincoat managed to baffle. As there was no way out of this, no obvious salvation, Mary felt calm and resigned.

Hit me, she thought, *but don't steal my prize, my magic charm.*

Popeye aimed blows at her arms and back, kicked her calf a few times, but she clung to the tins of food and they were reassuringly solid.

'Hit the bitch!'

Mary loved the children.

'Fuck the bitch!'

She loved the children.

'Kill the bitch!'

Popeye came away panting and pressed himself against the opposite wall.

'Just catching my breath, lads,' he gasped, 'then I'll fuck her. We'll all fuck her.'

'She doesn't make a sound, does she?' said the one with the hat.

'She will, Billy. She'll scream when I'm shafting her.'

They all laughed, even Mary, because she found something quite amusing in Popeye's grotesque imagination. He pushed himself off the wall and cocked his head to one side and stuck out his ribcage.

'Want some more?'

Mary raised her face.

Someone asked, 'Do you know?', and she was aware of a

thin figure somewhere in the corner of her vision. Someone else, one of the boys, breathed out a 'Jesus Christ . . . ' and the other voice asked, 'Do you know?' again, the thin man's voice, pitched somewhere between an ache and a shriek.

'Look at those fucking scars,' hissed Billy with the hat.

'Do you know?'

Mary, not understanding what was happening but sensing a shift in fear, seized the opportunity and ran. She heard Popeye behind her saying, 'No, we don't know,' most but not all of his cockiness gone, and this was followed by a swift and abrupt crack (head meets steel – guess which wins). She found Billy running with her but they were like animals before a forest fire, caring nothing about anything except the heat at their heels. From further away now came a yelp and another crack. Billy disappeared up a staircase connecting to the above deck, and Mary ran on alone.

Sophie's eyes nearly popped out of their sockets when she saw Mary closing the cabin door behind her carrying an armful of box that looked as if, could it be, could it be . . . *food*. Mary herself could barely speak with the confusion of ecstasy and terror she felt. At last she managed to say: 'Adam, Sophie, put your coats on and go out and play.' Mark was too ill to do anything but sit and stare and rock on his haunches. 'We're going to have a banquet.'

Adam and Sophie had never moved so quickly in their lives. It occurred to them that the sooner they started playing, the sooner they might finish and come back for the *food*.

Mary called after the two fast-disappearing children: 'Be back in about an hour, but be careful. Don't go too far and don't talk to any strangers!' She was delighted they were happy enough to pay no attention to her warnings. The thin man seemed just too distant to be a threat.

In fact, Adam and Sophie did not go far at all, only round the corner, where they sat in the rain and boasted who could eat the most food. Adam said he should have the lion's share as he was the biggest and a boy but Sophie objected, saying that Mark deserved most because he was so ill. Adam thought girls were silly, always being nice to weak people, but eventually he agreed that Mark should have a tiny, incy-wincy bit more than everyone else. Under normal circumstances, this argument would have been an excuse for total war, but today, with *food* so close like a peace-keeping force, it was merely a brief territorial skirmish.

Mary went to Mark's bunk and took his thin hand in her thin hand, and looking at him she had a brief, vague, chilling recollection of the thin man and of Billy saying, 'Look at those fucking scars,' and she let the memory drop.

'See that box, Marky? We'll eat tonight and you'll be all better soon.'

Saliva dribbled from the corner of Mark's mouth. Mary looked into his eyes for a moment (nobody home), squeezed his hand, smiled, kissed his knee, reached up, touched his hot cheek, and dabbed at the spittle with a fingertip.

She clambered into her raincoat and went round to Lil's, two cabins down the walkway.

She knocked. After some time, Lil opened the door and her expression slid from pleasant to indifferent.

'Oh, Mary, it's you. What can I do for you?'

Lil had a smear of blue under each eye and a smear of red over her lips. A man's voice came from within: 'Who is it, willow blossom?'

Willow blossom!

'I've got company,' she told Mary out of one side of her mouth so that the company would not know he was being referred to as company. 'Can't you come back later?'

'I want to borrow some things.'

'You're always borrowing things, Mary. I never see them again.'

'Yes, you do,' said Mary, as reasonably as possible. 'I gave you back your dish last month.'

'No, you didn't.'

There was no point in arguing.

But hands slipping round that fat neck and crushing the life out, oh God don't let it come to that.

'Who is it?' asked Company. Mary could smell incense escaping out through the doorway around Lil.

Lil answered over her shoulder: 'Nobody. I won't be a

minute, darling.' She fixed her eyes upon Mary, all pretensions to civility gone. 'Will you go away if I lend you what you want?'

'Of course. Can I borrow a knife and a pestle and mortar . . . please?'

Lil tutted and disappeared into the cabin. Everyone knew how Lil got hold of nice curtains and things for the kitchen and Mary decided she would rather become a stopper than stoop *that* low. Company loomed up half-dressed in the doorway, glanced at Mary, took her in with a sleepy nod, and returned into the darkness giving no other sign that he marked her existence. Lil came out with the utensils and plopped them into Mary's hands.

'Bring them back tomorrow. Clean.'

The door clunked shut. Mary heard Lil say, 'Useless bitch,' probably louder than she intended and heard Company laugh a lewd answer. She tried to forget it.

Back in her cabin, she ranged the tins out in precise positions on the table, laying the knife and pestle and mortar beside them. Her tin-opener no longer worked properly. She had to make a series of holes around the lid and cut herself twice in the process.

She put the circle of each lid in a neat pile to one side. Mouthwatering smells rose up to enchant her and her stomach grumbled, not unpleasantly. She solemnly slurped the contents of the ham tin out on to a dish. It was moulded in a foetus shape, plugged with aspic. Thin sauce seeped around it. The peas were the colour of seaweed, the carrots of a uniform size and orangeness.

She took the ham and sliced it into pinky-grey wafers, perfectly round. She placed four equal numbers of slices and tidy piles of peas and carrots on four plates (all but one cracked, a set *the Man* had given her years ago). The smell was unbearably tempting, heady.

Mary placed a setting on each side of the square table, a knife and a fork either side of each plate. Mark watched her without interest. His belly-button, pushed out by his swollen abdomen, was as large as the tip of a thumb.

Mary began to prepare the raspberries. Their syrup was dark red.

She had just finished by the time Adam and Sophie charged in, out of breath and wet-haired. They stopped and stared at the table, then at Mary. She had washed herself and, following Lil's example, had put on some make-up, the little she still had. Sophie said, 'Mummy, you look pretty,' and it was so matter-of-fact and yet the most beautiful thing Mary had heard in her life. She leant down and kissed Sophie and then Adam, who squirmed away and shrugged off his coat.

'Wash yourselves, you two. There's still some of this week's water left.' They ran to the basin.

Mary lifted Mark lightly off the top bunk and sat him at the table. He was weak and the feast in front of him seemed to dwarf him. Mary knew he would hardly eat a scrap. No matter.

Mary, Adam and Sophie sat down. Mary mumbled through a grace, then they set to.

Surely this was heaven. There were no words for their full mouths, no language for their tongues. The meal was a protracted moment outside time. Even the *Hope*'s turbines no longer turned for them. Perhaps the *Hope* was drifting on momentum alone, floating powerless on the waves and tides and currents of the unending ocean. Each cold-chewed mouthful sent her further along.

Mary slipped a few forkfuls past Mark's lips and he swallowed dumbly. Was she imagining it or did his eyes look less glazed? Deep inside them, was there a flicker of life?

Too soon, all the plates were empty and licked clean.

Such bad manners! thought Mary.

The service-light outside the cabin came on, announcing nightfall, and Mary got up to draw the curtains across the portholes. She found a candle in a drawer, lit it and put out the electric lights. In its flickering she thought the children resembled angels with their hair tinged gold and the glow of a kind of bliss on their faces.

'What's next?' asked Adam.

'Raspberries. Special raspberries. Clear up the plates, Adam.' He did so, hoping it might earn him a portion larger than his sister's, while Mary produced four bowls of raspberries swimming in syrup.

'Wait,' she said. 'Before you eat, I'm going to feed Mark.' Sophie gave a small 'Hmph!' but obeyed, because waiting for *food* always made it taste better.

Mary pushed spoonfuls into Mark's mouth until the syrup trickled thickly down his chin.

'All right, you can eat now, you two.'

For Adam and Sophie, there were seconds of mouth-cramming sweetness. Mary picked up her spoon and ate.

Later, when the children were tucked up and Mary had told them a story about a princess and a pea which she vaguely remembered *the Man* telling once, she said, 'Goodnight. And mind you go to sleep straight away, or the Rain Man will get you,' at which Sophie squealed in delighted horror and Adam expressed contempt for such childish nonsense. Mary sat in a chair and watched them and watched them, until tears of love sprang to her eyes.

After a couple of hours, Sophie woke complaining of a stomach ache and Mary hugged her on her lap, saying with a laugh: 'You've eaten too much, little piggy.'

Sophie began to cry and this woke Adam. He too had a stomach ache. Mark slept so still his breathing was inaudible. Mary felt a twinge in her own stomach. The candle, burning low into a mesa of wax, guttered and made the shadows dance.

A few minutes later, Sophie was sick down the front of Mary's dress, leaving a bitter red stain.

'It's just the raspberries,' said Mary. She felt weak and warm and sick and loving. Mark was no longer breathing.

Sophie shat blood down Mary's leg and died a few minutes later in her arms. Adam was whimpering.

It had come to this.

On the shelf was the mortar and in it there was a layer of dust like pale green sand.

Mary's guts contracted with the wrongness inside them. The candle went out and sudden darkness hid them all. Mary thought of *the Man*, how she had met him, how he had won her, how he had come to her one night, how she had loved the children he brought with him as if they

21

were her own, how she had promised to be a mother to them, how he had promised to come back one evening and never did.

We're coming, thought Mary Shitshoes. Wherever you are, we're coming, all of us.

No
Man's
Land

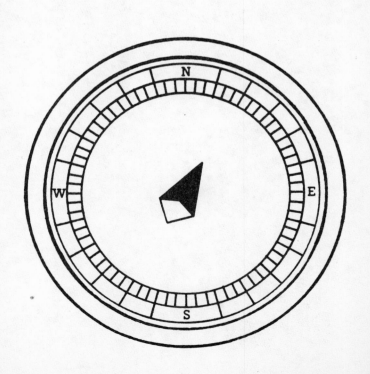

Charlie doesn't expect there to be an after-life or a resurrection like the priest says. Of course, we both go to chapel once a week same as everyone else and the Reverend William Chartreuse (I don't know about the name either, mate) preaches at us like this: 'If you're good, you go to heaven. If you're bad, you go to hell.' But that's too simple for Charlie. He says the Reverend William Chartreuse doesn't understand that heaven and hell can both be found on the *Hope* if you look hard enough, and it makes no odds whether you're good or whether you're bad, because either way you can win or you can get crapped on in life. Charlie says that Chartreuse should come down to the engine-rooms one day and then he'd learn about hell – not fire and brimstone and burning cauldrons of devil piss, but this giant room where few of the lights work and where there are two steel turbines, each larger than a blue whale and fed by oil-pipes the size of a dinosaur's dick. The engine-room makes a sound louder than the roar of ten billion souls. If Chartreuse came down here and listened hard, from then on his sermons would scare the bowel movements out of the good folk upstairs.

But that's only what Charlie says.

I didn't used to agree with him on this because I've always been a bit sentimental about God and all that. I get it from my mother. I can't help it, but when I think of heaven, I think of comfy rolls of cloud and beautiful people dressed in white singing Alleluia.

'But for eternity?' Charlie always comes back. When I imagine Charlie, I see him folding tobacco into a skin with one hand as easy as if he's been doing it since the womb and I hear him speaking with his American twang, so that's how I imagine him saying, 'But for eternity? That's a heck of a long time, pal. The human brain wasn't really designed to cope with thinking about eternity, but if I try, I try to think of a million years and then multiply that by another million and hope that comes close. I don't know about you, pal, but as far as I'm concerned spending that long in the after-life would be about as exciting as watching turtles mating. For ever. Slowly. I think all your heaven and hell stuff is so much crap, and romantic crap at that.' And then he grins like he knows something I don't.

He does. I found this out the other day. He told me.

At the end of my shift, 20.00 hours, I usually go up to Charlie's office. We call it his playroom, because he sure as hell doesn't do any work in there. He watches over us through double glazing, although the view isn't so good now it's all covered with smoke and oil and shit, but that means we can't see in very well either, so what we get up to and what he gets up to remain our own business. Mostly.

Aaron was wiping down the pressure gauges, with his permanent pearly grin fixed to his face, nodding in time to a beat the rest of us couldn't hear. He's painted his ear-shields black with bands of yellow, red and green across them. Mine are still regulation grey. I tapped him on the shoulder and he turned, dreads bouncing. I gave him the quitting time sign and he returned a huge thumbs-up with his thumbs like half-cooked sausages. Some of the lads, like Aaron, I see after work and I've sunk a few and talked with them the way normal people talk (you know, mouth, verbal), but there are a few – Creaky Stan's one, and Thompson, the older ones – whose characters are no more than nods, signs and grins to me. We understand each other perfectly but we don't know each other at all. It's funny.

I mean, I share a cabin with three other blokes and on the occasions our paths cross we're quite civil to each other. We've never had a fight, anyway. One of them, Paolo by name, is OK really, but he's just a kid and still into this stabbing and fighting lark. He's better than that. He'll grow out of it. What I'm trying to say is that, if you pushed me hard, I'd have to admit my only real friend was Charlie, if by friend you mean someone who'll tell you you're being a dickhead when you're being a dickhead but who's not scared to congratulate you when you do something worth congratulating.

But that's my business. As I was saying, I signed to Aaron that I was off to see Charlie (point up at the playroom) but I'd meet him later in the mess (energetic filling of mouth with imaginary food). Aaron grinned wider and gave another thumbs-up. He has hands like soup-dishes.

Charlie's playroom hangs from the roof of the engine-room, about a hundred feet up, and you can reach it only by a rusted ladder, not safe. He likes it that way. I climbed up, banged on the hatch and waited. Sometimes he doesn't hear but today he was quick off the mark and the hatch flew open. He signed for me to come in.

It was a relief to take the ear-shields off. They begin to cut off the circulation to your ears after a while and it feels as if you've got two hot pancakes stuck either side of your head. The scream of the turbines is still there in the playroom but it's bearable and you only have to talk a little above a shout. Ha! Just a little joke there.

'Pay-day early?' laughed Charlie.

'You know it, boss. I've come for my cut of that whisky you keep in that cupboard over there.'

'You mean this cupboard over here?' said Charlie, crossing behind his desk which had nothing on top of it except for a Newton's cradle. Its five tarnished balls (Charlie never cleans anything) were vibrating against each other to make a sound Charlie calls 'metal cicadas'. Whatever that means.

'That cupboard. Bottom shelf.'

Charlie produced two tumblers and a bottle, seal unbroken and covered in dust. I'd forgotten we'd finished one the day before. I don't know where Charlie gets the new ones from and I don't ask. Something about a gift horse, kiddies.

Charlie does the whole thing like a magician: empty bottle one day, full bottle the next. Out of nowhere, two tumblers. Watch closely, ladies and gentlemen. Flourish. Nothing up my sleeves. Two full tumblers. Ta-daa!

The booze kicked warm on my tongue and hot in my throat. I go through whole shifts looking forward to this moment and I don't know why Charlie favours me above the others in this way, but I don't ask either. The others don't seem to resent it. They even hint that I'm being groomed to take over from Charlie when he retires, but I've never once heard him mention anything about it. He's older than me by about thirty years. I was born and bred on the *Hope* and I expect to die on the *Hope*, but Charlie, he embarked like all the old people, drawn (he says) by the promise of something better on the other side of the unending ocean, and he knows things and shares them with me, like he thinks I can't live properly without knowing them too. He's not stupid. Some people think we're all stupid in the engine-room. They think we have to be stupid to work here and they might be right, but it doesn't make us sub-human. Just because we work with our hands doesn't mean we think with our hands.

So I sat back in the squeaky Styrofoam padding of the chair and stared at my swilling whisky and waited for Charlie to speak first, because he always does. He swung his boots up on to the desktop and pretended to examine his laces, letting me unwind and letting us both appreciate the booze. His fingernails were squared and dirt-free.

Finally he spoke: 'Do you know what horror is?'

'Being scared.'

'More than that.' It was a question.

'Being very scared.'

'Do you know what a pedant is?' And we both laughed. Charlie begins like this every time, like a teacher who's been preparing his lesson the night before. I managed to avoid school when I was younger, went straight down to the engine-room aged twelve because nobody knew who my parents were and charity on the *Hope* doesn't go too far or last too long. Mind you, Reverend Chartreuse offered me a job in the chapel but, though he's a nice enough bloke, I preferred the idea of helping to run the ship herself, of being where it all happens, over handing out hymn books and putting on a white dress to light candles. Charlie continued: 'Horror is being somewhere you don't want to be with something that doesn't want you there.' He looked at me straight, over the rim of his tumbler, over the ridged soles of his boots.

'I'd call that being in the wrong place at the wrong time.'

'You'd be right. But it's because that something *wants* you in the wrong place at the wrong time so's it can beat on you good. It wants you there because it wants to show you that it doesn't want you there.'

He'd lost me and I said so.

'OK, pal,' he said, putting his feet on the floor, setting down his whisky and leaning forward, 'I'll put it another way. You know old Creaky Stan, right? You know he walks like he's got a steel bar up his ass, right?' I smirked. That was how old Stan walked all right. 'I'll tell you a story about me and him and a few other guys you won't have heard of. This was way back, soon after the *Hope* set sail and we were just getting into the swing of things, learning the ropes and discovering that no one runs the *Hope* – she just runs herself and minds her own business and all we do is check the gauges and oil the pumps and make sure the turbines keep turning . . . '

And Charlie's story went like this.

Before your time there were rats down here, hundreds of the buggers, big ones as long as your forearm from tip to tail, bigger than the ones we used to have back in New England. They weren't exactly dangerous but they didn't make the job any easier. You'd reach up into the space above the vent-levers and one of them would be waiting for you, maybe give you a bad bite if you weren't wearing gloves, and then you'd need all kinda shots up your ass from Dr Macaulay. They hung around behind the air-ducts and you'd see this scaly tail dangling down in front of your nose and it'd jump ten years' growth out of you. One even got up here into the playroom, when Big Fred was running the show. He went crazy, completely bugshit, and throttled it with his bare hands. Came down the ladder with this dead rat in one hand to show us all. Worst was when you went into the store-room and found a mother rat in a bucket and she had given birth to a brood or litter or whatever you call a bunch of baby rats. She'd hiss at you like she was made of snakes and there were all these pulpy pink things sucking at her tits and it took two of us armed with crowbars to batter the bitch to death. That's mothers for you.

Did they have rat-poison in the ship's stores? Like fuck they did! No one had thought there would be rats on board their brand-new shining *Hope*. I'm not blaming anyone, but you wonder, don't you, if the people who design these things have a brain or not? They should have asked someone like me. I'd have told them what they needed on a ship this size. Industrial strength rat-poison, that's what I'd have said. Anyway, Fred went and got some cyanide off the black market, Bart's or somewhere, and dusted all the corners and dark areas and we had to wear face-masks for the next week just in case. We didn't see the rats for a while and then they came back with a vengeance, more than before, bigger than before (unless my eyes were playing tricks on me), as if cyanide was the greatest thing rats could ever want to eat. Rats' smoked salmon. We got a cat down here too, black one from the upper decks, some stray moggy a rich person didn't want, I expect. Black cats are supposed to bring good luck. Do you know how long it lasted? Three days. I came down for my shift one morning and Tommy – Thompson – showed me kitty in a box. Kitty had no head and no stomach.

As you can imagine, the situation was getting out of hand and we petitioned the Captain to do something. Fred sent him six messages and finally went and saw him, and the Captain said, 'It's your problem, you sort it out. And don't let any of the passengers hear about it.' The fucking passengers!

Then something peculiar happened. One day, the rats just upped and went. You don't notice things missing as easily as you notice things being where they shouldn't be and so none of us picked up on this for a bit, but Tommy mentioned it to me one evening and I had to agree. Not a rat in sight. Vanish. Poof.

A week later, Stan came running past me, kinda all het up. You know how you get to sense people moving behind you when you can't hear them? It's like a whoosh in the back of your head. Well, I turned round and saw Stan shinning up the playroom ladder and hammering on the hatch, and Fred let him in and a moment later they both came out, Big Fred with his Mickey Mouse ear-shields on. He looked an asshole in those ear-shields but it was his joke on us, you know, 'I'm not such a total bastard after all, mates.' You know Mickey Mouse, don't you? No? Never mind. Stan took Fred over to one corner. We were all watching now and, although they were quite a way away, I could see Stan pointing at something and Fred scratching his head and nodding and signing back to Stan that he would do something about it. Later that day Fred put up a notice saying there was going to be a pow-wow up in the playroom at the end of the shift.

We all piled in. There wasn't much space. In those days there must have been about forty of us, so it was standing-on-tiptoes-room only. Fred told us that Stan had found a rat-hole in one of the bulkheads. Came across it behind a floor cleaning unit he was supposed to be fixing. No one had used the unit for ages because there's not much point in cleaning the floor here, is there? Just gets dirty again in five minutes. At least, that's you lot's excuse. And Stan had probably just been taking a nap anyway. So, somehow these rats had gnawed through an inch of steel. I didn't believe it, no one believed it . . . you don't believe it, I can see. Not to worry. Put the heebie-jeebies up me, I can tell you, when I thought of how many thousands of rats had spent how many thousands of hours grinding their teeth and claws down to stumps, then bleeding to death or starving to death, all in the name of the rat cause. Brrr. A hole two foot square.

And Fred asked for a team of volunteers to go into that hole and flush the buggers out once and for all. Exterminate the lot. I didn't think anyone would be that stupid, but almost every man there stuck up his hand. We hated those rats. I was pretty green in those days and I wasn't going to be left out, so I stuck up my hand too.

'Only a dozen of us'll be going in there,' said Big Fred, and selected ten: Stan, Tommy, Ed, Falstaff, Benjamin (who was the biggest black guy you ever saw), a few others, all sensible choices, except Fred looked at me and asked if I wanted to be number eleven. Well, I said yes, but I didn't say it straight away. I asked Fred if he was sure and he said yes, so then I said yes. The rest of the guys went back down and Fred told us volunteers to go and look for weapons – hammers, bars, that kind of thing – and each get a flashlight out of the store-room. He leant back behind him and took a shotgun and a box of cartridges out of this very cupboard here. A couple of the lads laughed because they'd suspected he kept one there but they'd never dared find out for themselves.

'This is life insurance,' said Fred, 'in case one of you boys thinks he can do my job better than me.' And he laughed and we laughed, but it wasn't that funny.

By the way, in case you're wondering, yes, it's still here. Now, where was I?

Standing round that hole, feeling the shuddering of the turbines beneath our feet, you didn't need to know sign language to tell we were shit-scared. Our faces were screaming it out loud and clear. The edges of the hole were shiny-bright scratches in the metal and inside it was as dark as diesel. The light seemed to catch sight of those scratches and say to itself, 'I'm not going any further.' Fred had taped his flashlight to the barrel of the shotgun and he poked it in and shone it around. I couldn't help thinking the hole was way too big for a rat, they didn't need it that big, it was big enough for a human to use . . .

Fred squeezed through on his belly, the flash beam waving in front of him. Benjamin followed and barely managed it. I said he was big, didn't I? I lied. He was enormous. I was next. Fred had said he wanted me in front of him, supposedly because I was skinny and might be useful for getting into tricky places, but I think he wanted to keep an eye on me. I wasn't making any secret of the fact that I was terrified, pants-brown terrified. Then again, I don't think any one of us wasn't. You can't hate something enough not to be scared of it. I was carrying a shovel, its cutting edge sharp as a razor and clean as chrome, and I considered it the best weapon there was, after Fred's shotgun. If you couldn't cut the buggers in half with my shovel, you could flatten them.

The other guys slid through and we found we could stand up. In the light of the flashes there was this narrow passageway spread out in front of us, rising so high above us you couldn't see the top. The sides were reinforced with bolted girders separating the engine-room from the starboard gas-tank. I've seen this on the ship's specs. The gas-tanks (fuel-tanks, whatever you like to call them) take up the best part of the stern section, close on a billion gallons. There's the engine-room and the turbines sorta run through under the tanks out to the screws. The passageway is in fact a safety precaution. If one of the tanks should decide to rupture, it gives us about an hour's grace to get the fuck out of here before we drown in gas. It runs for the best part of a mile towards the stern. The turbines were even louder in there, kinda echoing in a confined space and getting through our ear-shields and making our ears sing. I felt sorta dizzy. And while I was feeling dizzy, an odd thought struck me, kicked me when I was down, so to speak. Why, if so many rats had been at work on the hole, were there no remains, not one corpse? Had they cleaned up after themselves? It seemed unlikely.

Fred prodded me forwards. I had been elected to take point, about which I should have been proud, but I could only think it put me first in the firing line if anything went wrong. I don't know why, but I was beginning to imagine the rats as an enemy army under a genius general who was steering us exactly where he wanted us. God knows, we should credit animals with more intelligence than we do. Remember when those whales attacked the ship last year? I didn't see it myself but people who did said the things were actually throwing themselves against the sides and knocking themselves silly. People said, 'How dumb can you get?', but you put yourselves in the whales' place. What if this huge iron and steel monster came flying over your home? I'd try to beat the crap out of it if I was them. The best defence is sheer terror, if you get my drift.

I mean, these rats had survived down here for several years with little or no food. I can't believe they made it up to the mess or the dining-hall or the food-stores or the greenhouses, but then again, who knows? Clearly they had something going for them, something that kept them organised and alive, something that ordered them to bite through solid steel until they died.

'I thought they were supposed to steal babies out of cabins when their mothers weren't looking. Isn't that the story?' I ventured. Charlie had filled my glass without me noticing and I was starting to feel comfortably numb.

'Now, I wouldn't put it past them,' he commented, 'but before I went into that hole, I'd have peed myself laughing at you.'

He continued his story.

So I set off along that passageway, me, little Charlie who only needed to shave twice a week, with eleven grown men behind me. We're used to small spaces on this hunk of junk, aren't we? But I was coming down with the dose of claustrophobia to end them all. The further we went, the more scared I got that we weren't ever going to get back out. I'm sure the other guys felt it too, like we were being swallowed and the only way out was either be puked up or wind up as lumps of shit. Don't laugh. That's how it felt. The girders stretched ahead as far as the flashlights showed and kept on coming up one after the other. Behind me other beams flashed up, down, around. There was no sign of life, no sign that anything could live there. I wondered if the rats hadn't all escaped out of that hole already, moved house and left the old one spotless, without even a turd to show where they'd been, ready for the new tenants.

We came to a pipe which crossed the passage at head height. I've looked for this on the specs and it's not marked, but I guess it's one of the water-coolant feeders for the prop shaft. Fred took out an oil-cloth from his pocket and tied it around the pipe so it was a marker buoy. We pushed on.

You know how I was talking about sensing movement rather than hearing it? It's a trick we all pick up down here. Well, I started getting that itchy feeling in my head but I didn't know why. OK, so there were folk moving behind me, but it wasn't them, I knew about *them*. It was something else that I couldn't see except in the corner of my eye. Shit, I don't know. I stopped and looked around. Couldn't see a darn thing. Big Fred had noticed it too. He looked at me all calm and steady, and it meant, 'Stay cool, don't lose it,' but I tell you, I was about to run back past the lot of them and to hell with the embarrassment. Cowardice don't mean shit in that kinda situation. But Fred grabbed my arm, Fred in his Mickey Mouse ear-shields, and I could willingly have fallen to my knees and worshipped him then and there because he gave me some of his strength. Dumb, huh? Yes, well. He might have been a mean fucker of mothers most of the time but when it really mattered you could count on Fred. That's why he was boss. He was the strongest link in the chain and – forget the old saying – if he held then the weaker links like me could sure as hell hold too.

So I walked on trying to look like I hadn't gone bugshit for a second and the itchy feeling got itchier, and it also got clearer, targeting itself like head sonar – you know what I'm saying? – and it was pointing upwards, upwards over our fucking heads in the fucking darkness. I poked the flash beam up and it was OK for about fifty feet and then it grew fainter and the darkness grew thicker. It loomed over us. That's the word. The darkness loomed and whatever was in that darkness (had to be the rats, didn't it?) was unseen and watching us and scurrying about in its excitement. I had that thought again about an army with a general. They had us where they wanted us, the perfect ambush.

It was then that I began to break out in sweat. The noise of the turbines was distant now and all I could hear was the pulse of blood in my ears. Must be like that in the womb, eh? Only there you're safe and snug, but between those cold slabs of steel rising up forever you were never safe. The back of my overalls was damp. The handle of the shovel was slimy wet in my palm. I had that thing in my guts like you're never going to be able to eat anything again. I had that taste in my mouth. And there was so much movement above us. You couldn't ignore it if you wanted to. Most of the guys' flashlights were trained upwards and in the half-light you thought you could see things flitting over the walls, scuttling like crabs, luminous swirls you couldn't make out properly, if they were actually there at all and not your mind playing games. We all wanted to turn back then. If one of us had – if I had – the rest would have gone, sprinting faster than jack-rabbits. We weren't wanted there. Simple as that.

After about a quarter of an hour of this – those things above us waiting for the right moment, waiting for the order to be given – we came to the end of the passage. To be more precise, I nearly fell over the end of the passage, because there was a drop of about ten feet into a chamber. Fred held on to me and I didn't look back at him but shone my flashlight around. I felt the others clustering behind me to get a look.

I've checked the specs for this chamber too and it's not there. I'm not saying it was built and then deliberately left off the specs. More like it was *not* built, or at least built accidentally, formed in the spaces between other chambers, the gas tanks, the side of the *Hope*, hell, I don't know. Negative space, do you see? It exists solely because it occupies a place where other things don't exist. A void. No man's land.

The floor was about six inches deep in water, its surface shivering with the vibration of the ship. It looked almost solid, jelly set in a series of tiny troughs and peaks. There were a couple of rats swimming in it, but I didn't mind them any more. They were only rats, not particularly big ones either, and they looked jittery – probably scared of us.

There was nowhere to go but down and Fred indicated he would go first. I blessed him for that. He knelt on the lip of the passageway and lowered himself over none too gracefully. His hands gripped the edge and then he dropped himself into the chamber. I shone the flashlight after him. He signed for me to follow. I copied what he'd done and landed with a boing of pain in my ankle-bones and cold water soaking into my socks. Benjamin came next and fell on his ass, but that probably did more damage to the ship than to his ass. One by one, the rest came, Stan last.

Something was wrong. Someone was missing. Fred took a head count and Falstaff wasn't there. I can't say I liked Falstaff. He was a notorious faggot and he'd tried it on with me more than once. It's hard to say no when the other guy is six foot four, wears an earring the size of a woman's bracelet, and has a scar as wide as a whore's pussy across his forehead, but I'd managed to stay virgin. Heh! Anal virgin, at least. I mean, not that I've got anything against them, understand, and we've got to take love where we can find it and all that stuff, but it's not for me, OK? And I just didn't like him as a human being, that's all. He'd been taking the rear – ha ha! Sorry – so nobody had seen him go. He might have run off but we didn't think so. It could have been any one of us and we just hadn't heard a darn thing. We were one down and we hadn't even met the enemy proper, but Big Fred wasn't stupid enough to send a man to look for Falstaff. Fred knew that something was up, and anyway, if Falstaff had simply chickened on us then he was on his own, full stop.

I felt even more exposed in that chamber. There was so much blank space above us and, as far as we could tell, nowhere for us to run except back up the side and through the passageway. Robinson signed that we should do just that. Stan nodded, even though the whole expedition had been his fault. But Fred wasn't looking at them. He had sloshed off to one end of the chamber, his body haloed by his flashlight, the shotgun pointing forwards in the crook of his arm. He crouched down to inspect the wall. We joined him.

He was peering into a hole slightly bigger than a man's fist, scratched at the edges like the one in the engine-room, which meant something had bored through here too. I smelt ammonia, piss, whatever, coming from outta that hole – unhealthy and biological. Perhaps we were in one of the drainage tanks where all the johns in the entire ship poured in. Perhaps it was due for a flush and feeder pipes were about to rain down on us. Imagine being drowned in piss. That struck me as quite funny, which gives you some idea of how bad things were.

Charlie had gone quiet, as if he was turning a page in his head which he would rather have left flat. While he was telling the story he was staring into space, watching the scenes in his head and recreating them for me, as a good storyteller does. I was convinced this was only that, a story, no more.

He snapped awake and fixed his eyes straight at me.

'I know what you think heaven is,' he said, 'clouds and angels and shit. What do you think hell is?'

'Rocks and devils and burning and lots of shit,' I answered. There was no point in dreaming up a more sophisticated version to impress him. Charlie knows me inside out and what's the point of pretending he doesn't?

'Yup. Because that day, I found the next best thing to the real thing.'

He lost himself in himself again and carried on the story.

As we were standing around feeling threatened and incompetent, like you feel when someone's looking over your shoulder when you're taking a leak, a dozen rats, maybe more, burst out of the hole as if they'd been shot out of a gun, and you could hear their squealing through the ear-shields. I'll admit I fell over in shock, dropping my flashlight and shovel and getting the crack of my backside full of water, but those little fuckers weren't hanging around. Their eyes were big and wide, like *this*, and they crossed that chamber in two seconds flat, no bullshit. We were terrified that they were terrified. I remember getting to my feet and backing away from the hole like the others. It didn't even cross my mind to pick up my shovel. I saw Benjamin muttering to himself, a prayer most likely, to one of the black men's gods, eh? What was worse was seeing Big Fred scared, although you wouldn't have known it for sure the way he levelled the shotgun at the hole and slipped his finger round the trigger.

Then I understood why there were no rat corpses at the first hole and so few rats down here. The rats hadn't just been trying to get into the engine-room.

They had been trying to get out of here.

Something in that hole scared rats shitless. Ate rats, dead or alive, bones and all. Even cleaned the place of rat turds. I did not want to know what it was.

The ammonia smell got stronger. My nose-hairs felt like they were burning.

Whatever finally came out of that hole might have been a rat once, but equally it might have been a fish or a bird or an insect or a snake. Christ, I can't even describe it really, other than it was white and covered in a pale grey slime like human spunk and it was about two foot long. Hairless, stumps for legs, a cluster of pink eyes at the front and a mouth full of steel teeth. No shit. Steel. Maybe it had learnt to grow steel teeth as normal animals grow bone. Don't ask me. God knows what might evolve in the deepest parts of this floating shitheap.

Whatever it was, it was mad as hell.

Big Fred shot it, though I think he only pulled that trigger in shock, and the thing exploded white pus against the wall. It had no skeleton. It was a fat sausage of flesh and pus and Fred popped it open.

But it wasn't alone.

Another appeared in the hole, stretching up its squidgy head to get a good look at us, and then it launched itself in our direction. It got Fletcher in the neck. Thank God Fletcher got in the way of Fred. I mean no disrespect for the dead, but if it hadn't been for Fred I wouldn't be talking to you today. Its teeth wrenched part of Fletcher's throat away and it burrowed into the wound, contracting its body to fit. It sucked itself in. Fletcher's face said he didn't know what was going on, didn't even feel it. The tail-end of the thing vanished, squirting blood out behind it, as Fletcher sank to the floor, his flash beam waving uselessly. His eyes rolled up. The front of his overalls was soaked with blood. If he was screaming, I couldn't hear it. In fact, the whole thing happened in this appalling vacuum of silence, the way nightmares do.

More things squirmed out of the hole. Some plopped into the water and began swimming like they were nicely at home there, thank you, nicely at home anywhere. Other shot themselves into the air, whirs of white and teeth. Fred managed to blast one in mid- leap and it became a spray of globules spattering him in the kisser.

A heavy weight thumped my shoulder and tumbled off, and I looked up without wanting to look up. They were falling from above too. The one that had bounced off me flipped itself over and made a beeline for my foot and I stamped on it. *Stamp!* Like that. You should not exist, you slimy bastard!

They fell like snow from a night sky and landed on our

heads and faces and necks. Robinson had one removing his ear and another working at his nose and his mouth was drawn wide with a scream I was glad I couldn't hear. Stan was swinging a sledgehammer at one in the water. There was a spurt where the hammer hit and he drew the head up with the thing stuck to it, flattened in the middle but solid at either end and a stream of fluid coming out of where its asshole must have been. It was wriggling and I swear if Stan had given it a chance it would have torn into his face, half-squelched to death as it was, but he brought the hammer up and brought it down on to another thing at his feet and the two things mashed into each other so you couldn't tell which was which.

Flashlights flickered beams crazily around the chamber, showing up thing after thing falling down headlong, teeth bared. White, black, white, black. I was hypnotised by the sick beauty of it.

Out of nowhere, one plunged into my face and I thought that was it, I was about to die in that shitty, filthy place with those unreal things. My fingers slithered on its skin. I felt it tense itself to strike and wondered how much it would hurt, and suddenly the thing was off my face and its smothering stink was gone. Benjamin, his eyes so white they seemed to glow in the blackness of his face, had plucked the thing off me and was holding it at arm's length.

I remember this bit clearest of all, because that thing squeezed itself out of his hand, and do you know what it reminded me of most? Toothpaste being squeezed out of a tube. And it slithered up his arm, white on black, and it headed for his armpit and it vanished into him in a second flat. Benjamin lifted his arm slowly and inspected the hole in his body as if it was no more than a surprise attack of bad body odour. You know, just slightly confused. Hey, what da fok's goin on? Then he jerked. The thing must have reached his heart. He virtually jumped over on to his back. Then he was making spastic movements in the water and I couldn't watch any longer. As I turned away, I found Fred grabbing my arm and pulling me with him. The glare of his flashlight caught one of the things on the floor and he loosed off a cartridge at it without pausing to consider. I had a vague idea that someone else was running after us, maybe two or three. Fred let go of me long enough to pump the shotgun and fire again, a soundless flash of flame followed by an explosion of white flesh and liquid, then he pulled me along once more until we made it to the entrance to the passageway.

Of course, it was ten feet up, but Fred boosted me over the edge with ridiculous ease and threw the gun after. I picked it up and pointed the flash beam down the passage. I prayed there were none of those things along there, but God's intercom wasn't on. I saw at least half a dozen scuttling in my direction.

I pumped the gun as I'd seen Fred do, took aim and fired, but I knew sweet nothing about guns and I missed and damn near broke my wrist on the recoil. The beam arced up vertically and the gun leapt out of my hand. At the same time, Fred scrambled up and over, caught the gun, pumped, fired, and pointed at the entrance with his free hand. I saw Tommy appearing, hauling himself over with his face looking like it was thinking about something else, nothing to do with the present. He groped for a handhold, with his body jack-knifed over the rim, stomach to the floor of the passage. I saw a flash of light behind me and guessed that Fred had taken out another of the things. I reached for Tommy and pulled at his sleeves, and as he came over I saw Stan's hands, one clutching his flashlight, a blinding circle.

Tommy and I did try to pull him up as quickly as possible but we were dazzled and when you're as scared as we were no part of your body seems to work properly except your bladder. Sounds like I'm making excuses, doesn't it? Don't mean to do myself any favours. Shouldn't ought to. In that passage, dark everywhere, the floor wet with blood and water and God knows what, it was a miracle we got Stan out at all.

He was quite calm about it. We pulled and we slithered as we pulled and at last he came up from out of the chamber. If we had been quicker, he might have been OK, who can say? But there was one of the things attached to the back of his leg, steel teeth sunk into his flesh and pulling one of his tendons free.

Tommy produced a bowie knife from his belt and took a slice off the thing's back. He took two more chunks out of it before it let go and fell off.

We got to our feet and propped Stan between us. Fred took in the situation at a glance and set off ahead, gun poised. Nobody else was coming out of that chamber, it was obvious. No man, at least. All we could do was follow Big Fred, the man with the gun, and move as fast as possible.

And if I'd known at that point that Fred had run out of cartridges, I wouldn't have gone a step further. Fred realised this, I think. At least, he never told us this tiny, unimportant fact – 'Uh, sorry, guys. No shells.' – until much later.

For minute after minute we limped on, with every step expecting to feel something fly at our backs or flop on to our heads and bite.

Fred stopped short. The flash beam was pointed dead in front of him.

There was the pipe with his oil-cloth tied round it and on it squatted one of the things, the biggest one I'd seen yet, coiled over the pipe with its tail-end hanging down and twitching and twisting. It was looking at us with all of its eyes, looking at Fred to be exact. From its teeth dangled a large gold earring, with the ear still attached.

'Kill it! Kill the motherfucker!' I shrieked, knowing Fred couldn't hear me, knowing also he felt the same way.

'This is the weird part,' said Charlie.

'The *weird* part?' I exclaimed.

Fred and the thing weren't moving, were just staring at each other. I saw Fred's pus-splattered face and I saw an understanding in his eyes. They were sharing something, our boss and their general. They were facing off. What passed between them wasn't for ordinary joes like Stan or Tommy or me, and it was a secret which I for one could live without ever learning and be happy.

The moment ended and the thing dropped Falstaff's earring and ear at Fred's feet, the way a dog offers its master a bone, only Fred wasn't its master (nor its dog). He bent to pick the earring up, found me looking at him, and left it where it was. His eyes were dead.

The thing slithered along the pipe and up the wall, disappearing into the darkness. Fred signed for us to move on.

The vibration of the turbines got deeper and louder and for once I was glad to feel it. Stan wasn't getting any easier to carry and his attempts at walking were pathetic by now. He had lost blood, lots.

A wedge of weak light appeared in the distance up ahead and it got bigger and brighter and I felt like I was waking up. We got to the hole and Fred slid into it, then we pushed Stan through. Tommy made me go next and he kept guard with his knife, but somehow we all knew the danger was over.

We took Stan straight up to Dr Macaulay. He was a good doc, not like this new jerk, and we told him exactly what had happened. We were too rattled even to think of inventing a cover story. And he listened good and nodded and we made him swear never to tell anyone and he promised. He did the best he could with Stan and Stan knows he's lucky to be walking at all.

Then we went back down and got hold of a rivet-gun, the one we're supposed to use for repairs. I hesitated, signing to Fred that some of the others might be alive back there, but he shook his head slowly, avoiding meeting my eyes.

We riveted the steel over that hole tighter than a nun's pantyhose.

'You think this is a pile of horseshit, don't you?'

'Do you want me to be honest?'

'Yes.'

'Yes.'

'Fine. That's your privilege.' Charlie rolled one of his cigarettes in that slick-fingered way of his and struck a match. The whisky bottle was half empty or half full, depending on how you want to see it. I was floating in a pleasant haze.

'Go and look at the hole,' he said, 'far corner, you can't miss it.'

'Wouldn't convince me.'

'Have I ever lied to you?'

'Well . . .'

'OK,' he said, waving his cigarette at me, 'perhaps I did make it up. Perhaps I didn't.'

I asked Stan about his leg later that night, and he said he'd broken it falling off a ladder and it had never healed right. But then, he could have been lying.

Now then, I believe there are places where you don't go, where only a wrong turn can take you, and I don't cling to my religious idea of hell any more. Sometimes, when I see that sheet of steel pinned to the wall with melted wedges of rivet, I think about Charlie's squidgy creatures and I laugh.

But not too loudly. It those things exist behind there, they don't want to be here just as much as we don't want to be in there.

Because before I left the playroom, Charlie said this: 'When I grew old enough, Big Fred threw himself overboard. He was letting me take over, I guess, but maybe meeting that thing on the pipe had been too much for him. Too much like him. Maybe being boss isn't such a great deal, huh?'

Maybe.

And maybe there is a secret better left riveted beyond my understanding.

Perfect

Cadence

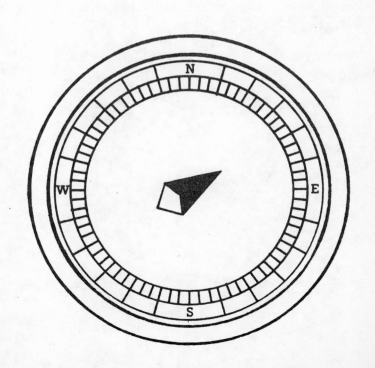

Punctually at six the orchestra struck up the lolloping oom-pa-pa of a waltz, the four violinists scraping out the melody for all it was worth. Dancers took to the floor on cue, as seagulls will take to a shoal of fish. The men were beautifully uncomfortable in tails and white tie (a white that had seen better days; now the colour of sea foam) and the women uncomfortably beautiful in shot silk and faded crêpe-de-chine. The women crackled as they moved, the men's shirt-fronts creaked. They knew the old dances perfectly and each couple waltzed like clockwork figurines, stiff, formal, elegant. They whirled in individual patterns, locked in a larger pattern of which none of them was wholly conscious, embraced as they were in a world stretching no further than the partner in their arms. They danced easily and swiftly. Stiff knee joints were forgotten; twinges of lumbago were ignored; arthritic fingers found courage to clasp other fingers. The tune was impossibly sweet, almost sickly, a surfeit of major chords and perfect cadences. No harmonic was left unturned.

And above, the great crystal chandelier showered light to all corners of the ballroom and the chairs ranged along the sides reflected the light feebly in their gilt. On one sat a woman, unaccompanied. She had a thin, fine-boned face that wore old age with dignity. Triple rows of crescent-shaped wrinkles on either side of her mouth promised frequent smiles, as if she was about to offer you one any second now if you went up to her and asked her to dance. No, thank you, that smile would say with so much grace that you would find it hard to take offence or feel the paralysing embarrassment you thought only adolescents felt. No, thank you. I don't dance. You might want to sit and talk instead, but the smile would turn down your offer just as politely. No, thank you. Might you simply sit beside her and watch the dance? It is so kind of you, but no, thank you. And you would go away feeling neither frustrated nor disappointed but somehow happier.

They had left open the curtains at the far end of the ballroom, where an expanse of picture window showed the *Hope*'s roofs, her funnels, her blackened spires like angular stalagmites, her ziggurats of upper deck piled high on lower deck. At the bows, the setting sun was hovering above the sea, a billowing circle of fading orange cut out of the drab sky. The sun edged the towers and canyons of the ship, the homes and lives of a million souls, with gold. On clear days the *Hope* had a baroque beauty which was as deceptive as it was attractive.

The woman of smiles took in the view through the sweeps and swirls of the dancers and the view pleased her.

The dance came to an end and the dancers applauded politely before dispersing to the sides. Signor Bellini, the important conductor, took a bow and modestly requested the orchestra to stand and take theirs. Everyone allowed themselves a five-minute rest. Restrained chatter filled the ballroom.

These displays of civility pleased the woman.

Angel flew and sank. One moment she was riding a pillar of fire over a desert, her body singing with the achievement; the next she was watching herself plunging backwards into an emerald sea, beams of sunlight darting down towards her in the depths.

Angel laughed and cried. One moment she was starring in the funniest play ever written and the audience were hanging upon her every word, her every gesture, waiting for her to release the joy from themselves; the next she was at a funeral, banners black as ravens' wings flapping from hats and sleeves.

Angel lived and died. One moment she was a creature of light – time, the universe and eternity lived together in the nail of her little finger; the next she had wallowed in night, bottomless, colourless, lightless.

She swam up into a room of brightness and fantastic figures brushed past her and around her, weaving hypnotic shapes.

Each time the figures passed her by, they left fluorescent after-images. She knew this place. She might know it if she saw it.

The dreams switched off abruptly.

It was morning. Dawn seeped sickly grey through the porthole. Push had gone without leaving any indication of where he might be found. Angel was sprawled over sheet and blanket, her body pale. The clock beside the bunk ticked with excruciating slowness as if moving its second hand was the greatest of efforts. Angel was cold with sweat. The shakes were starting and she dreaded the next few hours, hours made of minutes made of seconds that passed like hours.

From last night's cocktail of reality and hallucinations Angel remembered little except Push making her do something revolting to him and doing something painful to her body in return. She wanted badly for these to be hallucinations. But hadn't he also called her Perfection and My Only Angel? Hadn't he?

The cabin was distant, the walls and ceiling holding themselves out of her reach, as if in disgust. Angel pulled the sheet clumsily over her and curled up in the clammy warmth. She began to shudder.

The tune of the evening's last dance was still humming in her head as she made her way out of the ballroom surrounded by a crowd of the dancers whose foreheads were shiny and required constant mopping with clean handkerchiefs. One of the younger men, in his forties with a touch of grey at the temples, held the door open for her (someone always did) and she rewarded him with a smile. His eyes never left her as she walked along the deck and there was nothing but admiration in them. She sensed him watching and perhaps she held herself a little better than usual. She left the dancers' goodnights and kisses behind and crossed over a gangplank, pinching up her skirts with her right hand to keep the dirt off them.

The sky was pinned with a handful of stars.

As she reached her cabin, she had the same sensation of being watched. It was possible the man had followed her but it was also extremely unlikely. She felt no fear. Let them watch. Calmly she opened the cabin door, which was never locked.

Through the window could be seen a small landscape of decks and then a strip of sea to the horizon, whitened by moonlight. Her old cat Lucius jumped down unsteadily from the bed and greeted her with a reproachful yowl as he wound around and about her ankles. She picked him up and nuzzled his purring body. Sitting down, she switched on a lamp shaped like a mermaid combing her hair, settled Lucius on her lap and took up a book recommended to her by the librarian, *The Aspern Papers*. These books saddened her, belonging to a world she would never revisit, and yet she adored their exquisite eloquence, for the librarian knew what she liked reading and without fail would choose something to put her in this laughing-sad, crying-happy mood. Although she was finding the Misses Bordereau a little peculiar for her tastes, Venice in decay captivated her.

Lucius's ears pricked up and his purr stopped abruptly. From being passive and pliable, he became all stiff bones and nerves.

'Who is it?' the woman asked, either to the cat or to the presence that the cat had sensed.

There was no knock. The door swung in to reveal a frail figure. Before the poor thing – not much more than a child – pitched forward on to the floor and she ran over to cradle it in her arms, the woman of smiles glimpsed blood.

Angel spent the best part of the day in the same curled-up position on the bed, getting up occasionally to urinate or throw up in the basin. The crash had hit her heavily, probably because she had never dropped a whole six tabs before. She drifted in and out of conscious dreams, the premises of which were not of her making but the action of which she found she could control. People said what she wanted them to say, did what she wanted them to do, which was funny but nice. When each dream reached a sort of conclusion, she would wake up and curl up more tightly and go back to sleep and another dream. One was about Push and another was about her father. Neither of these was too bad but they were empty dreams, filled with bland ghosts and wandering no-hopers, something missing, cut out from their hearts. Angel felt sorry for them and, in so doing, for herself.

Gradually the shakes eased off and her thoughts began to flock together. She was starving. She had not eaten since yesterday morning and it was now . . . She peered at the clock through sleep-crusted eyelids and saw it was 18.25. Nearly twenty-four hours had elapsed since she and Push had come back here. Time lost. She must make a move . . .

But it was another hour before she managed to crawl into some clothes – jeans and one of Push's shirts. She felt like shit, like a slosh of organs and jelly, like her skin was the only thing holding her together. Catching sight of herself in the mirror which swung from a hook over the basin she saw dark matted hair and yellowy eyes and pale lips and nothing remotely appealing or perfect or angelic. She tried to smile and her reflection grimaced back at her with uneven teeth. Pushing her feet into a pair of sandals, she left the cabin and made for the Recreation Area.

There was quite a crowd at the Neptune's Trident. All the people she expected to see hanging out were hanging out. Wild Billy was lounging by the door to the Trident, smoking a cigarette and wearing his joke sailor's hat. Delia had a little girly on either arm – bewildered things – and had that familiar bollock-removing look on her face. Acid Cas was striking a bargain with someone Angel didn't know. It was funny, but Cas always seemed to come off worst from these bargains. From the doorway came pulses of light and sound, shadows of poses and postures thrown out, frozen in neon relief. As people queued to get in and pretended not to be queueing, Angel saw an aimlessness in everyone's movements that was matched by the drizzle and indifferent air of the lower decks, as if one bred the other. She nodded to Billy as she went by, then jumped the queue and flirted her way past the doorman. She wasn't a very good flirt but the doorman was in a good mood. Billy hadn't been his usual self recently, which he passed off to everyone as the result of taking part in the scrap to end all scraps, but that did not explain the hunted look he had about him occasionally. However, he managed to leer at Angel and she knew he was watching her backside as she went into the Trident, so she swung it around a bit for his benefit.

Inside, the light and sound took shape, becoming the rhythms and patterns of songs from records so old that the scratches often drowned the music with rusty squawks. It had got to the point where the squawks and needle jumps were an accepted part of the songs and the boogiers would scream with pleasure at each one. To Angel the words were nearly incomprehensible, the tunes more so. In her current state of shellshock it all made her head ache. The colours were unnecessarily bright. Faces swam at her from the press of people, some known, some strange, all mouthing things at each other. She pushed through to the bar. Eddy was on tonight. There were rings of sweat beneath his armpits as he handed out glasses full of varying mixtures concocted from the bottles on the table behind him. Few customers actually paid for their drinks. The bar operated on a unique barter system: you drank there, you were likely to be called up by Riot to do some 'business' for him, which meant fight if you were a man and keep the fighters happy if you were a woman (except in Delia's case). Places like the Trident operated all over the *Hope*.

Eddy greeted her. 'Hey, Angel!', then turned quickly to serve a customer.

She waited until he was finished and then said, 'Eddy . . . '

'Not now, darling,' he replied, fishing below the counter for a cloth. 'I'm worked off my feet.'

'Eddy, have you seen—?'

'Paolo!' yelled Eddy, as if he hadn't seen Paolo for weeks instead of minutes, and grasped his hand. 'How *are* you?'

'Eddy, have you seen Push?' He was not listening. She hung on for a moment, realised that the ranks had been closed, and pushed herself away from the bar with a cry of disgust. Hunger, for food, for the drug, was becoming imperative. She noticed for the first time how hot it was in the Trident. The girders in the ceiling were dripping with perspiration, the air was rank. She squeezed her way to the dance-floor and looked out over the sea of bobbing heads. She saw the porridge-head, Walter, making his way through the boogiers, on the prowl for boys most likely. People thought it was cool to have Walter around and give him celebrity status because he was a little bit simple and a whole lot crazier than they were, but Angel found him creepy, especially when he went on about God and Jesus and all that jazz.

'Angel, you look like death!'

If Angel could be said to have a friend, it was Gilette. Years ago, although not as long ago as she thought, the two of them had been inseparable. They had been nicknamed the Twins, neither remotely resembling the other but neither seeming complete without the other. As children, one dark, one blonde, they clattered along walkways and gangplanks, they traced the length and breadth of their deck area, they held secret meetings beneath the tarpaulin of a lifeboat on the outer rim (thrilled with the danger of being caught, a delicious flush of terror). The two of them took on the *Hope* – best of all took on the boys – and won. With every confidence they shared they grew wiser but not older and, when Angel watched her mother die, it was Gilette who held her and told her to cry. They ran and ran until they ran into puberty and then they tried to hold themselves together as the taunts came, chipping away at them maliciously – Didn't they like boys? Were they scared of willies? What was wrong with them?

In the end it was Gilette who took a boy along to one of their rendezvous. He was a spotted, greasy thing who swore a lot and kept cuddling Gilette and pawing her chest. Angel felt sick, not just at Ryan or Ron or whatever his stupid name was but at the casual ease with which Gilette had swept their childhoods away. They did continue meeting but Gilette always managed to bring the conversation round to boys this, boys that. The strange things happening to Angel's body at the time did not help, because it seemed to her that she was being twisted into swollen new shapes by the battle between Ought To and Want To, and that she was no longer her own mistress nor Gilette's perfect lover.

She still loved Gilette even now and envied the flamboyance with which she ensnared men and the flippancy with which she shrugged them off, but she resented her too, blaming her (irrationally) for the loss of innocence. When she felt Gilette put a hand on her arm and saw Gilette's face splashed with coloured light, she was torn between feeling she ought to cry and wanting to scratch her eyes out.

'Are you OK?' asked Gilette and her concern was so pronounced it might have been genuine. Angel could only examine her feet and nod.

'Bad crash, right?'

Angel nodded again, feeling the tears come and sniffling them back.

'Oh, baby . . .' Gilette tried to hug her but Angel shrank away. 'It's not so bad. You want to eat?'

Angel, weak and hungry, was close to breaking down, dangerously close to trusting Gilette, which was a luxury, like the drugs, she could not afford. She muttered that she was fine, thanks, don't worry about her, but Gilette was warming to the role of Protector of Angels.

'I'm going to get you something to eat. I don't want any bullshit, Angel. We're friends and friends look after themselves.' Angel wondered if Gilette had noticed the ambiguity of her last sentence but she kept her mouth shut instinctively. Swallowing your pride was one of the best ways to a full stomach. Before Gilette could do anything about food, however, Riot sauntered up, slipped his arms round Gilette's waist from behind, kissed her soundly on both cheeks and began to make exaggerated humping noises. Angel winced as Gilette squealed in pleasure. Riot was one of the so-called hard men, the leader, so you didn't tell him to fuck off however badly you wanted him to fuck off.

'Riot, Riot, stop it!' Without much severity. '*Stop it* . . . ' Again, laughing.

'Now this is a bottom that could take a lot of spunk!' Riot growled, before noticing Angel. 'Who's your friend, Gil?'

You know bloody well who I am, thought Angel. Are you doing this on purpose?

'Riot, Angel. Angel . . . ' Gilette squealed again as he nuzzled her neck, not taking his eyes off Angel.

'Pleased,' he said. When Angel did not reply, he murmured

in Gilette's ear (not so quietly that Angel could not catch it): 'Come on, Gil. There's someone I want you to meet.'

To her credit, Gilette said she couldn't leave Angel, but Riot insisted, so Gilette promised she would be back later. Angel asked her if she'd seen Push.

'You don't want to bother with him, Angel. Bad news. Find someone else. Riiiiot!' And she was dragged away giggling into the crowd. The music was depressingly loud. Angel let it roar over her like the sea she had drowned in on her trip the night before, and she was numb, and she was dead outside, so dead that she almost missed Push as he swanned by her (he had seen her but he had better things to spend his precious time on). It was, however, hard for him to ignore someone tugging on his arm. To the untrained eye the transformation of his expression as he turned round, from innocence to delight, was so marked that it might appear contrived, even unreal.

'Angel! Baby! I've been looking for you all over. I didn't see you there. Hey, you look beautiful. Has anyone ever told you that?' She let him plant his lips on hers. He held her face gently. His irises were screwed tightly around pupils no larger than a full stop.

'I want some . . . you know, shit.' There you go, be honest with him. Honesty's the best policy. Push made the drugs himself, using whatever was available, mainly salt and seagull-droppings. He was a devout advocate of the hallucinatory capabilities of guano.

'You want some you know shit, do you?' he mimicked in falsetto as he led her to one corner where the music was fractionally less deafening and the shadows would hide a man's face. He sat her down beside him.

'Why did you go this morning?' she asked.

'Business. You know the sort of thing. I'm a busy man. Busy, busy. And besides, you were sleeping like a baby. That was good shit I gave you, hey? I don't jerk you around, do I now? I respect you too much.'

'It's just . . . Well, I don't know. I think . . . No.'

'What is it, baby? You can tell me. We should be able to tell each other everything.'

'Do you like me?'

'Of course I do.'

'Really like me?' She took his hand. This startled him as much as it would if she had put her hand down the front of his trousers in public. Things, he decided, were getting way out of control. His expression transformed again as if made from mercury. His lip curled and his eyelids narrowed.

'Listen, bitch, stop bothering me, all right? I'm fed up with you. I'm sick of you. You bore me. Leave me alone. It's over. OK? Over.'

The music thundered in Angel's ears and beneath it she thought she could hear the angry rumble of the *Hope*'s engines, growing louder, and it seemed that the day everyone prophesied, the day when the engines would burn out and explode, had at last arrived.

'OK,' she said.

She brushed her hand across his face. She thought she brushed her hand across his face. She couldn't really tell because she was in the eye of a howling storm. She realised she had in fact raked her nails into Push's eyes and he was bent double in agony and screaming 'I'm blind! The slut's blinded me!' and although there was a lot of blood she could not tell if this was true or not, because Push was a bit of a liar, wasn't he? Her hands had only really brushed his face, hadn't they?

At that moment a record came to its end and the conversation, which would normally rush in to fill the gap like the Red Sea on the heads of the Egyptians, petered out as people sensed something was happening and looked unerringly towards where it was happening.

Push kept up an uncomprehending wailing and Angel stood with watery streaks of blood on her fingers.

'Christ, Angel, what the fuck've you done?' Gilette's voice, its revulsion undisguised. A drum-beat burst open a song over the silence and Angel was aware how people were watching her, how their dumbstruck curiosity was as insulting as the way Push had spoken to her. Words came from her mouth to be flung at the wall of eyes and faces, some known, some strange: 'Damn you! Damn you all!'

She found herself outside and running along the deck through the dismal rain and there was no sense of direction other than a need to go upwards, upwards and out of there, to climb staircases and scale ladders until the *Hope* dropped away beneath her and she would reach heaven. She climbed stairs past signs which read 'N DECK' and 'K DECK' and 'E DECK', and she had a vague idea that when she reached the top she would fling herself off into space, end her life in a final ecstatic free-fall, better than any birdshit drug. She would dive into the ocean as she'd often dreamed of doing and kiss the safety of its cold-comforting hands.

When she finally came to rest, exhausted, she was gasping in sweeter air and the rain was less persistent on her face. She took stock of her surroundings and was surprised to see no stoppers, no people at all. One of the funnels loomed over her, blocking out a large portion of starlit sky, and she thought the smoke pouring out of it must be the night's breath. She was not really allowed up here. That was an unwritten rule. You should be content with your own level. That was the way of the *Hope*.

And the sense of space was overwhelming, the sky vast, a monochrome dome cupped over the ocean, confining it and at the same time emphasising its unendingness, as if their edges never quite met.

Perhaps, thought Angel, we're sailing round and round in a circle inside the sky. Who would know, who could tell if we were?

She was giddy beneath the stars. She wished she could be up above the *Hope* and riding her like she'd seen horsemen riding in picturebooks, her legs like pylons astride the funnels and the ship's cables grasped in her giant fists. She was quite alone.

Music, faint and unlike any music she had heard before, broke in on her reverie. Without hesitation she headed towards it. She passed a row of potted palms looking sorry for themselves and then she came to a huge room of lights. She looked in through a porthole. She knew this place.

She had never seen so many old people in one room, but they did not scare her or revolt her as they were supposed to. The light, scattered from a shatter of diamonds suspended from the ceiling, glowed on the men's white hair and pink scalps and shimmered on the women's dresses. Couples pirouetted around the room, sweeping in and out of her line of vision. Their elegance was awesome. They swept by again and again, daring her, thrilling her, all for her, even though they did not know she was there.

The music came to an end and everyone clapped and knew, without having to be told, that it was time to go. A few yards from Angel a door opened and she ran and hid in the shadows, but kept watching. Of all the people leaving amongst the cloud of chattering voices one woman caught her attention, not just by her striking good looks but by the grace of her step, of her limbs. She walked away alone, although she seemed to take a part of every dancer with her, and Angel slipped through the dispersing crowd and followed her. Angel did not understand the urgency she felt.

The woman let herself into a cabin and Angel saw the door close and the lights come on. She padded up to the door and found she was trembling – in fear? excitement?

Push the door. Gently does it. A slice of light. The woman looking up (not hostile, not afraid). The flash of green cat's-eyes.

Things collapsed around Angel. There was darkness and she learned it was not a thing to be feared nor the oblivion she longed for. She felt herself floating up into the dome of the night, which had been waiting for so long to catch her.

There were hours of waking sleep and it seemed to Angel that every time she opened her eyes the woman's smiling face hovered over her and that her every slightest need was being attended to. A selfish part of her drew this attention into herself and suckled on it because it was a long time since she had been cared about (genuinely cared about). It was only right she should get her fair share of love. But in her more lucid moments she tried to thank the woman as humbly as possible, hoping she could pay her back in words, but the woman would hear nothing of it. She called Angel a poor child and said she would not let her move until she was much better.

Once, when the woman had gone out to buy something to eat, Angel propped herself up in bed and took a bleary look around the cabin. All the furnishings gleamed – polished mahogany and teak – and the drapes and the bedding were a rich dark blue, thick material such as she had never seen before. There was a lamp like a woman with a fish's tail. Angel studied it for several minutes, counting the scales. A large part of one wall was taken up by a mirror, in which she could see a small child engulfed in a huge bed. Someone had taken the trouble to comb the child's hair and wash her face and hands so that she was almost pretty. An old grey cat on one of the chairs was washing itself painstakingly, glancing up now and then at her to make sure she fully appreciated the efforts being made on her behalf.

Another wall was almost entirely window but the curtains were drawn across it to keep the cabin in twilight. Angel briefly wondered what the view was like from so high up and longed to see for herself, but exhaustion pulled her back down into the bed. As she fell asleep it occurred to her that there was no other bed in the cabin and that meant the woman had nowhere to sleep, but the thought lost itself in other softer thoughts.

Dawn broke brilliant and blue and the woman drew the curtains. Angel woke with it, feeling as if she had slept for a hundred years. The woman was sitting in an arm-chair, her back straight, reading a book perched on the back of the cat on her lap. Angel lay on her side and watched through half-closed eyelids in the hope that she could go on looking for ever, undisturbed, but the woman glanced up, shut the book and smiled a smile brighter than that morning's sun.

'Feeling better?' she asked, and Angel remembered Gilette asking, 'Are you OK?' and marvelled at how differently one question could be asked.

'Yes. Thanks. How long have I been asleep?'

'On and off, about four days.'

'Four days!' Panic reared up – parties missed, appointments blown – but it subsided quickly. So what about parties and appointments?

'Hungry?'

'Starving.'

The woman set about preparing breakfast in a small, immaculate galley kitchen and Angel followed her movements, the economy of her grace, like a dancer.

'I saw you dancing the other night, before I . . . came here.'

'No, you didn't,' said the woman, trying to sound reproachful.

'Yes, I did. You and lots of others, in a big room with a big light in the ceiling. You were there, weren't you?'

'Yes, Signor Bellini's ballroom.' Bellini – that was Paolo's surname, wasn't it? But Angel did not want to think about Paolo or Eddy or Gilette or Riot or anyone. Gabrielle continued: 'I was there, but I wasn't dancing. I don't.'

'Not at all?'

'Not any more. I used to—' And she stopped, as if she had said too much. Angel wanted nothing less than to upset her saviour, so she tried a different tack.

'What's your name?'

'Gabrielle. Call me Gabby.'

'I don't like Gabby. I think it sounds a bit silly. Can I call you Gabrielle?'

'If you want.'

'I'm Angel.'

'Yes,' said Gabrielle. 'This monster is Lucius.' She pointed at the cat, who was sitting expectantly on the counter. 'He's the last in a long line of distinguished cats.'

'How many do you have?'

'Only the one,' she said, tickling him behind the ears. 'I measure my time spent on the *Hope* in cats. The first I had was Black Ferdinand. I took him on board with me, but he disappeared after a few months. Poor thing. I hope he had a happy life. Then there was Margot and Wilfred and— I do go on, don't I? Ask me to talk about anything other than cats because when I start, there's no stopping me.'

'Oh,' said Angel, scared to say or ask anything more in case words broke the spell and she would suddenly be sent hurtling downwards back to the lower decks and the crowds of people who knew her and cared nothing for her. She contented herself with looking out of the window at the

Hope and the sea glistening in the sunlight. She had left a life somewhere down there in the canyons of decks built high and stifling on top of each other and she wished that life would stay there for good. Here, surely, conversation would be kindly and pleasurable and honest . . . if she was allowed to stay. She dare not ask, in case a refusal came like a sentence of death.

Breakfast smelt wonderful and tasted better. Angel cleared her tray in five minutes while Lucius sat beside her on the bed offering to help her out should she get stuck. There was tea in a fluted bone china pot (Angel poured it gingerly, frightened it might shatter in her hands, those same hands that . . .), and there was bread still warm from the ship's bakery, and there was, miracle of miracles, fresh fruit grown in one of the greenhouses. But with each heavenly mouthful Angel became more and more nervous that this was her final meal here, a parting gift.

Gabrielle removed the tray and Angel thanked her, believing she could never thank her enough. The older woman looked tired and Angel would not have been surprised if she had not slept once during the past four days, keeping vigil over a complete stranger.

'Please,' Angel said, 'you must have a rest. I feel fine. I'll get up and you have the bed. I'm fine. No, really.' In the end Gabrielle relented and lay down ('Just for a little while') and fell asleep with the cat lying fitted into the curve of her body. Angel, wrapped in a crimson silk dressing-gown, paced about the cabin for a while, feeling lightheaded, then sat in the arm-chair and picked up the woman's book. It was called *Jane Eyre* and Angel, having read the first few pages, decided she didn't have a clue what was going on and nodded off.

'You must think I'm absurdly old-fashioned, enjoying the dances like that.'

'No, I don't. I like it. It looks nice.'

'It's terribly difficult, you know. You can't just go out there and whoosh about with a strange man without knowing all the movements, steps and patterns. Oh! To listen to me, you'd think it was maths or geometry or something, and it's really nothing of the sort. But it needs more than knowledge alone. Any idiot can learn a few steps by rote just as any idiot can learn a times table. Well, except me perhaps!' She laughed a generous, self-deprecating laugh. 'To dance well, you need much more. You need . . . ' Gabrielle's smile became apologetic.

'You need to love it?' Angel suggested.

'Yes. I can't think of any other way to put it.'

It was afternoon, following a morning spent asleep and a lunchtime spent by Angel on tenterhooks, as she dreaded the blow that must fall eventually – 'You have to go now.' It had not fallen, yet, and when it did, she was sure it would come in the kindest, gentlest manner possible.

Gabrielle and she chatted like old friends about their disparate lives, a lot about the injustice of the way of the *Hope*, a little about life on the land. This last was a bizarre fantasy to Angel and a subject Gabrielle seemed uneasy about, as did most old folk. She said she vaguely remembered embarking, but it was about thirty years ago.

'One thing I remember well. There was a ticker-tape parade, thousands of bits of paper dropped from the very top of the ship down on to the passengers and the people on the quay as they were waving goodbye. They used black paper, which was unusual, but *très* chic. I thought it looked more like a shower of ashes. The whole thing was terribly unusual. It didn't feel like a time for celebration. I felt that the whole ceremony was for me and for me alone, private and not particularly joyful. When I've mentioned this to other people, they agree and say they felt the same. It's hard to know why. Perhaps it's best not to talk about it.'

As the day wore on, Angel relaxed slightly. Perhaps if she kept talking long enough, she might be allowed to spend just one more night.

'Why did you give up dancing?' she ventured.

Gabrielle scratched the top of Lucius's head and looked puzzled, not as if the question was unexpected but as if she had been asking herself the same thing every day and had not reached the answer, which lay locked in a part of her that said, 'You're too old and your time has been and gone. Who are you fooling?'

'I don't know why we make decisions like that. We just do. It might be pride, or a feeling that the old must give way to the new.'

'New! They're all over a hundred years old in there!' Angel exclaimed, with more derision than she intended but it was hard to break with the habits of a lifetime. Immediately she regretted it and apologised, to receive another of the famous smiles.

'No need, my dear. Yes, they're old, I'm old, and yes, there's no new blood to take our place when we've gone, and I think that when we're dead all the dances will die too, but that may not be such a bad thing. They belong to the land, to the life which the *Hope* is meant to be leaving behind, and to return to them would be going back in a circle, getting nowhere.'

And then Angel made a request she had been meaning to make for a couple of hours now: 'Teach me.'

As she said it, she considered what her friends would say if they found out, how they would think her some kind of deviant pervert, and she had a foreboding of the pains of withdrawal to come, and she glimpsed for the last time her old life like a dirty rag at the bottom of a bucket, and she remembered Push – had she blinded him? – and she understood that the desire had been there all along and had to be voiced, just as Gabrielle's answer had to be: 'Yes.'

Days come and go in pain as the hunger burrows its way out of her system and Gabrielle cradles her when she needs it and makes her laugh when she needs it. When the worst is over, she begins trying to persuade Angel that the dancing is not for her and she really should go back to her home and people her own age, but the effort is half-hearted, nobody can pretend otherwise, and only makes Angel keener to learn.

So the lessons start. Gabrielle has the knack of a good teacher, although she would never have suspected she did, and knows the right times to push or tease or coax or cajole or scold or congratulate her pupil. For her part, Angel is an apt learner and, while she will never have Gabrielle's innate grace, she finds a dignity within herself which she never believed existed, she has been keeping it under sedation for such a long time.

The lessons are long and Angel is exhausted at the end of every day. Gabrielle says this is because Angel is putting in too much effort and not enough precision. Angel complains occasionally, throws a tantrum, screams she will never get this right, and Gabrielle weathers out the storms, before drawing Angel close and telling her to behave and kissing her. Lucius follows all this with half-closed, knowing green eyes.

Angel has never been happier.

It will be in the middle of the fourth dance of the evening. A few people will see the woman of smiles entering the ballroom with a companion. The woman of smiles has not been there for a while, her absence has been noted with genuine concern, and there are rumours she has died, but she will walk into the room as if she is waltzing, with a young and frightened girl on her arm. When the dance ends, more and more people will take notice of the pair of them standing in the doorway and the conversation will become hushed and excited. The girl is beautiful, a little pale perhaps, but with dark and shining hair tied up and brilliant eyes and hands gripped tightly over her stomach and a nervous tilt in her posture, a slight hunch of the shoulders. Her dress is old and ill-fitting, one of the woman's cast-offs. She does not belong here and yet she cannot be more welcome.

The handsome man with the grey temples who held the door for Gabrielle several months ago will come forward, bow, and request the pleasure. Angel will turn to Gabrielle and Gabrielle will nod in approval and the man will lead Angel to the centre of the floor. The orchestra will strike up.

But nobody else is dancing. They will watch the couple, they will watch *her*, and Angel is both thrilled and terrified. Her shoes are pinching, a pin at the back of the dress is threatening to come loose, and she fears she will forget everything. Then they are away, the man leading, and Angel will feel dizzy and dislocated, just as she felt when she first arrived at the upper decks and saw the ballroom. But the learning and the lessons will take over. The music will rise and swell and fall and rise again. The audience will sigh as they observe her first unsteady steps and her blossoming confidence, and something like hope will find its way into their old quick-beating hearts.

Gabrielle, the woman of smiles, will smile.

Faith,

Hope,

Charity

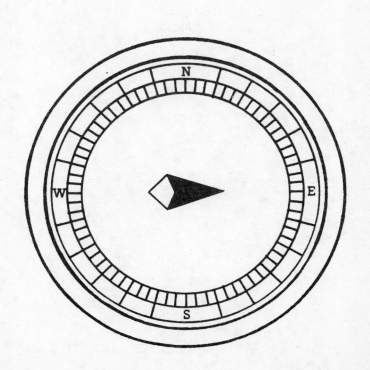

The Reverend Chartreuse was a great man, a greater preacher.

''Though I speak with the tongues of men and of angels, and have not charity, I am become as sounding brass or a tinkling cymbal . . . ''. What was Saint Paul telling us? What? I've lain awake many a night, listening to the people passing to and fro and felt the engines of this . . . great . . . ship, and I have asked myself that very question. Have not we all? What is charity? Some people have interpreted it as meaning love. What nonsense! Charity is simply charity, the giving to the less fortunate.

'So I pray to God and I say, 'Look, Lord, I have given money to the poor of this ship, to the homeless, the stoppers, the disenfranchised children – the *children*, Lord – and I have done Your works and been guided by Your mighty hand, slow to chide. And what of it? What of this charity, Lord? Does it profit me?''

'And you, good people, you place your offerings in our collection boxes at the end of the service, don't you? From the love in your hearts and your love for the Lord of Hosts, you do, and expect no return. Bless you. But does it profit your souls? Does it profit . . . your . . . souls? Paul would have us believe that throwing off all worldly goods, all the trappings of earthly life, is not charity! He says, ''And though I bestow all my goods to feed the poor, and though I give my body to be burned, and have not charity, it profiteth me nothing.''

'Good people, Paul is misled, Paul is confused, Paul is *wrong*.

'But he lived in primitive, less enlightened times. We have seen supreme acts of charity in our day. I'm thinking of the Philanthropist who built this . . . great . . . ship, a man who loved his dream to death. I can tell you, I have it on good authority that his soul is in hell right now, even as I speak, in Satan's parlour where all suicides are destined to go. Charity profited that man's soul? I say no.

'And so we must not take the Bible at face value. We must shift its focus to suit our times. Man should ever seek the truth, the truth between the lines. I take it upon myself to enlarge upon Paul's words, to see them in the way of the *Hope*.

'For we have set forth on a voyage, a long voyage, as the Pilgrim Fathers did many, many years ago, with no certainty that any of us here this morning will live to see the other shore, no consolation that we are anything but links in a chain of generations stretching across the ocean to a promised land of better things, milk and honey. It is a role that we do not cherish but one that we can accept in Christ and the Lord, if Christ and the Lord so wish it. We need faith in the Lord, good people, and I *know* that we have faith in the Lord. Your presence here, at the Lord's altar, in my chapel, proves to me your faith. But more than faith, we must live in hope, hope for that promised land, hope for those better things!

'I leave you, then, with this: "And now abideth faith, hope, charity, these three; but the greatest of these . . . is . . . hope."

'We will now sing, "Eternal Father, strong to save, Whose arm doth bind the restless wave."'

Arthur Wade the organist was so entranced by the Reverend's sermon that he began pounding out the wrong tune.

When the service was over the congregation filed out of the double doors, which were made of brass decorated with ornate curlicues and bas-relief iconography, on one side a hard-edged Christ with streams of spun metal radiating from His head and on the other a crude Mary, more like a man than a woman. The brass had a clumsy, pitted texture, but perhaps that was deliberate on the artist's part.

Arthur closed up the keyboard and locked the lid. Chartreuse shook every member of the congregation warmly by the hand, giving each a slight nod and a smile. Old Charlie and a couple of the lads from the engine-room stopped to chat for a moment and Chartreuse and those in the queue behind them got restless almost immediately, but soon everyone was out and Chartreuse was threading his way through the pews towards Arthur.

'Well?' he said, and it occurred to Arthur for the umpteenth time that Chartreuse was able to convey hideous implications of fire and brimstone in a single, quiet word. Then again, it was only fitting for a priest to have that kind of power.

'I'm sorry,' was all Arthur could find to say. He could not tell the priest of the spell cast by his sermons, how they banished mortal fears and doubts and unworthiness and replaced them with an overwhelming love for God, because spells, he knew, were the tools of the Devil and of unbelievers.

'Can I do the Lord's work properly if there is . . . incompetence undermining my efforts? Can I?'

'No, you can't,' Arthur replied lamely.

'No. But I can only forgive you, as the Lord would wish me to. We all make mistakes, do we not?'

Arthur was a crumb, a speck, a seagull dropping.

'So, Arthur,' Chartreuse continued, 'check the music before you begin playing. I know, I know, you were listening to me and I appreciate that, but you are doing the Lord's work too . . .'

The Lord's work! Arthur quivered inside.

'. . . and the Lord loves you for that and for what you are. Just pay attention. Carelessness is sloth and sloth, as we know, is a deadly sin.' Chartreuse paused. 'That's all. Off you go and I'll see you for Evensong.'

'Yes. I'm sorry. Thank you, Reverend Chartreuse. Thank you.' Arthur set off with a determined stride. This evening would be faultless, he vowed, if he had to practise all afternoon.

Walter was lurking in the shadows below the pulpit. He gazed at Arthur, his dumb, cow-like eyes overhung by the thick lobes of his forehead and a stringy fringe of hair. He made Arthur shudder. A half-wit stopper, Chartreuse had found Walter outside his cabin one night, so the story went, and had taken him in and instructed him in the basics of reading and writing and taught him about the Lord and calmed his pathological heart with the balm of Holy Truth, but Arthur doubted the Reverend had done the job properly because Walter seemed perpetually on the point of raising one of his cracked and scabbed hands and bashing everyone's brains out. Arthur averted his eyes and hurried through the double doors.

'Walter,' said the priest softly, and Walter sidled up to him like a whip-scared dog.

Agnes had not waited for him. She had gone straight to the cabin after the service. Arthur feared her recriminations almost as much as he feared Chartreuse's, Agnes not having the Lord's authority weighing behind her tongue but possessing to a near miraculous degree the art of cutting Arthur with the precision of a surgeon. She had put Sunday lunch – two small herrings each and some insipid vegetables – on the table as if nothing was amiss and Arthur sat down opposite her and examined his hands. She had assumed an armour of silence.

Halfway through lunch Arthur chose the most innocuous topic he could think of, knowing full well that whatever he said would bring her anger to the boil but it was best to get these things over and done with as quickly as possible.

'Good fish, dear.'

Agnes stared at the tangled bones of her fish, pursed her lips so that they resembled a cat's anus, and said nothing.

'Very good fish,' said Arthur Wade to his wife.

'You're lucky to get anything.'

Inwardly, Arthur sighed and prepared himself.

'I was so embarrassed,' she went on, absent-mindedly picking her teeth with a fishbone. 'I started singing and everyone laughed at me. I know they did. Maureen winked at me, the insolent woman, and afterwards Jean cut me – *cut me*. I hope William gave you a right seeing to.' William. She used the Reverend Chartreuse's Christian name as if he was her son or something.

'He did,' sighed Arthur, 'and I promise I'll get it right tonight.'

'You'd better. Someone in my position simply cannot afford to be made to look foolish, particularly in front of her friends, can she?'

'Of course not, Aggie. You are leader of the choir.' There

was no such position as leader of the choir and no choir to speak of. It was just that Agnes Wade had the loudest, if not the most tuneful, singing voice.

'Of course not. Of course not. You know, Arthur, sometimes I think you do it on purpose.'

Arthur had seized the opportunity to stuff some potato into his mouth so he could only mumble, 'Do what?'

'You know what I mean. Make a fool of me. And don't talk with your mouth full.'

'No, I don't,' said Arthur, swallowing hard.

Agnes raised her hands, palms facing her husband, seemingly to push him away. 'We'll leave it there, Arthur. There's no point in having an argument because *some of us*' – she glared at him – 'tend to fly off the handle when they get into arguments, do they not?'

Arthur finished his lunch, washed the dishes, went to the chapel, and practised at the organ until his fingers bled.

When Evensong was over, Arthur having performed perhaps his best ever, notably the introductory bars to 'Jerusalem', the congregation, which was made up of most of this morning's handful plus a few old folk who did not get out of bed early enough and the odd stopper hoping for a handout, filed out past the Reverend. Agnes was among them. She had barely acknowledged Arthur's existence for the duration of the service.

When the ritual handshakes were over, Chartreuse called him into the vestry. He told him to sit down while he changed, then pulled off his robes and hung them on a hook alongside a row of unused cassocks and surplices. He unbuttoned his dog-collar and the stud pinged to the floor and rolled through a grating. This prompted Chartreuse to say, 'Damnation!' under his breath. He was a slender man with auburn hair growing back from his head dramatically like flames. As he put on an ordinary shirt, Arthur glimpsed the ridges of his stomach muscles and felt quite conscious of the roll of gut nudging out over his own belt.

Chartreuse slipped on a white jacket and looked to Arthur rather elegant.

'Arthur.'

'Yes?' said Arthur, eager now the silence had been broken, hopeful for a word, a single syllable of congratulation for his fine organ playing.

'You're a good man, Arthur.' Chartreuse laid a hand on his shoulder. At that moment, Arthur would willingly have crucified himself for the Reverend. As it was, he felt as if he had been raised from the dead. 'I love you as a friend and I cherish you as a Christian and a committed churchgoer. I'd like you to run a little errand for me.'

Chartreuse went to the far end of the vestry and opened a large box which had been shoved into one corner, next to a door Arthur had never seen unlocked. Taking out a package about the size of a biscuit tin, wrapped in brown paper, he handed it to Arthur.

'Would you take this to the side and throw it overboard?'

'Of course,' said Arthur.

'The contents needn't concern you. Some paraphernalia I don't want any more. All right?'

'All right, Reverend Chartreuse. Thank you. I'll do it right away.'

'God bless you, Arthur.'

'Thank you, Reverend Chartreuse.' On the point of closing the door, Arthur added: 'Marvellous sermon today.'

'Thank you, Arthur,' said Chartreuse, sounding genuinely grateful.

It took Arthur the best part of an hour to reach the starboard side of the outer rim. The sun had sunk into the ocean, leaving a dim pink stain behind. Arthur held on to the rust-rough railing and leaned over as much as he dared, for the sea was frighteningly far below. The drop made his head spin. The white horses below were no bigger than pins.

Arthur hefted up the package, hearing its contents clink secretly, and hurled it over. As it fell, the wrapping tore and he saw familiar metallic shapes, dozens of them, tumbling out and glittering and scattering. Crucifixes. Metal crucifixes the size of a hand. Soon the cloud of them grew too small to see, a vanishing dot, gone. Arthur had never seen anything like them before. They were dull and discoloured, not pretty at all.

Supper would be on the table by the time he got back. Agnes was too much a creature of habit to allow her displeasure with Arthur to interfere with her running of his life and he knew he would be taking a risk going home by way of the chapel, but he thought he should ask the Reverend about the crucifixes. Had he really meant to throw them away? Might he have made a mistake? We all do, you know. In his heart of hearts, Arthur was also hoping for another blessing, one for a mission well accomplished. He set off for the chapel.

The chapel took up three flights of deck. Its windows, lit from within, conformed to the standard shape of window on the upper decks but had the adornment of illustrations from biblical events. Abraham and Isaac, the Burning Bush, the Conversion of Saint Paul on the Road to Damascus, and others, were drawn with thick black outlines and coloured in bright primaries, crude and childlike. Arthur thought it was grand at night when these images were cast large on to the walls opposite, washes of colour spread like God's word, so reassuring to Arthur's most humble faith. The Passion, the Red Sea, Joshua Fighting the Battle of Jericho . . .

The doors were open a crack, a good sign. The Reverend had not gone to bed yet. Arthur stepped into the bright chapel.

'Reverend Chartreuse?' he called, and suddenly realised how large the chapel was when empty and how this size deadened sounds. There was the organ, its pipes reaching up to the roof. There was the altar, clean and white with a glittering cross on it.

'Reverend Chartreuse?'

A scuffing sound came from the other end, from the vestry. Arthur walked down the aisle, its thin carpet swallowing his footfalls, his hand brushing his hair back nervously. He heard the scuffing sound again and heavy breathing that could not have come from the Reverend. He approached the vestry.

The door sprang open and Walter lurched out with a sack slung over his shoulder. Seeing Arthur he stopped and there was nothing recognisably human in his expression, not hate, certainly not comprehension. Arthur tried to speak, tried again, and succeeded: 'Walter, where's Reverend Char-treuse?'

Nothing in Walter's appearance altered perceptibly. Arthur might as well have asked him to recite the whole of the New Testament.

'Walter . . . ' said Arthur, attempting to sound threatening. As the chapel organist, surely he had some of the Rever-end's authority about him. 'Where is he? The Reverend? Man . . . with . . . white . . . collar? See?'

'Dunno.' Walter's slightly parted lips had not even moved.

'What are you carrying?' It was hard to sound stern when at any moment you expected to be swatted flat and he would never have dreamt of talking to Agnes in this manner.

'Dunno.'

'I wish to see the Reverend. Is he here? That's all I want to know. I have important business to discuss with him.' Not really a lie, was it?

'Not here.'

'Eh?'

'S'not here.'

'I can find that out for myself, thank you.' Arthur made to enter the vestry but Walter shifted his bulk to block the way and Arthur retreated.

'Not here.'

'I shall tell Reverend Chartreuse tomorrow about your behaviour, Walter. You can be sure of that. You're hiding something and I think the Reverend will want to know. He's a patient and just man, but I think this will try him a little too far. He may just throw you . . . out . . . of . . . ' The words trailed off. Walter had taken a step forward so that their faces were a few inches apart and a wart on his chin loomed large, blurred double, in Arthur's vision. Walter grinned mirthlessly, revealing a single diseased tooth hanging from his gums, and out came his breath like a pernicious fart. Arthur coughed politely.

'Say they know not what they do,' Walter said and looked quite satisfied. That was it, as far as Arthur was concerned. Turning, he took to his heels and reached the end of the aisle faster than a newly wed couple. He was at his cabin door before he could allow himself the luxury of wondering what in God's name Walter's last words had meant.

Walter seek and Walter he shall find yeah yeah bet you take Jesus take Jesus lovely little pretty baby Jesus he dead don't cry

Walter lumbered along his route to the outer rim.

His known no know route

The sack bumped against his back and every hundred yards or so he needed to readjust it, shift it around and heft it again, to ease his aching wrists and shoulders. His thoughts, of obeying, of pleasing, of loving, sang in his tiny brain.

Lo we come bring out your dead not dead but sleeping

At the outer rim he slung the sack overboard to go the way of the crucifixes, disappearing from sight long before hitting the water. Then he strolled back to the chapel along walkways knee-deep in mist, service-lights flickering, shedding lattice-work patterns of swirling white down on to the walkways below. The few people around after dark kept themselves to themselves and certainly were not going to bother Walter.

Holy Scripture all down in writing Rev say so say and nothing to organ man too late what's done is done Holy Writ all down in writing who'll know he'll know

'Do you know?'

From Walter's left, a voice, a hiss.

Serpent head bruise heel crawl belly

'Do you know?'

Walter stopped and the owner of the voice revealed himself from the fractured shadows.

Serpent scars in coils criss-crosses the mark of the serpent the mark of the beast Amen Amen Amen Hail Mary full of grace

The owner of the voice was as thin as a hermit, cheeks puckered inwards as if he was sucking them in for vanity's sake, and the skin of his arms was a waxy wrapping for etiolated muscle and bone. The arms were raised, either to hug or to pounce.

'Do you know?'

What Jesus know Jesus love is all you need to know
yeah yeah but Christ way

'Say they know not what they do,' said Walter.

A blur of movement between them. The thin stranger could have been flicking ash off Walter's sleeve. Walter screamed in primitive agony, staring at the gush of blood where half of his arm had been, and the stranger clasped Walter's face, palm flat against his nose, two fingers depressing his eyeballs. The muscles in the thin stranger's arm tensed beneath their flesh-coloured wax coating so that every fibre was visible, every rope of vein, every sinew. Effortlessly, he raised Walter up until his twitching feet were several inches off the deck and said: 'Sorry.'

Three days later Agnes told Arthur about Walter's death.

Sitting at the mirror in their cabin's bedroom annex, which amounted to four plain walls surrounding a double bed with just enough space to walk round the sides, she was giving her hair the regulation hundred stout brush strokes. To judge by the thinness of her hair, this practice of a lifetime had done more harm than good. Arthur was in bed reading the *Book of Common Prayer*, not concentrating on it because he was hoping Agnes might fiddle with him tonight. The ceiling light dimmed and brightened again.

'Heard about the simpleton?' said Agnes, as if it had only just occurred to her.

'You mean Walter? What about him?' Arthur recalled their encounter in the chapel and his mind conjured up a series of violent scenarios: Walter pulping his head, Walter stuffing him into a sack, Walter carrying his body God knows where, perhaps tipping him into a furnace and leaving him to burn for ever . . .

'Dead.' As far as she was concerned, that was the end of the conversation.

'Dead? How?'

Agnes sighed. 'Well, if you insist on knowing, he fell off a walkway and landed at the bottom, his head all caved in and one arm snapped clean off. Can't say I'm particularly sorry for him. He was an . . . unusual sort. But maybe it was all for the best. I mean, he can't have been aware of very much in life, can he? Not like you or me. Well, maybe not you. What I'll never understand is why William kept him around all the time, but then he is a kind-hearted man, William.

'They haven't found the arm yet,' she added.

'The Lord giveth and the Lord taketh away.' It was all Arthur could think of to say, as he remembered the way Walter's expression had changed from brute ignorance to appalling understanding in the space of a few seconds, as shocking as your dinner suddenly coming alive and saying it didn't want to be eaten.

'Indeed,' said Agnes, hoping Arthur didn't want her to fiddle with him tonight.

Reverend Chartreuse held a memorial service the next Sunday for 'a dear, simple friend whose value to me was as personal as it was exceeding great'. All the hymns were of the slow, solemn variety and Arthur made only one glaring error (and several minor ones).

It was after the service, while he was closing up the keyboard, that a scrap of paper fluttered out into his lap from where it had been wedged between two pipes. Greasy brown smears ran along the folds and inside Arthur found words etched in crayon:

> ARFER
>> THE REVREND HAV SUFRED THE
>> LITEL CHILDEREN CUM UNTO HIM
>>> WALTER

What on earth was Walter doing writing to him? Arthur had cleaned the organ thoroughly last Saturday, so the message must have been sent within the past week and, since he had never exchanged a word with Walter until he found him coming out of the vestry that night, it had to have been then, between his leaving Walter and Walter's death a few hours later. It was written on official chapel notepaper, which struck him as particularly odd as they had run out of the stuff years ago. Did the Reverend have a secret cache?

79

Walter had taken Arthur into his confidence about something, even going to the immense effort of writing it down and hiding it here, but what was it? A warning? A cry from the heart? A joke, perhaps? The rambling mind of a half-wit had construed the words of the Bible and made a hybrid sense out of them, supplanting Reverend Chartreuse for Jesus Christ (not so great a stretch of the imagination, thought Arthur). He read the message over again and he was troubled by the language, by the fact of the message's existence, words from a dead man. Indefinable doubts kept nagging at his brain. The back of his scalp itched and, scratching it, he discovered the short hairs there had gone stiff.

'Arthur.'

Arthur snapped the paper into the breast pocket of his shirt and he twisted himself around on the stool.

'Yes, Reverend Chartreuse?'

Flame-haired and a face so benevolent, so benedictory.

'Haven't you gone yet? I'd like to lock up.'

'Yes, of course. I was lost in thought. Your sermon. Most moving. We ought to rejoice that Walter has gone to the Lord's bosom, and yet it's so sad to lose anyone, especially a friend.'

Chartreuse filled his eyes with tears, quite a feat considering he had been weeping for most of the service. If he detected anything peculiar in Arthur's tone, he ignored it.

'I wasn't aware you knew Walter.'

'Oh yes, we chatted now and then. But I mustn't keep you. You must be terribly busy. You're probably going downstairs to bring comfort to the less fortunate.'

'That I am, Arthur. Off you go, then. Bye.'

Chartreuse waited until Arthur had reached the doors, then switched out the main lights and ducked into the vestry. Arthur paused, fearful of what he was about to do, fearful of the danger of discovery, fearful of the breach of faith involved. He gripped the door-handle set just below Christ's navel. He could easily slip away, be none the wiser, but what was it Reverend Chartreuse had said? 'Man should ever seek the truth.'

Arthur clanged the door shut, remaining inside the chapel.

He did not move for several minutes, to make sure Chartreuse thought him gone.

The luminous glow from the vestry reminded Arthur of the colour of the faces of yellow fever victims. He stumbled over a discarded hassock, stifling an exclamation, and scraping echoes skittered and sniggered into the far corners, into the altar-cloth, into the dog-eared hymnals. As Arthur drew closer the glow assumed the rectangular shape of the doorway, through which he could see the spare cassocks hanging in their rows, white folded in black. It was not too late to turn back. Surely.

Walter's message: THE REVREND HAV SUFRED THE LITEL CHILDEREN CUM UNTO HIM.

What had disturbed him so much about it? The misspelling, the scratchy lettering, the awkward misquotation, raw like an open wound.

SUFRED.

He would show it to Reverend Chartreuse. The priest would understand and would allay his fears and would bless him and absolve him. This was what Arthur had intended to do all along, yes. To tell it to the priest.

The vestry was empty.

But beyond, the locked-shut door in the wall opposite was unlocked and open. And Arthur heard voices, one high and panicked, the other low and even (Chartreuse's). Arthur could not make out what they were saying but there was urgency in both of them. And fear.

There was the box which had contained the package of crucifixes. Arthur knelt down beside it and peeked through the crack in the door. Inside . . .

Two naked figures moving together, violent, jerking. One on its knees, hunched over the other, as if protecting it from harm. The other spreadeagled on the floor. Bound hand and foot. To a makeshift cross. By shreds of white and black cloth.

The kneeling figure: 'Say it! Say it!'

The crucified figure: 'Jesus fuck me . . . '

'Louder!'

'JESUS FUCK ME'

'Say, "Father forgive them for they know not what they do." Say it, damn you!'

A spear-point of metal in the hand of the kneeling figure, a smaller cross, rammed into the back of the crucified body, which was writhing, and the spear-point was a crucifix like the ones Arthur had hurled overboard – what was he guilty of now? – and two people were screaming and Arthur found that one of them was him.

The kneeling figure shot his head up and fierce blue eyes glittered beneath flames of red hair.

Stumbling. Falling backwards. Clutching cloth (white and black cloth) and feeling it tear. Running into darkness. Hearing the sound of surf breaking against a million shores, tide rising, the sea reaching and retching waves which were the size of whole cities, whole *Hopes*, bring them crashing down to crush the land, grey foam on a night-time ocean . . .

Agnes complained she had not slept a wink for all his moaning and groaning. Arthur murmured an apology and for once she let it stand. He did not eat his breakfast. Weak tea with reconstituted milk and mackerel paste on dry biscuits had lost their customary appeal. He took a stroll along the deck, taking aimless turns again and again in the hope of losing himself but, as he had suspected might happen, he eventually found himself outside the chapel. Its windows were lifeless by day, the images sleepy, muddied. He let himself in using his key. It seemed as if the suffering Christ and the Holy Virgin were watching his back with blind eyes of brass corroded by salt. He sat in a front pew, resting his forehead on the rail, but no prayers would come. His forehead went numb but he did not have the energy to raise it, even when he heard footsteps approaching.

'Arthur.' The voice radiated a soothing power. 'I'm not going to hurt you.'

'Go away.'

'Arthur, I know what you've seen. I won't try to justify myself because it is the Lord's will and God moves in a mysterious way, His wonders to perform. His wonders, Arthur.'

'I don't want to hear it. I don't want to hear anything.'

'Of course.' He felt Reverend Chartreuse sit down beside him, so close that their elbows brushed. 'Of course, Arthur. You're very upset, but it's only because you have no under-standing of what you've seen.'

'How many?'

'How many what?'

'Boys. How many boys?'

'I'm not sure. Maybe thirty. Not only boys. Girls too.'

'And what about Walter?'

'Yes, poor Walter. So loyal, so useful.'

'Loyal and useful to blasphemy.'

'No, no, Arthur, not blasphemy, nor sin, but the message of Christ writ loud and clear. It came to me in the night, a voice calling out amidst the sound of the engines, telling me that there were better ways than preaching to save the souls of the innocent.'

'Not Christ . . . '

'Yes, Arthur. Don't you see? Those children, Walter found them for me on the lower decks. Except the last one, I had to find him for myself. Drifters, orphans, losers, ignorant of the word of God. Walter took them to me and I showed them Christ in all His glory, I gave them to Him, delivered them unto the Lord, in a state of rapture. "Except ye be converted, and become as little children, ye shall not enter into the kingdom of heaven." Matthew. I saved their souls, Arthur. I made them angels. You can't comprehend the wonder of it when I feel the souls leaving those young bodies, feel them stiffening in death and know that death is only the beginning for those . . . pure . . . souls. It is rapture. There is no shame in that feeling. God has told me to feel no shame.'

Arthur said, 'Amen' without meaning to.

'And now,' continued Chartreuse, 'I need another man like Walter, another willing to do the Lord's work.' He paused for effect. 'Do you know of anyone, Arthur Wade?'

The question hung between them for a full minute.

'I . . . may do,' said Arthur. Chartreuse touched him gently, warmly, on the shoulder and left him alone.

Arthur heard Walter's note crinkle in his pocket, disfigured words the truth of which could not be twisted, moulded or altered to suit the times. It was Walter's admission of guilt. Even a half-wit could feel guilt and it was not that surprising since he had been indoctrinated into a religion that celebrated guilt, worshipped guilt, made a perverse love out of guilt. With Walter's confession Arthur had the power to condemn or exalt Reverend Chartreuse. He tingled with the thought. The Reverend was a great man, a greater preacher.

Arthur Wade sat and pondered the future and prayed for guidance.

Reading

Habits

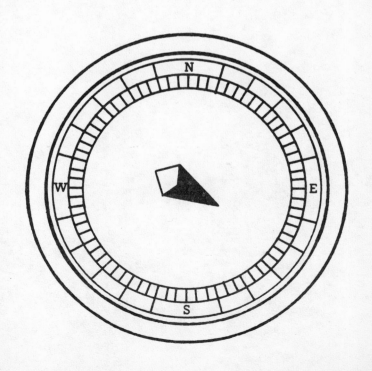

It had been twenty years before the librarian decided books were a load of crap, years spent sorting, coding, rearranging, stamping, filing, shuffling, reading . . .

He would go mad if he did it much longer. He huffed on his spectacles for the fifth time that morning, his breath cold steam, and rubbed around the lenses with his mitten. Didn't they know the cold was bad for books? Balancing the specs on his nose, he found he could see even less than before. His eyes had got worse over the years while the specs had stayed the same. And that was another thing. Why had they not allowed for an optician's on this bloody boat? Silly buggers, they should have asked him to design the thing. He could hardly see to read, and what was the use of a blind librarian, eh? Tell me that. About as much use as an atheist priest.

The trouble with books was that, contrary to popular belief, you could not lose yourself in them. Reading was a shallow experience at best. While the reader was meant to be a passive spectator, he could in fact play God – jump from page to page, re-read favourite bits, miss out whole chapters, close the book if it was boring, never pick it up again if it was really boring. And although books brought a form of immortality for the author, the books themselves were far from immortal. Paperbacks browned with age were shrugging off their cardboard skins and losing pages like an old man loses teeth. Hardbacks parted company with their bosom companions, the slip-covers, to reveal scratchy cloth bindings. Moreover, in twenty years of reading, how many plots and characters could the librarian remember? Really remember? They were no more immortal than him.

Twenty years was a lot of your life, a lot of time spent sitting and growing fat and bald and not screwing around or pulling the birds in one of the bars, not that there was much to pull, the odd tart with laddered tights or hags old enough to be his mother's mother. That cow with the inane grin who came in so often, she was all right in a wrinkled sort of way, and he could have fucked *her* at a pinch – tits like dewlaps, no doubt, but beggars can't, etc., etc. But she was only interested in books and he only recommended to her the weedy, romantic-type novels, Austen, Brontë, James, the sort of thing old biddies lapped up. In time, he might wean her on to Dickens or one of the great satirists, Swift, Thackeray, but it was unlikely she could cope with their vitriolic attacks on civility. At least she was a regular.

Christ, but this was a big place! Huge, and not a porthole in sight, stuck in the middle of nowhere with black walls and inadequate lighting. Rows of shelves receded into the distance, so high you needed a ladder to reach titles only halfway up, and hadn't he nearly broken his neck on more than one occasion? They didn't pay him much danger money. Come to think of it, they didn't pay him much money at all. He could have got a decent job, entertainments officer or some such useless nonsense. Damn it, he could earn more working behind a bar! But no, he thought he could put his education to some use down here, cataloguing and cross-referencing, dividing and sub-dividing.

The heaters had been on the blink for two months now and his repeated requests for a janitor had met with bluff disregard. He was only the librarian, wasn't he, and who read books these days? Answer: old people and odd people – the two characteristics usually went together. And though there were enough of both on the *Hope*, even they had better things to do. So why build a library on this bloody boat? He could have told them (if they'd asked him) to save their money, use the space for a massage parlour or a strip club or something of that ilk.

How did that joke about janitors go? He couldn't remember a sod these days.

He fumbled with the date-stamp, numb fingers unwilling to do what they were told. He could not even lick them to turn pages in case they got frozen to the paper. The stamp slipped from his hand and left half of the date in one corner of the flyleaf, no bloody use to anyone. Sod it. *One Day in the Life of Ivan Denisovich*. Who's going to want to read that again? All that snow and comradeship, it made him sick. Miserable bastards, the Russians. There was one on N deck, Alexei Something-or-other-onov. Never smiled. Wife dead, screwed around a lot, drank vodka as if he wanted to kill himself, often to be found with a floosie on his lap, and he never smiled! Was he *ill*?

Careful, careful. Thinking about floosies was giving him a hard-on, and he wouldn't be able to do a thing about it until the library closed.

Three people were wandering through the rows of shelves, letting their eyes pass over the titles, waiting for one to leap out and catch their attention. It was a fact, the librarian noted, that the more lurid titles went out the most often, all the Gothics and the science fiction. He detested Gothics and science fiction.

Eventually two of the people left without even glancing inside a book. They had probably come to relieve the boredom for an hour, because libraries gave you an excuse to wander round and look vacant and there was no one to see you except that dickhead librarian with his thick-rimmed specs and an upper lip like a bird's beak. The third, however, came up with a paperback edition of *Romeo and Juliet* in his hand and plonked it on to the librarian's desk.

'At last,' said the librarian humourlessly.

'Is it good?' asked the man. He was shaped like an avocado, had a carefully clipped moustache and spoke with an Italian accent.

'If you're into death, families and sex, yes.'

'Excellent. I believe it is what I need.'

The librarian stamped it, controlling his hands enough to render the date almost legible.

'I myself can do without the first two,' he remarked.

'Thank you. Don't you want my name?'

'To be honest, I gave up taking down names four years ago during an efficiency drive. You return the book or you don't, I don't give a toss either way. It's not my book.'

The Italian looked at him, perplexed. Was this an insult

or not? Did this man know who he was talking to? But the librarian's face showed not a trace of insubordination or malice, just a frank incuriosity. Signor Bellini gave him the benefit of the doubt, thanked him curtly and left.

'Bloody wop,' the librarian muttered.

It was 16.47, too early for official closing time, but who was going to check? He switched off the desk lamp and got out of his old leather-covered chair. God, his back was stiff. They could have got him a decent chair, couldn't they? He only had to sit in it all day, they might have thought about *that*.

He took one last stroll along the central aisle, glancing right and left along every row to see if there was anyone who had crept in without his noticing, some stopper wanting somewhere to bed down for the night or a brat.

And by Christ, there was someone! In the D section (Dante to Dumas), a stooped, limping man with a rag tied round his head and broken shoes and a great iron on his leg. The librarian was suddenly hot beneath his jacket, very hot, and his breath came faster than steam from an old engine. He gave an odd squeal. The convict had seen him and spoke with a tongue that was gravel, coals, salt-licked wounds, broken stones.

'Hold your noise! Keep still, you little devil, or I'll cut your throat!'

'Help,' the librarian said timidly, wishing he had a guardian angel to hear him.

'Tell us your name! Quick!'

'Er . . . ' It was strange how, in moments of acute stress, one could not do the simplest things. The other night a whore had asked him if he was looking for a good time and he had been unable to answer her, as if the idea of looking for any sort of time had been whisked out of his brain. She had smartmouthed him and he had walked briskly off, not sure if he even remembered his own name.

'Once more! Give it mouth!' snarled the convict.

But he hadn't said anything!

'Show us where you live. P'int out the place.'

P'int out? Where did this man think he was?

A churchyard, sprung about with nettles, tombstones of

crumbled stone, and beyond, flat and featureless marshlands. The librarian knew this place, but only as somewhere he'd never been. And he was inhaling its salted air and the sweet scent of decay, with a nose as sensitive as a cat's or a child's, not deadened by years of smoke and grease. The ground was springy and he felt unsteady on his feet, which were used to the steel walkways and bare floors and the ponderous roll of the *Hope*.

'I, er . . . I'm not sure what you mean by home. Sir.'

'You young dog,' said the man, licking his lips, 'what fat cheeks you ha' got.'

'Fat! You insolent pig!'

'Darn me if I couldn't eat 'em,' said the man and for no accountable reason shook his head, 'and if I han't half a mind to't!'

This was absurd, quite absurd. The librarian didn't have to stand here and listen to the ravings of a madman.

'Now lookee here!' said the convict. 'Where's your mother?'

'It's none of your business, but she's not here, if you must know.'

That had done the trick! The convict started, and ran off a few yards before looking back over his shoulder with eyes that would have curdled the librarian's blood, had he not been running in the opposite direction, short legs pumping the spongy soil, and *thwack*!

He found himself on his backside on the floor of the library, nursing a bruised biceps. Columns of books rose up over him, titles gleaming on bindings. The *Hope* vibrated the fat of his buttocks.

What the hot holy hell had happened?

The librarian rose shakily to his feet and brushed dust off the seat of his trousers. Twenty years of solitude had finally caught up with him. He had cracked. Taking a nervous peep behind him, he saw only books (Dante to Dumas). But he had recognised the convict and the churchyard, though he had never been near either in his life.

'Magwitch,' he said to himself, and inspected his watch. 17.03. The bars had opened.

*

The bars had closed by the time the librarian was pissed enough to contemplate his brief, disturbing encounter. With every glass, the possibility that he had nodded off and dreamt the whole thing became increasingly desirable. Not just desirable, but probable. He had often gone to sleep mid-sentence in a book and come to ten minutes later with the unshakeable conviction that he had been in a small boat for days grappling with a huge fish or that the pigs had taken over his farm. Some books sent him to sleep so often he had given them up halfway through – *Paradise Lost*, for example. What monumental tosh that was! And *The Divine Comedy*. He hadn't managed much of that. Reading Dante was like reading the ship's safety manual, but less funny and less useful.

But the smells and the feel of earth beneath his shoes! The convict had appeared so solid, so vivid . . .

'Penny for them?' A tart. Christ, she was ugly! He thought he said, 'Fuck off,' and either he hadn't or she was especially stubborn, because the next thing he knew was that he was in her cabin and she was undressing him and undoing his flies and he threw up on her head.

'I feel like a rat's bottom.'

'You look like one.'

The ship's doctor, Marcus Chamberlain, had the librarian lying on his back on a narrow couch, naked except for his Y-fronts, which could have done with a wash. Looking down his body, his tits and his blotchy pink belly, he wondered how clean his feet were. Dr Chamberlain was feeling his skull and seemed to know what he was doing. He was fresh-faced, seamlessly handsome, and his hands were cool and dry.

'Have you banged your head recently?' He sounded as if he had discovered a clue.

'No.'

'Oh. No, of course not.' Disappointed. 'Banged any part of your anatomy?'

'Only my arm. And that was after I'd had the . . . hallucination.'

'Um. After. Well, that's no good, is it? Domestic problems?'

'No wife.'

'No domestic problems. I've got it! Alcohol. You've been hitting the hard stuff, haven't you?'

'No. Yesterday evening was the first time in months I'd gone on a real binge.'

'But you've been drinking heavily?'

'No.'

'Steadily?'

'No.'

'Oh.' Dr Chamberlain took out his stethoscope, clamped it into his ears, placed the other end to the librarian's chest, frowned, turned it over and listened again. 'That's better. Your heart sounds OK. Overwork?'

'Hardly. I just sit at a desk for eight hours a day.'

'And you say this hallucination was from a book?'

'*Great Expectations*, yes. Word for word. I looked it up this morning. Pip meets Magwitch the convict in a churchyard, and—'

'Yes, yes. Put your clothes on. I can't see anything wrong with you, but I'm going to prescribe a course of pills.'

'What pills?' asked the librarian, struggling with his shirt in his eagerness to hide his body.

'Hang on, I'm thinking.'

'Are you a trained doctor?' he asked suspiciously.

'Yes I am!'

'Really?'

'Well . . . no, actually. I was apprenticed to Dr Macaulay, and he died before I could finish my training. But I've read all the books.'

So have I, thought the librarian, and for some reason he was scared by that.

He spent the rest of the afternoon fidgeting at his desk, expecting Magwitch to skulk out suddenly round the corner of the D section, his leg-iron scraping along the floor, coming to terrify the life out of Pip once more. And what if Miss Havisham turned up in her mildewed bridal gown and told him to play with the vicious Estella and in the end caught fire in front of him, her hair crackling as it shrivelled to black stumps? At the thought he shrank inside his jacket and cursed Dickens for his hyperactive imagination. The pills Dr Chamberlain had eventually given him had been no more than Valium, but he had popped a couple all the same. They made him drowsy but they did not ease his queasy stomach or his crawling sphincter. Business was slow, even for the library. Rumours of some juvenile antics, a gang war or whatever, kept most sensible people on the lower decks indoors. The old and the odd were a cautious breed. That was how they survived to become old and odd.

A sound made his ample backside leave the leather seat. A small pile of books on the desktop toppled. It was a loud tapping that came from the B section (Bacon to Byron). He didn't want to investigate, not really, because that was for idiots, and he had visions of Magwitch sounding out the metal frames of the shelves with the end of his iron, which was enough to send anyone fleeing. The tapping, quick and irregular, came and went again as he stood at the desk, knuckles white on the wood.

'Can I help anyone?' he queried tremulously. 'Whoever it is, I can jolly well hear you and I don't think it's very funny.' He paused. 'Are you looking for a book?'

The bookshelves were like the towers of a forgotten city, layer upon layer of different lives crammed high on each other, and you wouldn't be surprised if ghosts lived there, in that city, whispering along its streets and through its alleyways and in its parks, lost children wanting to go home.

'Hello?' The librarian took two steps from the desk, to prove he was no coward. The B section was close, a few yards away. The tapping had stopped again.

'Hello? Who's there?' The questions covered up his next couple of steps forward. He was beginning to think it was one of the little sods who sneaked in when they could and ran around rearranging books and trying to find the dirty ones, although the ones with suggestive titles often turned out to be rather mundane and by and large lacking in pornographic thrills: *The Naked and the Dead*, for example, or *A Streetcar Named Desire*.

Without realising it, he had rounded the corner of the B section and saw nothing but books, thick, thin, hardback, paperback, jacketed, bare. He leant against the shelves to steady himself.

Icy fingers grasped his hand and he moaned, 'Oh, God,' expecting to see Magwitch clutching on to him, eyes mad and wide, asking for food and shelter or else he'd eat him alive, but there was only a child's face and a sobbing voice: 'Let me in – let me in!'

'What the hell is—'

'Catherine Linton.' Obscure, as if through an old window pane, he glimpsed the shivering girl and recoiled in horror at the desolation in those eyes. He jerked his arm back and wounds appeared in the child's wrist, her skin slicing on thin air and blood sluicing out.

'Let go of me! Let go, you little shit!' he cried. Why was he in bed, in the dark, on a windswept night? Why was he wearing this ridiculous nightshirt? 'Bugger off, you little terror! I know your sort, you're only here to cause trouble.' He never had liked children, least of all wanted one of the brutes as his own. The girl kept wailing.

'It's twenty years,' she mourned, 'twenty years, I've been a waif for twenty years!'

'And you can stay one for the next twenty!' he yelled back.

And the girl disappeared, sucked away like water down a drain back into the pool of night. The librarian scanned the floor for bloodstains, checked the books (not that he cared, of course, but they might have been damaged), and returned to his desk. He spent the next hour sitting there, glancing left, right, over his shoulder, up above, then closed up the library two hours early and went to bed.

Dr Chamberlain had a joke that he was a man of considerable patience – the Captain, the priest, folk from the upper decks. Get it? Patients. In fact, his patience was less than considerable and this librarian was just about pushing it to its limit. Chamberlain recommended that he go to a psychiatrist, not a physician, although the librarian had pointed out testily that there was no psychiatrist on board this floating asylum and they ought to have consulted him first, he'd have told them what kind of medical help they needed to keep a million people healthy, certainly not an inexperienced quack who couldn't recognise a serious case when he saw one.

Dr Chamberlain smoothed his hair back and asked the librarian to leave. There was nothing he could do for him.

The librarian visited the chapel next and met the unctuous Reverend Chartreuse, who was all tea and sympathy as he listened to the librarian's story and said he would do what he could, until he discovered the librarian did not attend chapel services with any degree of regularity (not at all, if the truth be told), at which point he grew somewhat formal. It took a lot of persuading to convince him this was genuine demonic infestation, plus a promise to attend chapel for the next four Sundays, a promise the librarian had no intention of keeping, before Chartreuse agreed to come down and exorcise the library.

Armed with a phial of holy water, the Reverend stalked the length and breadth of the library, muttering some dog Latin formulae and sprinkling the floor until he ran out of water. He smiled, said, 'See you next Sunday!', and departed. The library seemed none the better for its divine spring-clean.

The librarian contemplated putting a 'Closed Until Further Notice' sign on the door, but 'Further Notice' was a huge cop-out. He might never come back at all and he might even be missed by someone – that grinning old woman, for example.

He sat behind his desk and waited for the library to spring its next trick on him.

He waited three days. On the afternoon of the third, after the day's sole visitor had left bookless, singing came to the librarian's ear.

It was a song of swollen buds and rich folds of red petals and spring shoots so green they were almost phosphorescent. He stood up involuntarily and had to stoop to ease the pressure of his trousers against an erection that had sprouted like an overnight mushroom. He hurried as best he could towards the source of the song, the T section (Taine to Tzara), but his progress could most kindly be called a waddle. The rhythm of the song was repeating itself faster and faster, building up to a soaring melodic climax, and the librarian was wincing as his erection enlarged at every step and threatened to burst his zip.

Buds and petals and shoots.

He fell into a woodland world where thick-bracketed branches blotted out the sun, and life – mammals, birds, insects – thronged in every bole of every trunk and every tussocky hole in the earth. He was in a dark glade and at its centre, framed by the intertwining trees, was the most beautiful woman he had ever seen.

Tennyson, he thought, you randy old bugger.

The singing died as she saw him. In her finespun-thread hair was twisted a gold tiara and clinging to her was a dress of translucent material that, in covering up her body, drew attention to that which it hid, breasts, nipples, the curve down towards her thighs, the shadow where they met, oh Christ!

The woman fell at his feet and kissed them, crying: 'Trample me, dear feet, that I have followed through the world, and I will pay you worship. Tread me down and I will kiss you for it.'

The librarian groaned and exploded into his Y-fronts, nearly fainting with the ecstasy.

The vision was gone and he was sitting on the floor, spent, sticky, shamed, guilty, embarrassed.

But at last he understood what was happening.

The librarian began giggling.

A few people, not many, were puzzled by the new and erratic opening hours of the library. Although they were not regulars as such, they had grown used to the place being open without fail 09.00 to 17.00 and now it irritated them to have to plan their visits to accommodate the two hours a day, not consecutive, during which they were allowed access to browse and at the end of which they were unceremoniously hustled out. Complaints to the librarian brought only stubborn intractability, a blank stare, sometimes downright rudeness. It was none of their business and if they didn't like it they could start up a library of their own. Gradually they stopped coming altogether. Nothing could have pleased the librarian more.

Every day he ambled along the shelves choosing his

read for the day. Spotting a book he wanted, he would stand by it and concentrate, not too hard because it didn't work that way, but hard enough to winkle the story out of hiding. Usually he got what he wanted but the library could make up its own mind and often chose something else from the same section that suited his mood better. The story would live and he would live in the story.

Feeling bored? Try one of the thrillers; cars, girls, guns, chases, girls, more girls.

Feeling depressed? Tumble into *Tom Jones* and a simpler era when love conquered all and Tom conquered all women.

Feeling frisky? *Lolita*.

Feeling bright and witty? Engage in the intellectual cut-and-thrust of dinnertime conversation in Peacock's funny little novels.

Feeling a bit too bright and witty? Travel up the sombre Congo towards the heart of Conrad's darkness.

The librarian fought the greatest warriors, feasted on the finest food, fucked the most beautiful women. It did not matter whether he lived or died, whether he was one character or dozens, for at the end he would wake up, the day's adventure done, the back cover shut in his head, exhausted and content.

He was living the books he had read and all their tastes, sensations and pleasures were his. The world of the *Hope* became as much a dream as the world of the books. He had to eat, sleep and shit in the real world, but these were minor inconveniences and barely registered. He didn't notice when strangers started to wrinkle their noses as he passed them by, either on the way to or back from the library, but he didn't much notice the need for a shower or a shave either. Sometimes a stranger might wave in greeting and he realised it was someone he knew and he was compelled to grunt something back, but he took to going around without his specs on to prevent that sort of thing happening too often. And that was another blessing, because he didn't have to ruin his eyes by reading Lilliput print now. No more headaches and unsightly red pressure-marks on the bridge of his nose.

Pretty soon he was sleeping in the library on a narrow camp bed so that he could start in on another book as soon as he woke up. It was a pity he could only live books he had already read. He tried a Gothic novel once to see what it was like – *Frankenstein* was supposed to be tolerable, wasn't it? – and found it was no use. Nothing happened. No matter. As the doctor had said, he had read all the books he wanted to read and some of them were worth reading several times over.

He woke one morning in the library with his face cold and his back tender. He would have to do something about getting a decent bed down here. Sometime. Maybe.

The only decision he made that morning, apart from the decision to piss in a corner instead of in a toilet, was to close the library permanently. What good was an open library if none of the ungrateful bastards came any more? Screw them. He scrawled a sign saying 'Closed For Good' on a piece of scrap card and tacked it to the door. He turned the key and put it in one of the desk drawers. There.

All that remained was to choose the book of the day and get stuck in. He decided to try for *Robinson Crusoe* as he felt like a little sun, sand and sea air, man back to nature, that sort of thing. He made his way to the D section, recalling how this was where it had all begun. Since his encounter with Magwitch, he had been back to read *Great Expectations* all the way through, right to its eloquent and bittersweet ending. He selected Defoe and relaxed, concentrating as hard as he needed, not too hard.

He was in a forest. There was a leopard, a lion and a she-wolf, and then he met a great poet whom he was to follow as the evening thickened.

This was not *Robinson Crusoe*. The librarian was not unduly worried. The library had chosen something else. So what?

A city. And there was weeping here, so much pain it filled the air like a colour in the sky, red or purple. The air was electric, thunderous, crackling with the cries and the wails. He was being led somewhere. Downwards. Into circles.

He knew this place.

The promiscuous. He belonged there, all right, but they were going further down and all he wanted to do was to return to the daylight, bask in it just one more time, but the air was black now and the crowds all around were vague, tortured outlines.

He knew this place.

The gluttons. He belonged there too, but the descent continued, his guide – Virgil – explaining and cautioning in an elegant, poetic tongue as they trod spiral paths. The librarian began to choke on the air and it tasted of sin and stank of putrefaction.

Virgil said, 'Here,' only that wasn't in the book. Strange.

The sullen. The librarian's feet would not move and looking down he saw he was knee-deep in slime and the slime was rising. No, it wasn't rising, he was sinking and it was up to his thighs. Around him the surface heaved and bubbled. There were faces straining to stay above it, hands breaking free now and then to claw in supplication before being dragged under again.

The slime was at his crotch.

He belonged here. Yes, he could admit that. He deserved this for ever.

But he did wish he had finished reading Dante.

The library was empty and quiet. On the door hung a sign, letters scrawled on scrap card:

Situation Vacant
Apply Within

The

Rain

Man

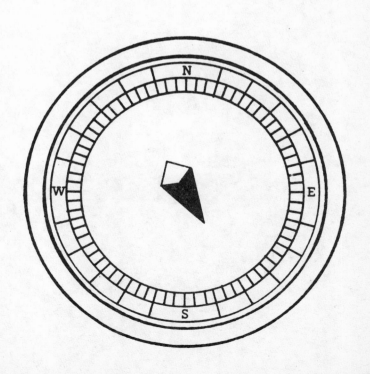

Hey, you. Got any spare change? No? Got a minute, then? Let me tell you about the Rain Man.

No, wait, hear me out. I've got all the time in the world, haven't you? I wasn't always a stopper, you know, although I've stopped here now and I quite like it. I once had a good job. I worked hard. In the kitchens, yeah. I was a chef and a damn good one too. Head chef. People used to come into the kitchens after the meal sometimes and they'd thank me like I'd worked a miracle or something. It's very confusing if you do your job well and people come in and act like you're the new messiah or whatever. Food of the gods, they'd say. Manna from heaven.

Well, I began believing my press, so to speak. I began to think there was more to it than a thousand and one things to do with fish, maybe God had smiled on me and said, 'Thou art the best thing in cooking since sliced bread and thou shalt cook the most divine meals ever.' I was on a mission from God.

There was this man used to hang around the kitchens every so often, asking for food, left-overs, bit like I do now, so it's a sort of poetic justice, isn't it? Because I treated him like dirt and told him to piss off and take all the crusts he could and never come back, only he did come back every so often and I sent him packing each time with enough food for a bird to survive on . . . just. He was an odd-looking sort, bony, bent, old floppy hat, and always so sad, a big runny nose and big bags under his eyes, like he was about to cry any minute.

One time he came back and he had a bag under his coat. I had gone out the back to throw out some rubbish and the seagulls were hovering overhead waiting and the flies were pretty bad because it was a warm day after a wet night, and he came up and showed me the bag.

'Special fish,' he said, and I've only heard that sort of excitement in children's voices when they're about to get a present. You know, 'Pleeeease, pleeeease.'

'What's so special about it?' I asked. I was thinking about chicken Parisienne, wine sauce, melons from the greenhouses ripe to perfection, so ripe they crushed cool on your tongue, I was thinking about anything except this moron's special fish.

'Tastes like heaven,' he beamed, 'and it's all yours. To thank you for being kind to me.'

'But I haven't . . . ' I began, then decided I hadn't anything to lose so I took the bag from him and gave him the sack of rubbish to sort through. Fair exchange, no robbery.

'Take what you want,' I said, feeling generous. The seagulls were dead pissed off.

I left him and went back into the kitchen and laid those fish out on a slab and they were like no other fish I'd seen in my life. I don't want to know where he got them from. There were two of them and they were bright orange and they were fish-shaped, and after that any resemblance to fish was purely coincidental. They had bits sticking out here and bits sticking out there, stalks and fins with no obvious purpose, as if nature had had a laughing fit the day she threw them together or else she'd been playing Pin the Tail on the Donkey blindfold thirty times on each fish and missed every time.

I set to work with my gutting-knife and took off all the bits until I had a small pile of them and I thought they would make a nice garnish, then I slit both fish open, and guess what? No guts, no organs, no stomach, nothing. Just white flesh and even raw that flesh looked delicious. It was so white it glowed.

What's this got to do with the Rain Man? Everything and nothing. Let me tell you about me before I tell you about him, OK?

It was getting near rush hour and I had to decide what I was going to do with Mr and Mrs Fish. You ever been in the kitchens? Let me tell you about it. The rush hour starts just before dinnertime. There's steam everywhere, the ovens are blazing so hot they singe your eyebrows if you stand too near, cauldrons of food all come to the boil at once. The entire kitchen is a seething mass of cooks running backwards and forwards like crazy to get things done, because it's the most important people on the boat eating out there – they're the only ones who can afford that kind of food, unless the Captain's treating some of the less well-off at his table and when was the last time that happened? – and they're eating what we make for them. That's power, I can tell you. In the kitchens we get into this state of panic because it's the only way we can operate. Four hours pass like four minutes.

I was getting wound up to it myself and I was desperate to serve up these fish, since I'd never seen anything like them and I was sure no one had ever eaten anything like them. I went for grilling them lightly, butter on one side (they still have a mountain of butter down in the stores) and maybe chestnut sauce. I had some chestnut sauce left over somewhere.

Sorry. Thinking about food like that makes me come over all funny.

I sliced Mr and Mrs Fish finer than fine so that as many people as possible could get a taste and I grilled the slices lightly. They went this brown-gold colour that made my saliva spit into my mouth just looking at it. I was tempted to try a piece then and there, but that selfsame moment the two Portuguese who work there got into an argument about whose turn it was to stir the soup. They speak perfectly good English but they pretend not to because they're a lazy, shiftless lot. If you ask them to do something, it's, 'Don' unnerstan', don' unnerstan'.'

And then the diners started filing into the dining-hall and I didn't have the leisure as all the junior chefs were asking me questions at the same time.

'Should I take the parsnips off now?'

'Do we want aubergines in the ratatouille?'

'The chicken's nearly ready!'

'No salt, no salt!'

'We've got courgettes instead of aubergines.'

'Chicken's ready!'

'Have you written the menu yet?'

'Actually, I don't like aubergines myself.'

'Chicken's burning!'

I really believe they couldn't take a dump unless I told them just where to do it, how to take their trousers down, how to sit, don't make too much noise.

I called the fish 'Poisson spécialité de bateau' on the menu. Everything sounds better in French, don't you think? I keep a pocket French dictionary in the kitchens for just that purpose. I can make dogshit sound like a new brand of caviar.

Twenty-three portions I made. Every one was ordered. I suppose people like a surprise. They certainly got one.

How was I to know it was lethal? I mean, take the puffer fish, that's in my recipe book as a delicacy, only it's got to be prepared exactly right or it'll kill you dead. I don't know if there was a correct way of preparing Mr and Mrs Fish, but if there was, I hadn't found it. I sometimes wonder why I never tried it myself. I wouldn't be here talking at you if I had, and maybe I'd be better off.

I'll give you some idea of how lethal that fish was. One of the waiters nicked a tiny piece off one of the dishes as he took it into the dining-hall, a piece no bigger than a coin. He came back in and told a junior chef how it tasted amazing, slightly scented and it sort of crumbled in your mouth. Nectar, he called it. We found him out the back three hours later, his face black and swollen like he'd been hit a hundred times and blood all down his shirtfront and the legs of his trousers. Just crawled out back, lay down and died. The seagulls had started in on him already.

The Captain sent me his compliments. He didn't have the fish himself because he doesn't eat fish. Isn't that peculiar – a ship's captain who can't eat fish? But so many people had said how wonderful it was that he sent his compliments, told me to come out so's he could congratulate me personally. Well, I went out and they all clapped and I felt better than a miracle-worker, I felt like *God*.

And three hours later twenty-three of those people who'd clapped me turned black and died. It started towards the end of the meal. A couple said they weren't feeling well. A woman fainted. Dr Chamberlain was called, which was about as much use as calling an arsonist to put out a fire. He said something about swollen glands, not much he could do, but he would prescribe some pills if they came to see him in the morning.

I knew something was wrong and it was something to do with Mr and Mrs Fish and I was scared, dead scared. Going out back and finding that waiter, that nearly blew my head. I went from being God to being a murderer in the space of a few hours. The juniors, they didn't know what had happened, but they knew something had gone wrong and they thought I'd done it on purpose, put rat-poison on the fish or something, and the way they looked at me, I couldn't stand it! Even the Portuguese! They looked at me like I was a mad animal, slobbering and growling, and in the interests of public safety I should be kicked and shot dead.

Well, I saved them the trouble. I put on my coat and I got out of there. I'd been up at the top, right up, so the only way left to go was down. I spent that first night huddled up on Z deck or even lower, if you can get lower than Z deck, just crying and shivering and too scared to show my face in case anyone saw me and said, 'Hey! There's that psycho chef who murdered twenty-four people!' Crazy, of course, because no one on the lower decks gives a toss what happens on the upper decks. A few of them die, so what? It's the same the other way round too. But I didn't know that then, so I wandered from place to place down here, crawling over rubbish-tips by day, sleeping under walkways by night. It always rains down here and it's always dark, you noticed that? Don't see how you can't notice.

I wasn't too good at getting food, though, and I was on my way to starving to death when I met Money. Yeah, that was his name, Money. He hadn't got any, of course. It was a joke. I think. He'd wink and say, 'I'm called Money so that if I'm raped, the guy who rapes me can say he's come into Money,' and he'd wheeze like mad because that was how he laughed. Wheeze, wheeze. He wore about six layers of clothing, you know, vest, shirt, another shirt, jumper, cardigan, this great big coat, and he never took any of them off. I hated to think what he might have growing under his armpits. Me, I tried to wash now and again, but you tell me where a stopper can take a bath. I usually waited for a rain-storm, then I'd strip off and run out starkers and dance around freezing my nuts but getting clean. Well, less dirty. Don't do that so much nowadays.

Money found me when I was on the point of jumping off the side of the ship, or on the point of thinking about jumping off the side of the ship. I'm a coward, really. If I'd had any guts, I'd have jumped overboard when all those twenty-four people turned black and started spewing blood. That would have been the decent thing to do but I had too much self-respect then and not enough later. Either way, I would never have got round to topping myself. I'd simply have sat and starved, waiting for my bowels to pack up and all sorts of gross diseases to set in.

Money sat down beside me and offered me his bottle. God knows what it was, though I can tell you now, that rumour about us drinking distilled engine-oil, that's all crap. We would if we could figure out how to distil it, but as it is, we make do with what we can steal from the stores or beg from passers-by. Like yourself. You sure you've nothing to drink on you? Ah well, never mind.

I pulled on that bottle like it was my mother's tit and he had to grab it off me, else I'd have drained it.

'Gimme that!' he said. 'Do a man a favour and he'll take another ten. I'm Money. Pleased to meet you. You're new to the stopping game, aren't you?'

'How'd you tell?'

'Clean. You don't smell enough. And your clothes are still white. Hey, were you a doctor?'

'Chef.'

'Chef! Wild! Not much chefing to do round here, is there?'

I had to smile. The man was as crazy as a cage full of lobsters.

'Not a lot. Pleased to meet you too.'

We sat together for a bit in silence and finished off the bottle. I tell you, that booze was the finest thing I'd ever drunk. Mind you, I threw up half an hour later, but you tend to do that on an empty stomach.

'Need something to eat?' Money asked, as if he couldn't tell.

'Ten steaks would go down fine.'

'And when was the last time you saw a steak, eh?'

I forget that a lot of the recipes in my book you just can't make on the *Hope* any more. We ran out of red meat years ago, though the fishery will keep us going for ever, I think.

'Never mind. Anything. I'd eat anything. I'd eat my own crap if I could do any.'

'Got you. Can you walk?'

'If there's food at the end, I could run all the way.'

'Good man. Come with me.'

Money took me up to this place he called Bart's. It's a shop, kind of pawnbroker, only it was shut so we had to bang on the door for ages until this guy Bart came out. Crabby old sod on crutches but he's got a heart of gold somewhere inside, so rumour has it.

'Money, Money!' he yelled. 'Long time. Got anything for me?'

'Let's get this straight, legless. You owe me a favour, right? All I want is dinner for me and the Chef here.'

Bart looked confused, as if it was impossible he could owe anyone a favour, but he signalled for us to come in. He can't go very fast. You have to shuffle to follow him, otherwise it would look rude.

The shop's full of junk, all covered in dust, things I can't see why people brought on board – dolls with cracked faces, ludicrous teapots like Arabian castles, some books probably lifted from the library, a wind-up tin monkey, an ugly statue of an ugly cat, a bowl of wax-fruit. But Bart knows what's valuable, what sells, what the upper deck people want when they've got too much money. He goes up once a month, sets up a stall and cleans up. He hardly ever comes back with anything except a pocketful of profit.

Anyway, he took us round the counter, his crutches thumping on the floor, and we went into a back room. He'd laid out dinner for one and asked me if I'd fetch another couple of plates from a cupboard. While I did, he and Money talked. Bart still couldn't believe he owed anything but Money convinced him. Something about stored-up credit. I think Bart had given way already since I was getting the plates out, wasn't I? Finally he said to me: 'So you're a chef, right? OK, cook us a meal.'

And he pointed me to a cupboard full of tins, all kinds of stuff, and I got to work on a two-ring gas stove. You can imagine this was all a bit of a come-down for me, God's chef, but I liked Money and Bart wasn't such a bad sort either and I desperately wanted to be accepted.

Not boasting, but I did a pretty fine job, all things considered. Frankfurters can be edible if you smother them in enough hot sauce. Bart belched when he had finished and that was a compliment, although not as fine as a standing ovation from a dining-hall full of gentlepeople, some of whom were clapping while poison *'poisson'* worked its way into their bloodstreams and their glands.

Bart said he was a public servant like I'd been, that it was his duty to make a living from the better-off. Money argued there was nothing degrading in begging, it was just another way of taking money from those who had too much.

'Begging, pfah!' spat Bart. 'Let me tell you about begging. It's laziness, sheer laziness. Man was meant to work for his living, earn his way, share out the money so that we can all eat and enjoy things. You stoppers,' – and at the time I was embarrassed to be included in this – 'you sit on your arses all day and get drunk and ask for money. Where's the skill, the thrill, the hard work in that?'

'We don't ask to be stoppers,' said Money, 'but if we are, we make the best of it.'

'Hah! Birdshit!' exclaimed Bart. 'I'll tell you, if I was running this ship, I'd have the lot of you castrated and put to work in the engine-room.' But he was grinning. 'Come on, Chef. What brought you so low?'

I told them my story. By the end, tears of laughter were running down their cheeks.

'It's not that funny,' I complained, trying not to laugh too.

'Twenty-three!' guffawed Bart.

'And a waiter!' wheezed Money.

'You've got to laugh!' said Bart. 'I mean, I only rip them off. You manage to kill them!' He couldn't stop laughing and

Money couldn't stop wheezing. They kept going until a deep rumble of thunder made them jump.

'Heh, the engines have finally blown,' said Bart in a low tone.

'What?' I said.

'It's only thunder, Bart.'

'One day it won't be,' growled Bart in his best doom-laden voice. He struggled up to his feet, wedging a crutch beneath each arm, and shambled into the shop and up to its window, which was a sheet of clear polythene with the shop's name stuck on in paper letters. 'Looks like rain, eh?'

Money and I joined him as the first heavy drops thudded against the plastic, gathering speed, more and more, drumming down until it was a continuous sound. I thought about stripping off and taking a shower but the others would laugh at me.

'Night for the Rain Man,' muttered Bart.

'Oh, come on,' I said, 'that's just a story to frighten children to sleep.'

'I know,' he said, looking out through the streaming window at the blurred deck.

We spent the night on the floor of the shop with the rain hissing down outside. Suffering from a full stomach and the effects of Money's booze (most of which, as I said, had ended up splashed over the deck), I slept the sleep of the just. When morning came we thanked Bart and left. In theory, the rain had stopped, but it dripped from the upper decks in broken streams almost as much as it had poured down during the night. We were soaked by the time we found some sort of shelter, a narrow alley covered over with a tarpaulin Money said he stole from a lifeboat on the outer rim. I still find the idea funny – somewhere there's a lifeboat so full of rainwater that, if anyone uses it, it'll sink like a stone. This alley was a regular stopper haunt. There were about ten of them – of us – huddling there. I was glad when the rain stopped for good and we could get out. When nine or ten stoppers are gathered together, believe me, you breathe through your mouth and you don't stay long.

Sit down, you must be tired standing there. I won't keep

you. Going somewhere? Right, so what have you got to lose? Time? There's plenty of *that*.

Over the weeks, Money taught me everything he knew about survival, which was a lot. I learnt how to catch and kill seagulls, and that's not easy. If you've seen one close up, you'll know they're big buggers, wingspan as broad as you are tall, and vicious to boot. What you do is you lay out a trail of rubbish, good stuff, crusts and rinds and what have you. One gull will always follow this trail to the bitter end, which is you, hiding round a corner with a chair-leg or stick of some sort. Then, you bash it – *Wham!* – and you keep bashing it until it stops trying to peck your hand off. Money says bashing it tenderises the meat, but seagulls still taste like shit and even I can't improve that.

I also learnt how to steal from the stores, which is dead easy if you're thin (and show me the stopper who isn't). There are vents leading round the back of the stores where the air from the refrigerators is pumped out. You crawl along these until you get to a grating the size of an upper deck porthole and you can lift that grating off and squeeze through. Those stores are big and there are about three hundred of them all over the *Hope*, but they're careful about checking the food stocks. So there's an unwritten rule in stopper law that says take only what you need for that day and don't go too often. If someone took too much or was caught, they'd find those gratings and close them up faster than you can blink, and we'd be lost then. You won't tell anyone I told you this, will you? I thought you didn't look the type.

Money also taught me how to beg, but he said (and it's true) that this is an inefficient way to live. You're not allowed on the upper decks. The crew beat you up if they find you, maybe kill you. So you stick to the lower decks and there's precious little spare change around here, is there? Look, are you sure you've checked your pockets? Well, there's no harm in asking.

Once, I went up to the kitchens to see how the boys were getting on without me. One of the juniors, a snotty-faced little twerp who couldn't manage bacon and eggs, they'd made him head chef, and he came out the back and saw me hanging around and told me in no uncertain terms to depart. He didn't recognise me! Isn't that great? I didn't mind. I was quite growing to like my life, sitting around the deck with my back against a wall, feeling like part of the ship, get? Well, it's a life, isn't it? I sit and watch the world go by. There are some pretty interesting sorts on the ship. You must have seen that woman in the red plastic raincoat. Actually, man I used to know, called Foster, said he'd screwed her, but I don't believe him. She used to pass us by quite a lot and I always thought she had a kind of . . . nobility about her and that getting screwed by anyone was the last thing on her mind. Money used to say to me how she hadn't a hope. Three kids to feed and no cash and she combs the tips every day and isn't very good at it. She won't last.

All right, all right, I'll tell you about the Rain Man. It's not as if my life story's not interesting by itself, but the Rain Man has something to do with it.

It was pissing down again one night, like when we were at Bart's, only this time we were under that tarpaulin with a couple of others, all snuggling up to one another, not because we were keen on each other or anything but because it's the only way to survive the night. Shared bodily warmth. Money repeated Bart's remark about it being a night for the you-know-who and one of the others, Foster, the one I mentioned earlier who said he'd screwed the woman in the red raincoat, he had a glass eye, different colour from his real one, and I think only pretended to be a stopper because he thought it was cool, and he'd spent most of the night telling us about the women he'd laid, he said: 'Story has it that the Rain Man is looking for his soul.'

Well, I mean, it's for kids, isn't it? I asked Foster if he'd ever seen the Rain Man.

'Um, no . . . not exactly. But I know a man who has, and he said when it's pouring the Rain Man wanders along every deck on the ship trying to find his soul, which was taken from him by the Captain.'

'Well,' I said, proud to get on to my own area of expertise, 'I've met the Captain and I don't think he could take anyone's soul. Or their sole!' And I laughed, only none of them got it because none of them knew like I did that the Captain doesn't eat fish.

'I don't mean literally,' said Foster impatiently, probably thinking I was the biggest peckerhead he'd ever met.

'Shut up and go to sleep,' growled Money. And we tried.

I was actually in the process of nodding off, my ears ringing with the din of the rain, when I felt Money get up and saw him kneel beneath the end of the tarpaulin to take a leak. As I watched, he stopped fumbling with his flies and his body went all sort of rigid, as if he'd found something alive in his underwear, but he wasn't looking down any more, he was looking out along the deck into the rain. Then he shuffled back and shook me.

'Chef! Chef! Come and look!'

I crawled over on all fours wishing I could be allowed just one minute's good dreaming and Foster came too and the other man and we looked.

'It's him!' hissed Money.

I couldn't see a thing at first, only sheets of rain falling, dripping, spattering, then the rain took shape, a man's shape, a man in a long coat walking slowly towards us, taking each step carefully like he didn't want to slip and fall. His head was turning all round, like this, you know, left and right and up and down, as he walked.

'Looking for his soul,' whispered Foster.

'Shut up!' said Money.

The Rain Man got nearer and nearer and I tried to make out his face under the brim of his wide hat. It was mostly in shadow but he had a big nose, that I could tell. It was strange, I tell you, but the rain didn't seem to bounce off him. It sort of went through him, but that's not right . . . He wasn't a shape in the rain, he *was* the rain. He carved his outline from raindrops, it swept into his body and became him, and he was fluid, no more, a walking waterfall shaped like a man.

Yes, go on, laugh. I would.

The Rain Man walked right by us but still I didn't get to see his face. I swear as he went by each step went sploosh, sploosh, the sound you make when you walk through a deep puddle, and water cascaded away from his feet and left miniature tidal waves behind instead of footprints.

'Christ! Let's see where he goes,' said Money.

'Are you mad?' said Foster.

'Well, what harm can he do us? He's all water.'

'About time you took a bath, Money,' I said.

The other guy thought it wasn't such a good idea and said he'd stay behind to guard the shelter, like someone was going to attack it, I ask you! Actually, I didn't think staying behind was that bad an idea because although I took Money's point about the Rain Man not being able to do any harm I didn't really believe it, not in my bones. Don't think Money did either, but that's the kind of guy he was.

We came out and the rain drenched our hair and was pouring into our eyes before we'd gone two steps, so much you had to squint,. and I thought we'd lost the Rain Man but Money yelled, 'This way!' and me and Foster took off after him.

It was hard to stand up, let alone walk straight, with the walkways slippery beneath you and the stairs treacherous. We were headed downwards, see? Water trickles downwards and so did the Rain Man, going down staircase after staircase to the lowest of the lower decks. And I don't think I'd ever seen so much rain and it seemed like all the rich bastards upstairs were emptying buckets from half a mile up and laughing as the water picked up speed to come splashing down on our miserable heads. We nearly lost sight of Money but suddenly he stopped and just beyond him I could see the Rain Man had stopped too. We were right at the bottom of the *Hope*, up to our ankles in water, which was collecting too quickly for the bilges to pump it out straight away.

Now, as Foster and me got close, we saw Money go up to the Rain Man and something in me wanted to scream, 'Don't touch him! Don't touch him!' but I didn't know why and I don't think Money would have heard me anyway. It was like he was hypnotised, like he just had to tap that Rain Man on the shoulder and ask him who he was and what he was looking for if it was the last thing he did.

Which it was. Money put out his hand and the tips of his

fingers sank into the Rain Man's back and water splashed out, as it does when you stick your hand under a tap. This spray of water came out into Money's face and he jerked back, squinching his eyes shut. When he opened them again, tears came flooding out but his eyeballs were gone and his eyes were only sockets.

Money opened his mouth and water flooded out of that too, a great gush, his head emptying out, and it was coming out of his shirtcuffs and over his waistband and from the bottoms of his trouser-legs. His clothes were shrinking inwards and his shape just kind of . . . deflated, see? His head wrinkled in. All this water coming out, it was *him*.

In about a minute, his clothes sagged to the floor. They were dark wet, a heap of six layers of clothes, empty, floating apart. That's all that was left of Money.

I know he doesn't count for much in the big picture, but Money was my friend, perhaps my only friend, and I know he was only a scummy parasite stopper to most people but that didn't matter to me. And I stood there in shock and felt tears coming down my face, hot in the cold rain.

Excuse me.

The Rain Man walked his slippery walk around a corner and I was too shocked to follow but Foster went after him. I think he wanted to see the Rain Man's face almost as much as I did.

Eventually I got my act together and gathered up some of Money's clothes for myself (I think that's what he would have wanted). Of course, only his outer clothes. I didn't really trust his shirt or vest. I stuck these under my arm and tried not to think about the water squeezing out of them. I followed after Foster. Round the corner, and I couldn't see anything, except something small bumped against my boot and then I spotted another bunch of clothing and then I looked down at my feet and there bobbing in the water was Foster's glass eye.

I picked it up and pocketed it, expecting Bart might give me a good rate for it.

The Rain Man was waiting for me at the end of the walkway, not looking for me but standing there with his back towards me in this hunched position that said, 'Come on, come and get me.' I went up close but not close enough to touch him because I wasn't that stupid. The water was up to my shins.

'Face me,' I shouted over the rattle of the rain. 'Let me see your face.'

He didn't say a thing but he began to turn round nice and slowly to stop himself from falling over. When I saw his face, a giant key clicked into place inside my head.

The Rain Man was the man who'd given me the fish all those months before. I didn't know what to say or do. I didn't have the right to scream vengeance at him, because I hadn't exactly treated him like royalty when he came to the kitchens for scraps, and I certainly wasn't about to beat him up. So I stood there with the rain falling into my eyes and mouth.

The Rain Man smiled. His eyes were bloodshot as if he had been crying for years on end and the bags beneath them were flowing out tears. His skin was kind of runnelled with lines eroded into it, down his cheeks, nose, the backs of his hands, so he seemed old and ill. And in his smiling mouth I saw nothing but water streaming from roof to tongue, one continuous stream like a curtain.

He held out his hands to me, water filling the cups of his palms.

Then he dissolved, just like that, a rush of water falling splash, sending a wave to break against my shins, ice cold and lonely. Even his clothes. Nothing left, except the water in the bottom of the ship and he was part of that now, to be sucked out by the bilges and pumped into the sea and then to be breathed up by the sun and become cloud and wait for the next storm, the next rainfall, when he could come down and take shape and live for a while and belong, until another rainstorm washed him away.

I envy him that. Belonging.

Sorry to have taken up so much of your time, but I like to tell people about the Rain Man. It's like I *have* to tell someone and every time I do, I feel a little better. But I'll never be completely well.

See you again sometime, maybe?

Goodbye.

Carnal

Appetite

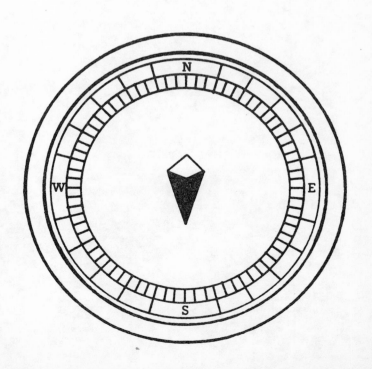

Eddy and Diane were something of an item. In fact, in the eyes of their peer group, they were as good as married. They had been going out for seven months, three weeks and two days.

Ask Diane and she will tell you it was love at first sight. She went down to the Neptune's Trident one night to escape from her parents and there was this barman; gorgeous-looking guy. That instant she knew they were destined for each other. She sat at the bar all night and he chatted with her between customers. By the end of the evening, she was his, body and soul.

Ask Eddy and he will tell you about a horny-looking girl who came down one night and just hung around and hung around, kept ordering drinks and talking to him. He was just being polite but it was clear she was meat for cutting, you know what I mean? After closing time, he took her back to his cabin. You can guess the rest. Tell you one thing. Damn cherry, man!

Diane moved in with Eddy a week later, leaving behind her mattress in the corner of her parents' cabin and her screaming baby sister and a view of the ocean (at least, if you stood on tiptoe outside the cabin, you could see a vertical grey line that was probably the ocean). They had been together since.

She did not have a job, but Eddy made enough to get them by. Days, she would wander the decks, cadging stuff if she could, being really nice to the stoppers, going any-where except up to her parents'. Nights, she would sit in the cabin doing nothing, waiting for Eddy to come home. You might wonder what she thought about as she sat there in the semi- darkness, squatting on the bed, brooding and alone. Perhaps she was simply praying Eddy would come back alive. He got into scraps now and then, went to the pool with Riot, and he also hit customers who asked for credit or jerked his chain in any way. Perhaps she was scared he might end up in someone else's bed, that slag Gilette's most likely. Now, Eddy was pretty faithful – as faithful as you could expect – but he did not like Diane to sit in the Trident all evening. Cramped his style, he said. He meant as a barman, naturally. She went in for a drink now and again, just before closing time, and that was OK, but mostly she sat in that cabin and waited. You might think she went a little crazy doing that.

One evening Eddy came in a bit late but when Diane asked him where he had been, he said he had stayed behind for a drink with Riot and a few of the boys, planning.

'Not another fight,' she complained.

'You just keep it to yourself. I'm not meant to tell you anything and anyway it may never happen, but Riot says Lock and his boys, they've been pissing us off good and proper. Happens again, we stomp on them.' He pulled off his T-shirt, which had sweat-stains down the front and under the armpits, went to the basin and began sluicing water over his back and face.

'I'm scared about you, that's all. I don't want to be left alone. Eddy, I can't think of life without you, don't you see that?'

'And I can't think of life without you, baby,' Eddy said, through a burble of water.

Diane undressed. She had been wearing knickers and one of his shirts, the one with 'ALL A MAN NEEDS IS SIX INCHES OF STEEL AND SIX INCHES OF PORK' written on it in fabric paint. She slipped under the blanket, still slightly coy about her body even after all this time, all this intimacy, this knowing each other inside out.

'I'm sorry,' she said, 'I shouldn't have complained, but I'm glad you told me. We shouldn't have secrets, don't you think?'

'No,' he replied, rubbing his face with a towel, 'no secrets.'

He stripped off, removing his flick-knife from his back pocket and placing it by the bed within easy reach, and got in beside her. She snuggled close and, after kissing him, traced with her finger the line of a knife-scar he received in a scrap three years ago. It ran from his nipple to the middle of his stomach.

'Tell me again how you got this, Eddy.'

'Scrap. Defending a girlfriend. Four guys wanted her and I wasn't going to let them touch her. Took them, all four.'

'Was she pretty?'

'Not as pretty as you, darling.'

She touched the scar again.

'Did it hurt?'

'A bit.'

'Does it hurt now?'

'No.'

She gazed in adoration at his body.

'Spot, Eddy. Yellowhead.'

'Where?'

'Neck. You wash properly?'

'Course.'

'Want me to pop it?'

'OK.'

'I love you, Eddy.'

'I love you too, Diane.'

Eddy left early the next morning, some 'stuff' needing attention. The scraps frightened Diane. It wasn't good. Fighting didn't get anyone anywhere, especially if Eddy got stabbed or killed even though everyone said he was the best fighter. He had been kind of preoccupied last night, like he was thinking of something else. The sex wasn't bad or anything, it was always good, but she liked to talk during and after and he had not been in the mood. Told her to shut up and go to sleep. Poor Eddy, he must have had a tiring day. But she loved him all the more for his weaknesses: the preoccupation, the fighting, the bad moods. In spite of them, because of them, he needed her, he really did.

Diane turned over in bed and stuck her hand beneath the mattress, groping around until she found a tin box that had once contained her father's tobacco. The smell of the box reminded her of the cramped confinement of her parents' cabin. Through the haze of cloying smoke, while she was sitting in the corner trying to think of nothing, would come her mother's voice: 'Why don't you go out and do something, Dido darling?'

It meant that her parents wanted to do sex but that awful name, as affectionate as a gunshot, was enough on its own to get Diane out. She had tried to get interested in reading books, something to while away the time, but the creepy man in the library put her off right away. It was as if his thick glasses could see through her clothes and he was examining her tits, wondering what she was like in bed, dying to get his sweaty little fingers on her. So there was nothing for it but to wander the deck aimlessly for hours until the boredom got too intense and staring at things trying to appear fascinated got too difficult. It was different when you had someone as fantastic as Eddy to come back home to. When you only had tobacco-smoke and parents and, later, a screaming baby sister with smeggy nappies, every minute spent wandering was both relief and torture and when you got back in, waiting for you there was only a curt, 'And where have you been?'

The night she met Eddy at the Trident was the first time she had gone downstairs on her own after dark, suspecting that either she would meet someone and fall in love or else she would be raped and killed. Eddy was about the first man she looked at and it was perfect – love at first sight. She didn't know much about attracting men but she just kept talking to him and getting a bit tipsy and they went back to his cabin. Of course, she hadn't slept with anyone else before or after.

Her parents didn't make leaving their cabin easy. They didn't like feeling old or losing part of their power, even though they had the baby now to fuss over, mould in their own image, instil with guilt from the earliest possible moment – Christ, little Annie must have felt guilty the second she was conceived!

Through the veil of smoke, her mother said: 'You'll regret it, Dido. You need us.'

Her father said: 'And where do you think *you're* going?'

Her mother said: 'This is no way to treat us.'

Her father said: 'You're behaving like a spoilt little child.'

Her mother said: 'Aren't you interested in us any more? Don't you care about us?'

Her father said: 'Don't come crying to us when you need help, that's all.'

Moving in with Eddy was the best decision she had ever made.

The tobacco tin had a lion on the lid. She opened it, swinging the lion out of sight. Inside were the clippings of Eddy's fingernails and toenails, scaly and brown. She had one hundred and thirty-seven of them.

He was a bit of a slob, just cut his nails and left the clippings all over the floor, so when he was out she picked them up and put them in the tin carefully, lovingly. They were a little bit of him belonging to her and her alone. She had another tin somewhere with a collection of his body hairs.

Out of the tin in her hands she took a nail and held it between thumb and forefinger as daintily as a lady with a bone china teacup. She popped it between her lips and chewed.

Eddy was gone all day. Diane moped around, washed a few of his shirts, made the bed, went for a walk, tidied up the cabin, sat and stared at the wall, slept fitfully, watched the light going from dim to black through the porthole, saw the service-light go on, ate some tinned ham, washed herself, climbed into bed, waited.

He came back almost immediately after closing time, for which she was grateful. No council of war this evening. He told her about a girlfriend of Push's who they were having this big thing against, nobody allowed to talk to the deadhead, wasn't that funny? Actually, it wasn't so funny later on because she scratched his face and she might have blinded him, the doctor can't tell. Crazy deadhead bitch.

They did sex and during it she asked him to bite her. He did and she asked him to bite her harder, and then harder, until he broke the skin and she orgasmed with the exquisite agony. Afterwards, she examined the tear in her shoulder, a crescent of broken flesh weeping blood. She asked him to lick it better. Soon the bleeding stopped. The wound ached and throbbed but she didn't mind. She thought it looked like a smile, only upside down.

As the world grew fuzzy with sleep she kissed him, probing his mouth with her tongue and tasting her own sweet blood on his teeth.

'I love you, Eddy.'

'I love you too, Diane.'

Sometimes it scared her that she loved Eddy so much, maybe too much, for she had seen other girls ditched and broken-hearted. They let their hair go. They let their make-up run (when they could be bothered to put any on). They had red eyes. They went around saying it was all right, don't worry about them. They did stupid things like have screaming fits and throw themselves at their exes. They were prepared to sacrifice their last shred of dignity for men who didn't care about them. It was just as well Eddy loved her back. He always said, 'I love you too,' as if he meant it, although she had heard that men were notorious liars. They weren't even very good at lying but they did it all the same, as if they were content not to fool anyone but themselves.

She was lucky to have Eddy, if only for the nights, when he was all hers, all of him except his mind. She had his heart but she could never know his mind.

Lying awake, the porthole a glowing circle in the dark, hearing the occasional passer-by clang along the walkway, she asked: 'Eddy, what are you thinking?'

He woke up.

'Huh?'

'What are you thinking?'

'Nothing. I was asleep. Why aren't you?'

'Can't. I keep thinking about you, how I love you, that kind of thing.'

'Well, don't wake me up just to tell me that, will you?'

'But what do you think – about me, about us, when you lie awake, after we've done sex?'

'You don't *do* sex, darling, you have it, you have it.'

'Well?'

'Well, what?'

'What do you think?' Was he playing games with her?

'I don't know,' he said turning over on to his back with a sigh. 'I suppose I think how happy I am . . . with you . . . you know. I think about . . . things. The Trident, the gang, how we're going to come down on Lock, if it comes to it. Usual sort of stuff.'

She was silent for a minute.

'What do you think about me?' she asked.

'For Christ's sake, why do you have to keep asking?'

'Because I have to know!'

'You don't *have* to know. Can't you just accept things? Can't you trust me?'

'I do trust you.'

'Then shut up and go to sleep.'

She slid out of bed and walked across the cabin, shivering and naked.

'What now?'

'I want a drink of water, OK?'

She ran the tap and filled a mug. On her way back, she stopped and knelt down on Eddy's side of the bed. His breathing was heavy and slow. She picked up his flick-knife, walked round to her side and sat on the edge with her back to him. Wedging the mug between her legs, she pressed the stud on the knife and the blade arced out in a sudden flash of silver. She laid her left arm out on her lap, exposing the pale flesh of the underside of her forearm.

'What you doing?' asked Eddy, his voice muffled by the pillow.

'Nothing. Just sitting.'

She tensed herself and drew the blade across her skin. Eddy kept it so sharp. She hissed in a breath through her teeth. Her skin parted and a dark rivulet flowed out, dripping on to her thigh. She held her arm over the mug and let the blood trickle into it. It made a tiny plopping sound.

After a couple of minutes, she held the gash up to her mouth and sucked at it until the blood congealed. All the time she was wincing with the pain but she did not let out a cry even though it was worse than the bite on her shoulder.

She wrapped a cloth around her forearm, clasped the knife shut, and stirred the contents of the mug with her finger. Then she drank about half.

'Eddy?'

'Mmph?' This time, he could not conceal his irritation.

'Would you drink this?'

'What is it?'

'Water.'

'No. I don't want any.'

'Please, for me. If you love me.'

He propped himself up on his elbow and leant towards her.

'I'm not thirsty, OK? What's got into you? Stop hassling me and let me sleep.'

'Please. If you love me.'

Eddy deliberated. Perhaps this would be a good time to chuck her. No, he liked the girl, even if she did have some funny ways.

'All right. Give me.'

She handed the mug to him, making sure he had it tight in case it spilled. All she could see of him was the line of his cheek picked out in the light.

'I love you, Eddy.'

'I love you too, Diane. Cheers.'

Morning:

'Where the fuck's my blade? What you done with my fucking blade?'

'Nothing, Eddy. I haven't got it, honest. What would I want with it?'

'I don't know, all kinds of crazy shit. I know you've fucking got it! Give it to me!'

'Don't hit me, Eddy. It won't bring your knife back if you hit me.'

'Yeah, it will. Because you've got it, bitch. Nobody else could have got it.'

'Someone might have come in during the night, what about that?'

'Bullshit!'

Eddy thwacked his arm across the side of her head and she was flung to the bed shrieking. He hit her again as she lay there sobbing, a couple of pounding blows to the small of her back.

'Where am I going to get another, huh? Where? I'm going to magic one up, huh? Bart ain't got none, Push's on the critical, who am I going to ask? Tell me that.'

'I don't know, I don't know.' Racked with tears, pleading.

'Well,' said Eddy, straightening up and making it look like it was the greatest of efforts for him not to thump her again. 'Well. You find my blade before I get back, or I'll beat the living shit out of you. Got that?'

'Yes.'

The cabin door thundered shut. Diane lay crying for a long time.

He came back. Eventually. It was in the small hours and she had been lying awake all evening, every trembling minute spent framing an abject apology and listening out for his footsteps. He flung the door open and before she could open her mouth he said: 'You still here?'

'Eddy, I found your knife. Why didn't you just look for it this morning? I found it under the bed. Why didn't you look for it?'

'Where is it?'

'I'm sorry. I should have looked for it. I'm sorry. Please don't be angry, Eddy.'

'I'm not angry, darling. Where's my blade?'

The way he filled that doorway, it was so . . . impressive. She knew why she loved him so badly.

'Here, Eddy. I love you.'

She held out the knife towards him, the blade open, then brought her left hand up. Calmly, without ceremony, her eyes not leaving his, she hacked off the tips of three fingers.

'Jesus Christ!' breathed Eddy. 'Jesus, Jesus, Jesus . . . '

Diane stared at her abbreviated fingers as if they no longer belonged to her – three stumps of bone cradled in purple meat, leaking blood. Her eyebrows were drawn down, shadowing her eyes. She turned her hand this way and that to examine it. Blood pattered down on to the blanket.

'Jesus, Diane . . .'

She spoke dreamily, revolted and fascinated at the same time.

'It's for you, Eddy. For you.'

Eddy finally pulled himself together. He hurried over, tore a strip off the sheet and wound it around her hand. The three tips were lying on the bed, the skin grey and blotchy. The nails shone with varnish.

'Baby, it's going to be fine. Be calm.'

'Oh, I'm fine, Eddy,' Diane said in that scary, dreamy voice. 'Love doesn't hurt.'

The makeshift bandage was soaked through already.

'Jesus, Diane, what am I meant to do?'

'We should eat the pieces, Eddy.'

'Don't talk like that. That's crazy talk. We should go and see the doctor, that's what we should do. Jesus.'

He had forgotten she still had the knife until he felt the edge of the blade stinging his neck.

'We should eat them, Eddy,' she said and pressed the knife gently so that it nicked his skin.

'Put it away, darling. This is crazy talk. Put it away.'

'Do you love me, Eddy?'

'This is crazy talk, darling.'

The knife pressed deeper. There was a look in her eyes, wild, subtle, fearful. Eddy swallowed hard.

'Do you love me?'

'Of course I do. You know that. I tell you every night.'

'Boys lie, Eddy. I need proof. I need proof that you love me.'

'What do you want me to do?'

'I've already told you.'

'No, but that's crazy bullshit, darling.'

He supposed he might be able to grab the knife off her, twist it out of her hand, but he would have to move quickly. The bitch was deadly.

With the thumb and forefinger of her bandaged hand, she took one of the fingertips and held it up to his mouth.

'You drank me last night, Eddy. I've got the scar to prove it.' She showed him the scabby line down her forearm. 'Now eat me.'

Eddy remembered drinking that water and he thought it had tasted funny, but you couldn't tell with the water on the *Hope*. It always tasted slightly salty. He feared he knew what she had put in it.

'No,' he said.

She pushed the morsel against his lips, which he was compressing shut. He felt a warm trickle down from the knife to the neckline of his T-shirt. Sweat prickled in his hair.

'I'll cut your neck open all the way.'

'I'll have that blade off you in a second flat.' He was mumbling in order to keep his mouth closed.

'Try it.'

Why did he always get the nutcases? She'd seemed OK when they met, normal, bit nervy, but he'd put that down to her being cherry.

'Eat. If you love me.'

The back of his throat felt woollen and as he inhaled through his nose he could smell the nail-varnish.

'Stop this, darling. I love you. I love you. OK?'

Diane jabbed the knife hard. Eddy let out a yelp and she slipped the fingertip in.

Eddy retched and gagged, trying to reach out for Diane. On his tongue the cold pad of the fingertip was smooth and dry, ragged at one end, the nail hard like a beetle's carapace, the blood sickly. It seemed enormous, filling his entire mouth, touching the roof, his teeth, the insides of his cheeks.

Keeping the knife at his neck, she held her palm over his mouth and pinched his nostrils with her finger and thumb. His inhalations became panicky, urgent. A whine came from the back of his throat. Tears were crushed out from under his eyelids.

Still holding his nose, Diane raised her hand and kissed Eddy on the lips.

'I love you, Eddy. Now swallow.'

He spat hard. The fingertip flew out and smacked into her forehead. Her eyes swelled with shock.

'BITCH! FUCKING BITCH!'

He slammed her arm away, wrenching her wrist so that the knife tumbled away. Snatching it up, he pointed it at her and spat and spat and spat.

'YOU CRAZY FUCKING BITCH!' he roared.

'Eddy, don't talk like that. It's only because I love you so much—'

'Shut your face! You're deviant, that's what you are.' He put his hand to his neck and found blood. 'De-fucking-viant.'

'Eddy—'

'I'm going to kill you. You've got five seconds to get out or I'm going to kill you.'

'Eddy—'

'Four. Three.'

She scrambled off the bed and pulled open the door.

'Two. And take all this fucking shit with you!' He flung a handful of her clothing after her. Most of it fell over the edge of the walkway.

'But I love you!'

'Don't want to see you again. Ever.'

Everyone has tiffs, thought Diane miserably as she meandered along the walkway and nursed her wounded hand. And then they talk it over and they get back together again and it's like it was before, only better, because they need to know what it's like to hate each other so that they can love each other more. That's what Eddy doesn't understand. At the moment he can only hate me, but when he's calmed down he'll love me again. Better, even.

Her hand throbbed mercilessly and she supposed she should take it to the doctor. She doubted Eddy cleaned his knife much so there would be all sorts of germs on it and she might get an infection if she wasn't careful.

The deck was darkened, service-lights providing fitful interruptions that didn't seem to improve things much.

Diane wandered a bit more, then, feeling drowsy, she squatted down in the drifting warm air from a heating vent and tried to sleep.

Poor Eddy, she thought. Poor, poor Eddy. He was hers, heart and mind, body and soul. He just didn't know it yet.

She woke the next morning hungry and nauseous. Her hand was stinging badly now and the bandage was wet through. The tide-marks of the bloodstains reminded her of rose-petals.

She would wait until midday before heading back to the cabin. She might leave him a note. Sometimes it was easier to write things down. You couldn't be misunderstood and what you wrote could be examined and re-examined until it sank in properly. She decided that her and Eddy's problem was lack of communication and that it was her job to improve matters. A note would be a start.

She came across a stopper and got talking to him, as was her habit. He told her a story about the Rain Man, which she didn't believe, but something about his own life she found really interesting, the bit about gutting and slicing the fish that had killed all those people! Stoppers had big imaginations, she knew from experience, but this one was unusual. She found herself wanting to believe him, even if she couldn't. She wanted to believe about the gutted fish.

Finally she said goodbye and went to the cabin. She still had the key and so she let herself in. It was a mess and she set about tidying up right away. She was hampered a bit by her hand but she did a good job of washing the sheets, folding Eddy's clothes, putting her own clothes back in the drawers, wiping up the bloodstains.

Sitting on the bed with her knees hugged up to her chest, she predicted how surprised and pleased Eddy would be to come back and see her. He'd say he was glad she'd come back, he thought he'd lost her for good, please forgive him, he loved her. She thrilled with the idea. He would go up to the greenhouses and buy her flowers, even though they were hideously expensive. He'd say money was no object and there were some things more important than money. Red roses. For her. I'm sorry, darling.

Diane found the tobacco tin and consoled herself with

a couple of Eddy's toenails. She then recovered the other tin, the one with his hair inside, from the pocket of a pair of her jeans folded at the bottom of a drawer. The hairs were dark and stiff like wire. She had preserved them carefully, rescuing them from the pillow and the sheets and the plughole, separating them from her own, which she couldn't see any reason to keep. There were straight ones from his head, and the slightly curly ones from his chest and armpits, and the very curly ones . . . She giggled to think where *they* had come from. She stroked a finger through the collection, stirred them round in a circle to reveal the dented metal underneath, held them up to the light one by one to see them glisten.

If her mother and father could see her now, they would surely approve. When it came down to it, all they wanted was for her to be happy and here she was, deliriously so.

She gave the hairs names and invented little lives for them until Eddy returned.

Eddy was lying on the bed, stretched fully out and stripped naked. He was calm and, Diane thought, reconciled.

There were red roses all over the cabin, everywhere. She'd never suspected he loved her that much and he couldn't possibly afford them, but the sight and the sentiment were breathtaking.

When he'd returned, there had been frenzied moments of passion. Diane's love and pity had been powerful things, lending strength to her embrace and ecstatic fury to her caresses. He had melted in her arms. He had fainted in the light of her love.

And then there was the stopper's story . . .

Looking at him now, Diane, exhausted, satisfied, content, could only tell him again and again how much she loved him and his reply did not need to be spoken, she trusted him that much.

Of course, it could never be the same again for her and Eddy. She'd been silly to think that. You only had to read his body language: the fingers of his ribcage thrusting up through the hole in his chest as if in prayer; the sagginess at the top of his scalp where the hair was dark and matted and folds of skin were torn back and points of bone gleamed through; the missing organs . . .

Diane wiped her mouth. He was hers now, body and soul, heart and mind.

Dr

Macaulay's

Casebook

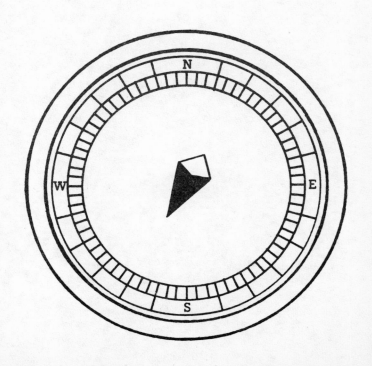

D r Chamberlain has read the last of Dr Macaulay's casebooks twenty-eight times in almost as many months and each time he closes the book he draws in a deep breath and exhales slowly. There really does seem to be no cure.

It is late. The surgery is empty and Dr Chamberlain sits in his clinically clean office. The furniture is simple: two chairs (one comfortable, one less so) divided by a formidable desk. There are books, mainly Dr Macaulay's casebooks, lined up along a shelf on the wall behind him.

Dr Chamberlain takes out Macaulay's last casebook and reads, for the twenty-ninth time, words written three years ago . . .

Tuesday, Week 1,783
One doctor for one million patients. It's patently absurd. They didn't intend for there to be any health care on the *Hope*, or if they did, they simply didn't anticipate the scale of the problem. The statistics thus far:

Cholera	897 deaths
Typhoid	325 deaths
Yellow fever	107 deaths
Cancer-related	142 deaths
Sexually transmitted	83 deaths
Respiratory	760 deaths
Old age	2,689 deaths
Unnatural causes	951 deaths
TOTAL:	5,954 deaths

Nearly six thousand, not counting those which I have not attended or attested to.

I have seen death in myriad forms – lungs coughing up black phlegm, faces so riddled with cancer they resemble a relief map of the Black Mountains, whole deck areas devastated by plague.

But to see a baby born choking blue on its own umbilicus and lack the necessary skills and equipment to save it!

And I am only one man.

What *was* going through their minds when they launched this ship?

Wednesday, Week 1,783

I have re-read yesterday's entry. It was an unforgivable lapse, but I will not erase it. Besides, I was forgetting Marcus, who is coming along excellently. He has a natural aptitude for medicine and has learnt almost everything I have to teach him. He will make an excellent assistant and, in time, my replacement.

The usual cases today. Minor ailments, wounds from fights and accidents, one serious case of dysentery. Two deaths. I am dispensing as much sympathy as I can but I am running perilously short of it. Luckily, I am not running short of drugs. I think people would rather have a pill than a doctor. Pills are uncomplicated, don't need to apologise, won't break the bad news to you (while trying to soften the blow), are always there when you need them, don't tire of you.

I stare through the window at grey seas and I wish I was small, white, smooth and round. That way I could be with every patient all of the time. The palatable doctor.

Thursday, Week 1,783

Among many, two patients today who could most politely be called eccentrics.

The first swore the *Hope* was about to explode and we should all man the lifeboats. Such paranoid delusions are not uncommon, particularly under these exceptionally claustrophobic circumstances. I have reassured him as best I can and prescribed a mild sedative, which will reassure him better.

The second is more singular, an involved and complex

psychological disturbance which I have chosen to study in some detail. I have asked him to return tomorrow.

I feel certain that you, Marcus, and your successors will learn more to your benefit from this case, if it proves to be as interesting as I suspect, than the endless list of trivial complaints and large-scale tragedies with which these casebooks have hitherto been filled.

Friday, Week 1,783
The gentleman concerned is a Mr Alexei Antonov.

The conversation that passed between us on our only formal consultation is set out below, a transcript of a tape-recording I have made. The transcript may be cross-referenced with the original, Tape No. 157D.

Alexei Antonov speaks excellent English with only a trace of Russian inflection. He is intelligent and forthright, in his fifties, with hollow, red-lidded eyes but generally in fine physical health. A great Siberian bear of a man, if that is not too much of a cliché. I do not believe he can easily be deluded and similarly I do not believe he has set out to deceive me. It is the very lucidity with which he treats his madness that I find so intriguing.

I must note his obsessive habit of running his hand through his hair, which became increasingly marked as the conversation progressed, so much so that a few strands had accumulated in between his fingers by the end. In consequence of this habit, the hair on the top of his head has thinned considerably.

'Sit down, please, Mr Antonov.'

'Alexei, call me Alexei, doctor.'

'Very good, Alexei. You don't mind if I record our conversation?'

'No.'

'Now, tell me again what you told me yesterday. What is the nature of your complaint?'

'It is not me, doctor. It is my wife. The ship is trying to kill her.'

'The ship?'

'The *Hope*.'

'How are these ... attempted murders taking place?'

'Not murder.'

'Can you qualify that statement?'

'No.'

'What, then, is happening, Alexei?'

'This ship is alive, doctor. She breathes, she thinks, her iron heart beats. Of course, we humans believe we are running her. We have a captain, a tidy man who steers our course and keeps law and order. He runs the ship, does he not? And we have a crew of stout sailors well-versed in the modern techniques of sailing. They act also as an unofficial police force. There are officers and petty officers and entertainment officers and engineers and janitors and chefs and the greenhouse-keepers and the food-store guards. They all run the ship, do they not? And the rest of us, the passengers, we live our days and scrabble to earn a living, to keep our heads above water, so to speak.

'But I truly do not think that the Captain or any of the crew run anything except the lives of thousands of humans.

'Imagine the ship as a dog with an infestation of fleas, and you will have some idea of my vision of the *Hope*.'

'I can see that. But it presupposes that the *Hope* is sentient, as you believe, and that we humans are parasites.'

'Correct. It is an apt metaphor, no?'

'No. The ship was built to carry humans. That was its sole purpose.'

'Is not a dog created in part to carry fleas? It provides them with a source of food and life, just as the meat of other animals provides the dog with a source of food and life. It is nature's way. A chain.'

'How is this relevant to your wife?'

'Pray, let me continue. Finally, the dog decides it wishes to shake off the fleas. It has been irritated too long. Naturally the fleas are dying anyway but new ones are hatched to replace them. There are diseases, accidents, killings, which kill off some of the fleas, but they are replaced. An exponential increase. The numbers are swelling. The dog must take direct action. The dog must scratch.'

'Your wife?'

'Ah. About three weeks ago, we were promenading along the outer rim, taking in a marvellous sunset, when the section of walkway upon which Pushka was standing collapsed, taking the railing with it. If we had not been walking arm in arm in our old-fashioned way, she would have plummeted straight down into the sea. As it was, we both nearly fell but I managed to catch hold of the end of the railing. My wife was clutching my arm, hanging on for dear life. She did not scream.

'"Pull me up, Alexei," was all she said. And I did. I would rather both of us had fallen than let go of my Pushka. I hauled her over the edge of the broken walkway and held her in my arms. I think I had been more scared than she had.

'I took her home and went back to the spot. I knelt down and examined that walkway and I saw no sign of rust, decay, any sort of corruption. The break was clean and straight, as if it had been cut neatly in half.

'I have not told my wife about these findings. At the time, I can tell you, I was considerably shaken. Half a bottle of vodka put paid to that, however. Ha ha.

'Then, last week, the porthole in our cabin shattered as Pushka was going to open it for some air. Exploded inwards into her face for no apparent reason. The noise nearly turned my beard grey. *Crack!* Like a gunshot. By a miracle, she only received a small cut on her chin. It might have been much graver, doctor, grave enough to require your attention, but God willed otherwise.

'"My goodness!" she said. And that was it. She has nerves of steel. Me, I finished off the rest of that vodka then and there.

'And now, strangest of all was what happened the evening before last. It decided me that I should seek help, your help, doctor, as one of the few sane men left on board. You have an excellent reputation, doctor, did you know that?'

'I only do my job. I hope I do it well.'

'Ha, ha, so modest. "I hope I do it well." Ha, ha. Well, then. Let me tell you.

'The evening before last, doctor, the cabin came alive.

'At dinner, Pushka and I were enjoying a quiet meal when I saw something move on the wall behind her. I believed it

143

was a shadow cast through the porthole by the service-light outside. We have had to cover the porthole with a sheet of polythene. It is unlikely it will ever be fixed by a janitor, eh? Perhaps, thought I, the sheet is flapping slightly and casting unusual shadows.

'I went over to fix it. The polythene was firmly in place. I looked at the spot on the wall. There were no shadows.

'My wife asked what was the matter. I replied that I thought I had felt a draught. Whether I had or I hadn't, I certainly felt a chill of some sort. I took my seat again.

'Pushka was telling me once again about her childhood in the Ukraine. I love the stories of her childhood, which was so innocent and uncomplicated compared with mine. My parents were Jewish, you see, and it has never been easy for us.

'Mid-sentence, Pushka stopped.

'"Lexi, what is it?" she asked. I was staring behind her. I believe I dropped my knife. I don't remember.

'"Lexi?"

'What I saw had to be real. My mind could not invent such a thing. The steel of the wall was running as if it were melting, and reforming into a shape. It flowed and grew solid. It made an arm with a fist the size of your head and it was poised to descend on my poor Pushka to crush her.

'I made some sort of inarticulate cry – I think grunt was the word Pushka used to describe it afterwards – and I leant over the table and pulled her towards me with little regard for her person or my own. The table tumbled over, scraping my shins, and with it Pushka fell into my chest. At the same moment that fist came down and smashed into the chair in which she had been sitting only a second before. The chair was left in ruins. I clutched Pushka to me and held her face away from that terrible, incomprehensible sight, not wishing her to share it. Luckily, before she could look round, the arm withdrew into the wall, leaving no mark of where it had been.

'"Lexi, what happened?" she asked.

'I did not know. I could not explain.

'And there you are, doctor. I cannot stay much longer, as

144

I must get back to my wife and protect her as much as I am able. I do not think I will be able to save her in the event, but I do not like to leave her alone.'

'What do you think I can do?' I asked.

'Tell me if I am going mad.'

'I can't say. To be honest, I think you would agree with me that your story is somewhat . . . improbable. The accident on the walkway I can believe, the porthole shattering too. This is an old ship and things tend to go wrong now and again. But the fist . . . Well, it's improbable.'

'Improbable. Ha ha. It is impossible! But I am not lying.'

'No, I don't think you are.'

'Then I am going mad.'

'The only help I can give you for that is to prescribe a course of tranquillisers. It's all I'm qualified to do. That, and advise you to stop worrying.'

'No, no, no tranquillisers. I can get my own tranquilliser, if I need it, in liquid form. Ha ha.'

'Then . . . there is nothing I can do.'

'I know. But come and see my wife. Assure her all is well, it is just her poor, mad fool of a husband who sees things that should not be there.'

'You told her about the fist?'

'How could I not? And she insists the chair simply broke when I grabbed hold of her. Fell over and broke. Ha, ha. It was made of metal and plastic, doctor, and it was mangled beyond recognition. Broke!'

'Very well. Let's go and see your wife.'

He took me down to a lower deck. Every time I go downstairs I am appalled by the conditions in which these people are expected to live. Every available surface is covered in soot and filth. The graffiti of desperate youths trying to make a name for themselves, however insignificant, is scrawled over certain areas. Stoppers line the walkways at regular intervals, asking for money or the time, or your time if they simply want to talk. The air is unclean and turgid and reeking of despair. Every time, I wish there was something I could do. Every time, I feel inadequate, as a physician, as a human being.

Meeting someone like Pushka Antonov, however, I have a

small lift of the heart. To endure such degrading misery and come through with such alertness in your eyes, such grace in your bearing, such dignity, is nothing short of miraculous. She was in her late fifties and still handsome, and had a manner that suggested ingenuity and resourcefulness. She certainly didn't appear terrified or victimised.

The Antonovs have made the best of their cabin. Richly coloured Armenian rugs hang over two of the walls and a photograph of a former General Secretary is dutifully pinned on the door to their bedroom.

I thought it would be intrusive to bring along my tape recorder and so did not record any of the conversation that took place in the Antonovs' cabin, but I will attempt to supply the gist of it as far as I can remember. The precise details are immaterial.

Pushka Antonov offered us tea. We both accepted and in the meantime I examined the hollow porthole. It would take an expert on these things but I could discern no obvious structural damage around it. The wall was neither warped nor buckled. The same held true for the patch of wall which Alexei was convinced had come to life.

When the tea came, it was bitter and dark brown.

'Thank you for coming, doctor,' she said. 'I know you are a busy man.'

'I wish I could do more than sit and tell you not to worry,' I replied. 'My experience in psychology is limited, in psychiatry non-existent.'

'These are bad times, are they not?'

'We have to make do.'

'But there is so much sickness here. You surely have seen that.'

'Too much. I'm close to giving up hope that anyone will survive the crossing. It is a long journey. Our stocks of food and medical supplies are dwindling . . . '

She reached across the table and grasped my arm with disarming intimacy.

'Do not give up, doctor. You must not give up. You must do everything you can, save as many lives as you can. It is the only way.'

'It's not the way of the *Hope*.'

'Maybe not, but it is the way of humanity.'

She turned to Alexei, who was sitting brooding.

'Lexi, my love, would you leave me with the doctor? Just for a little while?'

'I must be here to look after you and protect you.'

'Oh, you big old baby! I will be fine. The doctor will look after me. And we must talk alone.'

'Very well. I will go for a short walk, but I will not go far and I will be back soon.'

She gave him the tenderest of kisses and squeezed his hand and said something softly in Russian. I have never seen more devoted a couple. When he had gone out, she sat down opposite me again.

'No doubt Lexi has told you everything,' she said with determined humour. 'Fantastic, no?'

I used the adjective improbable, as before.

'Poor Lexi! His family have always been emigrants and immigrants, you know. His life has never been settled. Always travelling, always having to find a new place to live. That is why we came on board the *Hope*, to find a new place. And I don't think we will live to see that new place. It is sad. I do believe it has driven him mad.'

'You think he's mad?'

'Quite so. Come, let me show you. I am sitting on the very chair which he insists was smashed out of shape by his . . . phantom. Look.'

I looked. One leg of the chair had been broken and repaired with plastic tape, and that was it.

'And the porthole?' I asked.

'Maybe a young boy broke it, threw a stick or a tin can or something at it. These things happen. It gave us such a fright that we did not think to look outside until much much later. Besides, Lexi was too worried fussing over my little graze here.'

'I see. What about the walkway?'

'Oh, it still scares me to think about that! If it had not been for Lexi . . . But it was an accident, clearly. This is an old ship.

147

'That's exactly what I told him.'

'He loves me very much. I love him very much. I think he is feeling his age, feeling a little frightened that one of us will die soon and he wishes it was me and not him. He would do anything to spare me the grief of his death.'

'That's understandable.'

'What do you advise, doctor?'

'There is nothing I can advise. Look after him. Humour him. Treat him well. I suspect you have been doing that anyway. If he is a little over-protective, well . . . There are worse things.'

'Yes. But I feel so sorry for him.'

At that point, Alexei returned, his short walk having been very short indeed.

'Well, friend doctor,' he said, 'what is the diagnosis?'

'Rest, good vodka and a loving wife.'

'I have all three,' he said, giving her a great hug. 'Am I not mad?'

'I have seen madder,' I replied with a laugh.

'Thank you, doctor. You have done everything you can and I feel better for talking to you. Please, come and have dinner with us some time.'

'Tomorrow evening,' said Pushka. 'I will accept no excuses.'

'The cooking won't be fancy, but it will be excellent.'

Who was I to refuse such an invitation? I took my leave and promised to be back the next evening.

Looking back over what I have just written, I find it reads like a bad novel. There are many cases equally deserving of such attention, but in my defence I would like to point you back to earlier case-histories that I have dealt with in similar depth, such as that concerning Mr Quinnell in Week 1,095 and the incident in Week 945 when the inhabitants of a deck area, gripped with a sudden mass hysteria, came to believe that they were all ghosts and stopped eating since, they reasoned, ghosts don't need to eat. I could not persuade them otherwise. All but three died of malnutrition.

Certain matters demand such attention. There is an element of the Antonovs' situation that, to me, is endemic of life on board. I ought really to list all of Tuesday's statistics under this new heading.

I have chosen to call it the *Hope* Syndrome.

Saturday, Week 1,783
I will be happy to live without seeing again the events which I saw this evening.

I do not need to relate anything about the actual meal at the Antonovs' other than that the food was, as promised, excellent and the conversation intelligent and delightful. When you don't notice three hours passing, when you don't want those three hours to pass, that is a sign of happiness and a rarity on the *Hope*. With every minute of those hours I became more and more enraptured by Pushka's lively character and affectionate towards Alexei's bluff good nature. The conversation did not touch once on madness, nor did anyone mention the way of the *Hope*.

One remark of Alexei's I will repeat, in that it has some bearing on his condition. When I asked as tactfully as I could why they had no children, he responded: 'Ah, what kind of place is this to bring young ones into? What quality of life will they have? No decent food, pitiful education, breathing air you can see. No doubt they would end up running with some gang, sticking knives into each other for something to do. It's not a life.'

Pushka was nodding, in a way that meant she did not agree but she would go along with him if his feelings were that strong.

After the meal, over cups of coffee brewed so black it was almost solid, Pushka told me, at Alexei's urging and presumably for his own benefit as much as mine, stories of her childhood. Hardships, small joys, deprivations, triumphs of love – I can see why these stories so enchanted Alexei.

As she was speaking I noticed Alexei growing restless and agitated. Nothing she was saying could have induced this state of mind in him. When he wasn't drumming his fingers on his knee, he was engaged in the habit I mentioned in yesterday's entry of running his hand through his hair repeatedly. Pushka saw this too and stopped.

'Lexi, what is the matter?'

'Nothing. Pay no attention to me. The good doctor wants to hear your stories.'

'Is it the fist?' I asked. 'Can you see the fist again?'

'No, no.'

'Something is troubling you,' she ventured.

Without warning, Alexei pounced upon her, crying, 'No, leave her be!' and his hands were about her throat. I rushed to grab his wrists and it was like grabbing steel bars, but I pulled as hard as I could with markedly little effect.

'Let go, doctor!' he yelled. 'Can't you see the hands? They are strangling her!'

'There are no hands,' I replied. Pushka was choking hard and clawing at her husband, at the same time trying to form words. If she had been able to say anything, I have no doubt it would not have been angry or fearful, but calm, reasonable, soothing.

Alexei's face was a red mask of righteous fury. Reason alone would not put him off. There is a nerve just above the shoulder-blade which, if pinched correctly, induces temporary paralysis in the arm. Knowing I could not use brute strength to dislodge Alexei, I chose this alternative method. With a bewildered yelp he fell back and I interposed myself between him and his wife, who was ashen-faced and drawing quick, rasping breaths.

'There is nothing there, Alexei. Can't you see? Nothing! No arms, no hands. The ship is not trying to kill Pushka.'

Clutching his numbed arm, he glared at me from beneath brushwood eyebrows. His voice was roughened with a growl.

'Get out of the way, friend doctor, or to reach Pushka I will kill you.'

'Kill me, then. But look! Where are the hands? There are no hands.'

'Around her neck, idiot! Are you blind?'

He lumbered towards me and it was clear there would be no contest between us, but I was not about to let him lay a finger on Pushka. I would rather have died. I was preparing to do exactly that when I felt Pushka push me gently aside and stand in front of Alexei, dwarfed by his size. On her neck purple contusions had already appeared but despite the obvious pain she looked up at her husband with eyes clear of any flecks of mistrust. He raised his good arm. It hung poised before her.

'Lexi, I am unharmed. The hands are gone. There is no danger.' She repeated it in Russian, I gather, and Alexei made a reply in kind. For a full minute they stood there, facing one another a few inches apart, saying nothing, as if Pushka was daring him against the name of all the years of their marriage to kill her. Slowly, Alexei blinked, blinked again, and gave all the signs of waking up. Then he glanced abruptly at the wall. I followed his line of sight.

I cannot be sure – I will not commit myself on paper – but for an instant I thought I saw something moving on that wall, a slight swirl in the solid steel such as that of oil on water, shapeless, spreading and losing form. It was gone so quickly that it may have been a trick of the light. But I will never be certain.

'It is gone,' breathed Alexei. 'It is gone.' He clasped Pushka to him and buried his weeping face in her hair. I took my leave as hastily and politely as I could, but Alexei caught my arm and said quietly: 'Thank you, doctor.'

'I'm sorry about your arm, Alexei, but it will be back to normal soon. One of the few occasions I have been glad of my medical training.'

'No matter.'

He laughed and patted me on the back. Pushka braved a smile and I left them clutching each other.

To see so noble a man driven to such insanity . . .

I thought I saw something move in the corner of this office. It is late and I am tired. It was probably a rat.

But there are no rats on the *Hope*.

Sunday, Week 1,784

No surgery today.

I have not been feeling particularly well since I got up this morning. The events of last night haunted my dreams, made them ghastly and feverish.

I went for a walk along the outer rim to clear my head but

could not find the broken section where the Antonovs had their narrow escape. Naturally it was too far to walk all the way round the rim. Perhaps I was nowhere near the scene of the accident. Perhaps, that most unlikely of occurrences, it had been repaired.

I wish I could know for sure.

Monday, Week 1,784

You must have discovered by now, Marcus, that there are no drugs left except a few harmless sedatives and tranquillisers. In a few minutes, when I have finished writing this entry, I intend to take a whole bottle of Valium. I have it on the desk in front of me. Little white pills.

I have disposed of all the major drugs, the vaccines, the inoculations, the antibiotics. It took me all day to pour them down the sink. They will have drained into the ocean by now. I emptied pills into boxes and took them to the side and threw them overboard. It is one advantage of being situated so near the outer rim which I have never appreciated before. In the same manner I have thrown away all the syringes and surgical implements.

I have left you with the aspirin and the Valium and the disease, the *Hope* Syndrome. I am truly sorry for my cowardice. We should not foist our own failures on the successive generation, as if they have a duty to clean up after us or try to live with our mistakes. The sins of the fathers should not be visited upon the sons. I am sorry. That is all I can say.

A neighbour of the Antonovs came up at midday today and told me something terrible had happened in their cabin. He would not specify, but a thought sounded deep and clear in my mind: Pushka is dead.

Dogged by the neighbour, who clearly thought there was some kind of reward to be earned, I rushed downstairs. A crowd had gathered outside the Antonovs' cabin trying not to look as if they were attempting to see through the open door. I pushed my way through.

Alexei was sitting on a chair in the centre of the cabin, staring at his hands. Pushka lay on the floor, her body a twisted knot of limbs and torso. Her legs were pulpy, stretched nearly half their length again. One foot was inverted beside the other, like the fish chasing each others' tails in the astrological symbol. Her arms were bent behind her back, every thumb and finger broken. I could not see her head because it was wedged between the floor and her collar-bone. There was no blood.

I took Alexei's pulse, as there was no point in taking Pushka's. It was frantic and irregular. He lifted his face.

'Doctor, we could not save her. The hands. They crushed her to death an hour ago. I tried and tried to beat them off, but I failed.

'And, doctor . . . I was wrong. We are not fleas. We are worse than fleas. We are rats, trapped.'

I could say nothing. I left.

I have not reported this to the Captain. I don't expect you will either, Marcus. Nor will any of the Antonovs' neighbours, I think. The lower decks like to have as little to do with the upper as they can.

It is obvious, to all intents and purposes, that Alexei killed his wife. He is a big man and, enraged by madness, would be capable of such physical violence, and worse. One might be able to argue a case for him on the grounds of diminished responsibility, if the matter reached the Captain and a trial was called for. I doubt it would get Alexei off. I think he would prefer execution.

They have already given Pushka burial at sea. I hear that Alexei did not attend the funeral, but many did. She was a well-loved woman.

I believe, like Alexei, that the *Hope* killed her and it was not murder. When you catch a rat in a trap, when you slap at a fly or a mosquito, when you scratch your skin and eliminate thousands of mites, do you call it murder? Alexei's last remark reminds me of a case I had barely a year after we embarked. You will find it under Week 47, if memory serves. There is a connection but I only know it in my instincts. I feel as if I am groping around in the dark. The earlier case concerned Stanley Harris, an engineer. His co-workers brought him to me late at night with a wound torn into the back of his left leg.

The man was near fainting with the pain. While I worked on him they told me an alarming story. Again, you may look this up for the details if you wish, but as I remember . . .

The walls of the office are shifting slightly. They think I can't see, but I can. I haven't much time.

As I remember, a dozen of the engineers went in search of the lair of the rats that had been infesting the engine-room, intending to carry out a spot of extermination. Instead of rats, they encountered some inexplicable creatures with steel teeth. Only four of the men got out alive and to my mind their terror was too overwhelming for them to have made the story up. I thought at the time that they had suffered a kind of mass hallucination. Really, their working conditions are appalling and the racket of the engines is enough to drive anyone crazy. However, one singular aspect of the story has been borne out over the years. There are no rats on the *Hope* any more. In addition, I remarked in the entry that the awful creatures they found were acting in a manner similar to those of a living creature's immune system. Antibodies. I was less experienced then and the remark was intended to be flippant, but I am not so sure now.

This room seems distorted, as if my corneas are distending. In the corners of my eyes I am seeing all sorts of shapes. They form and then pluck themselves away when I try to look at them directly. Even the pen and the casebook are unwilling to serve me.

I have no time left. There is only one cure and it sits in the bottle in front of me.

I have taken all the pills. The light is dimmer now and my writing slurred.

Marcus, I have left you no option but to play the fool. You cannot save everyone. You cannot save anyone. The passengers must not be allowed to place their faith in you. You must not allow them any placebos.

The rats have deser . . . —

Dr Chamberlain closes the casebook, sits back and rubs a hand over his face.

He recalls finding Dr Macaulay the morning after the entry

154

was written, face down on the desk, pen in hand, his lips with a bluish tinge which made Dr Chamberlain think of the times when, as a child, he had chewed on the end of his pen once too often. Dr Macaulay's corpse was indecently rigid, not at peace even in death.

And earlier this evening, a young man was brought in clutching his face, streaks of blood running down his cheeks. Upon examination Dr Chamberlain found his eyelids had been torn off, by a jilted girlfriend, apparently. He had to sew up the eyelids without an anaesthetic. The young man's friends held him down during the operation, but he still writhed throughout, and Dr Chamberlain could not do a particularly efficient job. He doubts the fellow will see again. He gave him a whole bottle of pills.

What kind of provocation could there be for such savagery? he asks himself. We *are* rats, biting in frustration at the trap that has snapped shut on us.

He stands up, crosses the room, switches out the lights. The deck is quiet. Putting on his jacket, he goes to the front door of the surgery and opens it. The sea-wind gives him a cool shake of the hand. Outside someone is waiting for him in the dark to ask him a question: not 'Doctor, how long have I got to live?' nor, 'Doctor, what do you think it is?' nor, 'Doctor, can you give me anything for this?' but: 'Do you know?'

Dr Chamberlain examines the thin man's mutilated chest and wants to ask some questions in return: 'Did you do that to yourself?' and 'How could anyone inflict that much pain on himself?' The scars are jagged and ragged. The implement could not have been too sharp.

But he does not diagnose. Instead he accepts that there is a cure after all.

'No, I don't,' says the doctor.

Hands reach.

The

Last

Waltz

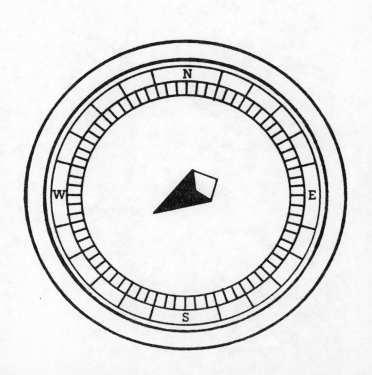

Signor Bellini woke to the sound of something going bump in the night. He turned over, mumbled something and was drowsing off to sleep again when he heard another bump. He sat up and listened hard. Maria snored lightly beside him. The sound came once more, from the cabin above, and once more, and became a series of bumps.

'Not again!' he groaned, then shook his wife and received a thick snort in reply.

'Maria!'

She pushed his hand away.

'Maria, my little *lavabiancheria*, the Montgomerys are at it again!'

The bumps had now been joined by a counter melody of squeaks, and then the little bass thuds of the bedstead were introduced. Bellini pushed back the covers and lowered his feet to the floor, testing the temperature with his toes and wincing. Summoning up courage, he put down both his soles and let out a compressed whine of complaint.

Maria muttered something indistinguishable.

Overhead a duet for two voices, tenor and soprano, had begun in earnest. The words were unclear but the volume grew steadily from *piano* to *fortissimo* and the gist of the libretto emerged in moans and cries. Bellini in his barber's-pole striped pyjamas pulled on a patched pair of socks and gathered his dressing-gown around him.

'Where are you going?' asked his wife without much enthusiasm. She spoke as if she was somewhere deep under water.

'I'm going upstairs to sort out this nonsense! Four nights in a row it has been. Four nights without a decent sleep. It is too much! I am going to complain.'

'At least wait until they are finished, dearest. It is only polite.'

159

'No, I will not wait! They wait for me, I tell you. They wait for me until I fall asleep, and then they start – bump, bump, bump – and so I will not wait for them. It is too much!'

He hurried into the main cabin and flung open the front door. Fingers of mist probed in. The cold tingled the hairs on his shins and shrivelled his testicles. Muttering, Bellini launched himself outside and stamped loudly along the walkway, hoping to wake as many of his neighbours as he could. Why should they be allowed to sleep and not him? He stamped up the nearest staircase and stamped along to the Montgomerys' cabin. Their performance was audible even out here. The tempo had reached a furious *molto allegro*.

Bellini banged on the door, unaware of synchronising his knocks to the Montgomerys' rhythm. The performance stopped dead, as if the conductor had tapped his baton on the rostrum. There were hurried scurrying noises, urgent whispers, and finally a man's voice: 'Who the bloody hell is it?'

'Signor Bellini,' announced Signor Bellini importantly. 'I have come to register a complaint.'

'Well, go and register it with the complaints officer.'

'It is not that sort of complaint,' said Bellini, raising his voice in order that everyone in the deck area might hear. 'My wife has been disturbed four nights running by the sound of your activities. I would advise you in future to consider repairing the fittings of your bed and lowering the volume of your . . . utterances.'

'I think you could keep your utterances down a bit too,' came the voice from inside. 'Do you want to wake the whole deck?'

'I believe,' said Bellini, clearing his throat, 'that you have already done that.'

'Look,' said the voice, coming now from just behind the door, 'why don't you piss off back to bed and mind your own business, OK, fatty?'

Bellini sucked in a lungful of air and inflated his chest to epic proportions. His hands curled up into large, pudgy fists.

'I HAVE ASKED YOU POLITELY. NOW, WILL YOU SHUT UP OR DO

I HAVE TO MAKE YOU SHUT UP?' Each word was a controlled explosion. Lights flicked on in nearby portholes and muffled voices raised muffled questions.

'All right, all right, signor. Keep your moustache on. We'll try to hold it down to a whisper. Now bugger off.'

Bellini thought that at that moment, in his rage, he might be able to punch a hole through the door and he drew back his hand to perform the function, but common sense caught up with him at last and with it his whole body deflated to its original size. After a pause he spoke again, emphatically reasonable: 'Thank you. Good night.'

He strode back along the walkway past curious faces staring at him through portholes and half-opened doors. He moulded his face into a beaming, satisfied, 'I'm in control,' kind of smile. It was only when he had got back to his cabin that he found his penis had been poking out through the front of his pyjama bottoms and dressing-gown all along. Shamefacedly he redressed the oversight.

He sat down on the edge of the bed and pulled off his socks, huffing with the effort of bending forward over his belly. He was rather proud of his girth, if the truth be known, because all the great opera singers were of a similar build. He himself did not have much of a singing voice but he nevertheless entertained fantasies of himself in *Don Giovanni* or *Rigoletto* pounding the air with his mighty vocal cords, taking a final sweaty bow, blowing kisses to a stunned and roaring audience, ducking the showers of flowers.

'Well, you certainly made your point, Gian,' sneered Maria. He looked over his shoulder at her.

'Still awake, my *balenetta*?'

'How could I sleep with you making that racket upstairs? It was worse than the Montgomerys. And next time, don't use me as an excuse!'

'We must stand up for the rights of the individual, Maria.'

'What about their right to make love without you barging in?'

'But we must respect each other's privacy! It is the only way to live.'

'I couldn't agree more.' With that, Maria rolled over, presenting her dimpled, pockmarked back to her husband.

Bellini raised his eyes to heaven and gave up a small prayer to the Blessed Virgin. Then he slid into bed and scrunched up the pillow beneath his head.

In the middle of a marvellous dream of standing ovations, the bumping started again and he shot upright.

'*Santa Madre di Dio!*' he cursed.

'Gian! You've woken me up again.'

'Not I, *carissima frizione!* The Montgomerys. I'm going to sort them out properly this time.'

With this, he thumped his feet on to the floor and was reaching for his socks when Maria said: 'Gian, I forbid you to go out.'

'But, Maria—'

'You go out and I will not talk with you for a month.'

'But, Maria—'

'And that is not all I will not do with you for a month.'

'Maria—' But there was defeat in his voice. He hustled himself into bed and sighed and dragged the covers over and sighed again. The noise from above increased as he lay staring into the darkness, sighing loudly every so often, planning revenge.

It occurred to Signor Bellini that the best way to fight noise was with noise. He was too Catholic in every respect to ask Maria if she would join him in a spot of sexual caterwauling and believed such behaviour could only bring shame to his respected name. Besides, it was not in Maria's nature to make much noise during their weekly love-making. Sometimes he wondered if she took any pleasure from it at all, although it was really none of his business. All he knew was that he could not make such a demand of her.

Bellini was one of the few people on the upper decks who could be said to be gainfully employed. Most of them drifted around idling their time away, as passengers will, waiting for the voyage to be over. They ate in the dining-hall, they swam in the three open-air pools, they kept themselves beautiful, they took long constitutionals around the outer rim, they sat out on the decks when there was any sun, they played games of deck quoits by day and games of sexual intrigue by night, they engaged in dull but polite conversation, they danced at Bellini's ballroom. For them, boredom was not a way of life but a way of passing time. Some actually enjoyed being bored. Bellini, however, believed he offered them a means to alleviate this boredom. Indeed, his ballroom was well attended every night and he made a tidy profit from their subscriptions. He supplied the needs of public demand and reaped the benefits – renown, money, a pleasantly situated cabin.

In younger and slightly slimmer days he had hoped to set up an on-board operatic society with himself as director, producer, musical supervisor and star. He had scores for all the major Italian operas and set about transcribing them into individual parts. It was a Herculean labour and it took him many weeks of ruling sets of staves across blank paper and filling them in with notes and words. He had never credited the expression about seeing spots before your eyes until then, when every evening as he was nodding off to sleep he would see breves, semibreves, minims, crotchets, quavers and semiquavers floating beneath his eyelids in bilious, splenetic shades of green and blue. This he did not allow to hinder his work. The Bellini Chorus was too important a dream.

Finally, encumbered with reams of home-made orchestration and poor eyesight, he put the word about that he was seeking singers to join him in his project. He held an audition. Three people turned up and one of them was Maria, out of marital obligation. The remaining two simply could not sing – the philistines! Bellini had to reject them out of hand and, much as it pained him, abandon the idea of an operatic society.

He then hit upon the idea of an orchestral society. Many of his acquaintances played some form of musical instrument with varying degrees of success. Perhaps he could band them together and provide the occasional diverting evening's entertainment of classical favourites (particularly favoured would be the overtures to major Italian operas). He put the new word about and held another audition. This was somewhat better attended than the last, although there was a preponderance of trumpeters who seemed unable to perform at anything less than full blast. Bellini employed a rigorous selection process along the guidelines that if you could play you were in. As far as the trumpet section went, he chose the one man who knew how to play softly and another who had some idea that softly existed.

It was a source of some satisfaction to him that so many music lovers had chosen to bring their instruments on board and that he had provided them with a creative outlet.

'It is my duty,' he would say in an off-guard moment, 'to use my talents to improve the lot of others on the *Hope*.'

During its fledgling rehearsals, the Bellini Orchestra only disagreed with its founder on one small matter – his choice of music. They decided democratically that they would much rather play waltzes and polkas and Charlestons. Democracy was as alien to Bellini as Wagner. He regarded it as a dangerous concept that denied the rights of individual superiority. In a fit of pique, he sacked the entire orchestra.

The next day he sent a note of apology to every member in which he agreed to let them play any sort of music they wished as long as he could remain conductor.

The old state room proved an ideal ballroom. It had been virtually unused since the launching of the *Hope*. People sauntered through it now and then to admire the grand chandelier and the gold-leaf patterns swirling around the ceiling, and then they would perch for a minute on the gilt chairs, worn out after so much sauntering. Word of mouth about the room's new purpose spread fast and the opening night celebrations were protracted and enthusiastically attended. If you asked Bellini now, he would tell you it had been his intention all along to establish a popular institution.

'You need to know what people want,' he would say, 'and fulfil that particular need. That is the way to success, *mio amico*.'

It came as a surprise to the orchestra when, on the evening after Bellini's fourth sleepless night in a row, just before the dancing was due to begin, the important conductor suggested a midnight rehearsal afterwards in his cabin for the brass section. The greatest element of the surprise was not the time of the rehearsal but the very idea of rehearsing at all. They had been playing the same stuff for over twenty years now. The horsehair of their bows had grown thin on these pieces. Their reeds had split and their brass had tarnished from the repetition of familiar tunes. No one needed his or her score any more, although some put it out on the stand for old times' sake (and to play noughts and crosses with their neighbour in the breaks between numbers). To rehearse? Was the *signor* feeling unwell? Straight away, a vote was called for. Their brass-playing brethren would surely not tolerate the unconstitutional demands of their conductor.

Then Bellini perverted the course of democracy by indicating that he wanted to see, in the privacy of his cabin, how loud the brass section could play. He felt they were not pulling their weight. The brass section immediately resolved that rehearsal was not such a bad thing after all, they were a little rusty and it would do them good to go over their parts without the rest of the orchestra. So, the matter was decided.

All things considered, Maria took the midnight intrusion of two trumpets, a French horn and a trombone extraordinarily well. In her billowing nightgown she raved at her husband and threatened all kinds of terrible things, but in the end it took him only ten minutes to pacify her, using all the tenderest nicknames at his disposal – *scimmietta*, *olocausta*, *scoppia*. He knew she was pacified because she merely shut the bedroom door on him rather than slamming it.

Bellini arranged the brass section around the cabin, chose a ponderous waltz for them to play, exhorted them to blow for all they were worth, waved his baton, counted them in . . .

Arnold Montgomery's father, David Montgomery, had always sworn he would die from choking on a fishbone.

'Since they got rid of that chappie in the kitchens, the one who killed old George Barnes with a poisoned fish – and not just George, mark you, but nearly half the upper decks – the standard of the food in this place has dropped appallingly. He might have been a psychopath but he could cook damned well! Never have thought of him as the killer-type, but there you are. It's always the quiet ones, eh? Take a look at this. Fillet? Ha! It's a mass of bones, I tell you. One day, I'm going to choke on one of these.' So saying, he would hold an inch-long bone up for inspection and Arnold would offer to check the fish over for him.

'Leave it alone, my boy. When I die, I want it to be either while I'm eating or while I'm screwing.'

In the end it turned out to be, as he had often predicted, while he was eating. In the middle of a tirade against the violence of youths on the lower decks, David Montgomery made a gargling sound, fell back in his seat, napkin flying, and jabbed a finger at his mouth. A large proportion of the other diners shrieked and ran out of the hall to stick two fingers down their throats, fearing a repeat of the food poisoning that had accounted for twenty-three of their brethren a year ago, but Arnold boldly ran round behind his father's chair and tried to introduce two fingers into his father's throat. He felt blunt teeth and slobbering tongue around his knuckles. He reached in further. His father raised several strong objections to this treatment, lips struggling to form words around his son's hand while his face turned red and then blue and then purple.

Arnold seemed to take a very long time extricating the fishbone. His thoughts, in fact, were not intent on saving the life of his dear old dad but on the old man's delightful cabin, a far cry from the hovel he and Tracy shared on M deck; on the number of times he had tried to persuade his father that he would be happier living on M deck, and that Tracy and himself were thinking of starting a family and wanted somewhere nice and large for David's grandchild to be brought up; on the insistence with which his father maintained they would have to wait until he was well and truly dead.

For anyone watching this domestic drama closely, it might have appeared that at this crucial juncture Arnold balled his hand into a fist inside his father's mouth, but surely it could not have been his intention to cut off the old man's breathing? Ridiculous! Fortunately, none of the other diners was interested enough to watch. Those that were not running outside to induce spontaneous vomiting were keeping their heads down and thanking God they had ordered the corned beef. And if Arnold *had* tried to suffocate his father . . . Well, he was only speeding up nature's course a tiny bit. And besides, he was all tears at the funeral and many of his friends commended him on his efforts to save the old man.

Arnold and Tracy were delighted to move, at the Captain's request, into David Montgomery's cabin the following Monday. Immediately they sorted out the old man's personal possessions, dividing them into things that seemed to be of value and things that did not. They took the rubbish and the valuables downstairs. The rubbish went on the nearest convenient tip, the valuables to Bart's, where a good bargain was struck. At least, Bart thought it was a good bargain. Arnold had been born into a wealthy family, so he had never had much of a head for figures.

In their transport of grief (or excitement), the Montgomerys overlooked one thing. The old man had been an inveterate hoarder of food. He used to go down to Bart's frequently and buy black market tins, planning for the day when the *Hope* finally ran out of food. The Montgomerys threw several boxes on to a rubbish-tip on P deck in the belief that they contained books or something equally useless. The boxes contained tins of food, and all but one was scavenged within an hour. The last, containing ham, peas, carrots and raspberries, was accidentally buried beneath the surface of the tip and waited a whole day to be found.

Arnold and Tracy celebrated their first night in their new cabin with a bottle of champagne from the old man's private stock, chased down with a spot of strenuous family-raising. This practice continued unabated for the next three nights, despite the poor condition of dear departed David Montgomery's old bed and the intrusion on the fourth night by that fat Italian from below. Likewise, this evening – the same evening that Signor Bellini decided to hold an informal brass gathering – Arnold had suggested a bit of provisional child-rearing and Tracy was quick to agree.

Roughly halfway through attempt number three, a sound came from beneath them like the heavens opening and the Trump of Doom blaring and God's mighty hand reaching down to earth. It fair put Arnold off his stride.

The fanfare continued for a full hour with only occasional breaks. For the most part it was musical gibberish, hinting at the tunes of the popular dances, but more significantly it was deafeningly loud musical gibberish. A clamour rose throughout the deck area and a deputation went down to bang on Bellini's door. Naturally, they could not make themselves heard and so went miserably back to bed and pulled the covers over their heads, praying for it to stop. At last it did and an apocalyptic hush descended. Even the ship's engines appeared to have quieted themselves down in respectful awe.

Then a still small voice spoke from one of the cabins: 'That bloody fat bastard!'

Signor Bellini raised his baton for the third number of the evening, that perennial favourite 'The Blue Danube'. There was a particularly good turnout tonight. Although that beautiful lady was missing, the one who often complimented him on his excellent conducting and smiled on him like an angel, several young couples had inexplicably decided all at once to observe and participate in the noble art of ballroom dancing.

If they are serious, said Bellini to himself, I shall have to think about setting up dancing classes. They look quite well-to-do. There will have to be a small subscription fee, of course.

He felt encouraged that the ballroom might have a secure financial future. Not having met Arnold and Tracy Montgomery face to face, he did not recognise them in the crowd and he could not have known that the young couples were the Montgomerys' friends. Had he done so, he might have smelled the proverbial rat and been on his guard.

Four bars into the waltz, he realised that the violins were a semitone sharp and the trumpets were a semitone flat.

If you can imagine a hundred cats in a room where the floor was wired up to a generator supplying 250 volt shocks in three-four time, you might have some idea of the quality of the Bellini Orchestra's rendition of 'The Blue Danube'. You might prefer to have listened to the crashing scratches and jumps of the music at the Neptune's Trident.

The dancers were torn between outrage and epileptic hilarity. The former gradually gave way to the latter and the ballroom was filled to the chandelier with elegantly dressed guffaws. Bellini banged his baton on the rostrum to no avail. The orchestra carried blindly on, themselves trying not to dissipate into a giggling heap. For one flautist it was all too much. She blew a shrill peep into her instrument and doubled over in her chair, gasping and crying with laughter. The music continued in perfect dissonance.

Bellini chose to ride it out.

I am a dolphin on the wave, he thought.

His baton waving grew quite energetic as the red of his face deepened to scarlet and then burgundy and his body doubled in size. The laughter behind him threatened to drown out the orchestra and it was all directed at him, the conductor. After all, when things went wrong you did not laugh at a group of people, you did not laugh at violinists or trumpeters, you laughed at the conductor, the important one, the man in control.

Bellini was thankful Maria had refused to come tonight, among the many other things she had told him this morning she refused to do in consequence of the midnight rehearsal. Furthermore, he hoped Montgomery considered however much he had bribed the orchestra as money well spent.

'It is war, my *prodigalità*,' Bellini told his wife when he returned to the cabin after the evening's débâcle. The young couples had departed swiftly after 'The Blue Danube' while the older folk tried to regain a semblance of dignity and order, although it was difficult for them to avoid the odd smirk. As for the orchestra, they played for the rest of the night with innocent precision, as if nothing had happened. Out of tune? Them?

'Yes, Gian,' said Maria in the manner in which she had been speaking to him for the past day, unenthusiastically.

'Out-and-out war,' he continued, dipping his legs into his pyjama bottoms. 'We are families at war. You, I, even Paolo, wherever he is, we are at war with the Montgomerys. I have been insulted.'

'Do not bring Paolo's name into this.'

'I find it hard to mention that ingrate's name at all.'

'Ingrate! Who was it who threw him out of the cabin?'

'I admit I did, but it was only so that you and I might have some privacy, and Paolo must learn to fend for himself.'

'And he must be grateful to you for that?'

'Exactly.'

'Sometimes I do not believe I know you at all.'

'There is much to know about me,' said Bellini smugly.

'Yes, Gian. Turn the light out and go to bed.'

He obeyed and, on the way back into the main cabin where he had been consigned to sleep on the floor, he remarked to her: 'It is like *Romeo and Juliet*.'

'No, it isn't.'

'I shall take the play out from the library tomorrow. I shall see if it has any message for me as to how to deal with those *bastardi*.'

Bellini knew the story of *Romeo and Juliet* from the opera by his better-known namesake but the Shakespeare version which he borrowed from the library the next day did not shed new light or open new doors for him, partly because he found the English hard to understand and partly because, as Maria had implied, the plot bore little relevance to his situation. The conclusion, however, with the lovers dead and entombed together, struck a resonant chord in his scheming brain. He slept on it, in as much as he was allowed to sleep.

Signor Bellini's movements during the following morning could best be described as furtive and mysterious. The furtiveness was that of a humiliated man scared to show his face in public. The mystery lay in the nature of the places he visited.

The night before, the orchestra had behaved themselves and the only dancers had been the regulars, but Bellini went home quickly when the dances were over, not daring to meet anyone's eye. Very early the next morning he went down to Bart's before it officially opened and persuaded Bart by waving a sum of money beneath his nose to allow him to make some private purchases. Bart was not a man to ask questions unless he was establishing whether a customer's credit was good and he discreetly supplied the *signor* with everything he needed.

With his purchases bundled under his coat, Bellini visited the individual members of his brass section and spent a short time with each, leaving with a handshake and a wave. It took him the best part of the morning to complete his rounds, up and down decks, traversing dozens of walkways and gangplanks until he was quite out of breath.

He joined Maria for a silent lunch.

In the afternoon he shut himself away in the bedroom, emerging at around 16.00.

'Been busy?' Maria asked as a formality.

'Yes, my dearest *ricettacola*, I have spent a very profitable day.' He gave her a peck on the cheek. His moustache prickled her. 'I am just going to make peace with the Montgomerys. I think this nonsense has gone on long enough.'

Maria stared at him with a mixture of astonishment and judicious concern as he walked out with a small toolbag under his arm.

Bellini knocked gently on the Montgomerys' cabin door. Arnold opened it and instantly banged it shut. He called from inside: 'Go away! Leave us alone.'

'But, my dear sir, I have come to make peace. This petty bickering between us is senseless and cannot be allowed to continue. We must respect one another's privacy. I have come to do you a favour but if I have interrupted you I will come back later.'

'We weren't doing anything. Did you say favour?'

'Yes. I offer to repair your bed. Perhaps that way, we will both get a better night's sleep.'

Arnold opened the door a crack.

'Are you sure about this? I mean, you really don't have to.'

'Will you be able to get a janitor to fix it? No. But I, I have some small skills as a carpenter and I will do what I can.'

'Well, come on in then.' Arnold swung the door fully open and held out a hand to Bellini. 'I agree with you, I think it's better that we don't fight. I mean, there's enough fighting on board the *Hope* anyway without two sane chaps like you and me butting heads, eh?'

'Quite right,' said Bellini, beaming as he walked across the threshold and shook Arnold's hand.

Arnold introduced him properly to Tracy, who smiled nervously. She had heard about the Italian temperament and expected anything but the amorous hug and kisses the *signor* bestowed upon her.

'Ah, *bruttissima*!' sighed Bellini and Tracy blushed and Arnold, who like his wife did not speak a word of Italian, chose to assume a proud and pleased expression. 'You are a lucky man, Mr Montgomery.'

'Please, you can call me Arnold.'

'Arnold. How distinguished. I am Gian.'

'Gian's come to make peace, Tracy, and he's offered to mend the bed.'

'Oh, that's wonderful. It is a tiny bit noisy, isn't it?' She gave a shy giggle.

'The screws are loose, that is all,' said Bellini. 'A simple matter. I will have it fixed in no time. Is it in here?' He indicated the bedroom and Arnold readily ushered him through. There were boxes, some full, some empty, strewn over the floor. In one corner there was a pile of framed pictures, only one of which had been hung up. This solitary portrait of a half-naked woman made the walls seem even more bare. The whole room was incomplete, undressed. Bellini put down his toolbag and jiggled the bedstead so that it bumped against the wall. He hummed and hahed for a minute, jiggled it a bit more, and stroked his moustache.

'Yes. It should not be too difficult.'

'This is awfully kind of you, Gian. I thought after my little trick the other night you would rather punch me in the face than do me a favour.'

'Ah, we must forgive and be tolerant. I did not mind so much your little trick.'

'It was quite . . . amusing, wasn't it?'

'What? Oh, amusing . . . Yes, very amusing.'

'Well?'

'Well what?'

'Will you fix the bed?'

'Oh, sì. But surely you do not wish to stand around watching me work? It will not be very interesting.'

'You don't need a hand?'

'No, not at all.'

'This is decent of you. Tracy and I were going to pop out for a bite to eat.'

'Do that.'

'You don't mind if we leave you here for half an hour?'

'Not at all.'

Arnold and Tracy made their goodbyes, having asked if there was anything they could get the *signor* and received a polite refusal, and left him to it.

'Such a nice man,' said Tracy as they made their way to the dining-hall.

'I thought he might want to kill me after what I did to him, but he's turned out to be a rather good sort.'

'And it's important that we get on with the neighbours.'

'Such a better class of people than we had down on M deck.'

Tracy slipped her hand into Arnold's.

'And the bed's being fixed! You're a clever old thing, Arnold.'

Arnold found it hard not to smile.

They returned to find Bellini putting the finishing touches to his handiwork. The bed did not look noticeably sturdier but he assured them it would not wobble and bump as badly as before. Arnold stepped forward to give it a test.

'No, no!' cried Bellini. 'I must warn you, my friends. The glue I have used will not be truly dry until midnight.' He winked and tapped the side of his nose. 'I would advise you not to use it until then. Perhaps you would care to come to the ballroom instead this evening? Complimentary, of course.'

'Well . . . ' said Arnold.

'We've got plans,' said Tracy hastily.

'Ah, plans. Never mind.'

'But any time I can return the favour, I will,' enthused Arnold. 'Just ask.'

'Of course.'

The two men shook hands again and Bellini embraced Tracy like a long-lost cousin. The Montgomerys saw that he was smiling a smile of deep satisfaction.

'I'm glad this matter is resolved,' he said.

'Yes, it's good that we can forgive and forget,' said Arnold, choked with sympathy.

'There is nothing that I have forgiven,' said the *signor* as he stood in the doorway.

'Surely you mean there's nothing to forgive, don't you?' suggested Tracy.

'Yes, that is what I mean. My English is not very good. The grammar is so hard. *Buona notte.*'

At a quarter to midnight, the brass section tramped into the Bellini's cabin, lured by the promise of another voluble rehearsal and the offer of a small consideration of money from the *signor*'s own pocket. All in all, it had been a profitable week for the members of the Bellini Orchestra. On this occasion Maria put up a protest of wild-eyed and stony silence, which was somehow more terrifying than her previous verbal outpouring of fury. Bellini doubted he would get a civil word out of her for a week or be allowed to return to the bedroom for another month, but he considered it a small price to pay.

The brass section sat in readiness, puffing into their instruments to warm them up and waiting for their great conductor to give the signal. The *signor*'s neighbours, they decided, were tolerant people who clearly loved music and so they resolved to give an especially rousing display tonight.

Bellini cocked his head, listening out intently for something. The trombonist's knee quivered in anticipation.

Suddenly, Bellini raised his baton.

'Two, three . . . '

In the cabin above, a few seconds before the Bellini Orchestra brass section began their attempt to outdo Joshua at the walls of Jericho, Arnold and Tracy Montgomery tumbled loudly on to their newly repaired bed in a tangle of arms, legs and clothing, only to discover that the mattress was no longer attached to the bed-frame. As they crashed through to the floor Arnold was thinking that the *signor* had not been as much of a handyman as he had claimed. But this was not the case. The true ingenuity of the *signor's* craftsmanship was evident in his introduction of three wickedly sharp wooden spikes, each over two foot long, the end-product of an afternoon's energetic whittling on pieces of wood bought from Bart's. These were fixed pointing into the underside of the bed in such a way that they were pushed upwards by the force of the mattress as it descended beneath the weight of two bodies. The spikes pierced the mattress and impaled first Tracy, then Arnold.

Arnold could not understand why his wife was screaming and why he himself could not move and why they were wriggling like baited worms. He found it hard to think, what with Tracy screaming and the trumpets blaring away down below and this peculiar feeling in his chest and stomach . . . It felt very wrong there; was it something he had eaten? Things were growing dim around him. He could see Tracy's contorted face in blurred close-up. Was that blood?

The brass section noticed how beneath Bellini's moustache a great 'I'm in control' grin had formed and they redoubled their efforts in order to afford him the greatest possible pleasure for his money. They were deaf to anything except their noise, as were the inhabitants of the surrounding deck area.

Maria thought the trumpets sounded like human screams.

Friend

Ship

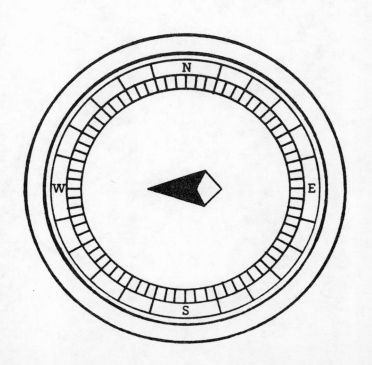

Pratt had chosen to be sexless because having a sex caused endless confusions and complications. For example, it limited your choice of friends. Being sexless you could have both men friends and women friends and not feel awkward in the company of either, scared neither to roar heartily or smile secretly depending on the sex of the company. A further compensation was that no one could criticise your choice of friends. A woman who associates mainly with men is a slut; a man who associates mainly with women is a pansy. Pratt was neither a slut nor a pansy, but poised elegantly somewhere in between. Pratt thought that Pratt might have had a sex once. Pratt's first name might have been James or Jane, George or Georgina, Paul or Paula, but that was a matter of the past, immaterial. Only the nameless, sexless present mattered.

In the nameless, sexless present, Pratt was watching a performance by a troupe of clowns, cavorting and leaping shapes in red-spotted costumes and gills of ruff around their necks, each with a cherry for a nose. They back-flipped and forward-flipped, leap-frogged and prat-fell, banged each other on the head, pulled each other's ginger wigs, sat on their baggy bottoms rubbing their bruised egos before jumping to their feet again and rejoining the fray. There was circus music coming from somewhere; Pratt was unsure of its source but nevertheless clapped joyously in time. Pratt punctuated the clowns' performance with whoops like commas and laughter like a full stop at the end of every gag.

When Pratt gave three big laughs, the clowns stopped their antics and looked up as if they had just heard thunder. The music was amputated in mid-note. The clowns scurried away into the walls, which parted for them like curtains, dragging their paraphernalia of ladders and squirty flowers and hoops. Pratt begged them to return, crying, 'Encore! Encore!'

and clapping until Pratt's palms ached, but nothing happened. The cabin was empty and chilly without the clowns.

Pratt drew consolation from the fact that loneliness was all in the mind. Being on your own did not make you lonely. Not seeing your neighbours did not make you lonely. Not going out for dinner did not make you lonely. It was so easy to have friends, friends of either sex, if you were on your own. The *Hope* sent you friends and friends filled your time, whiling away the hours of the present until the present became the past and the future became the present.

Pratt had a dachshund called Dotty. Pratt could not remember where Dotty had come from, nor how Pratt knew what breed of dog Dotty was, nor how Pratt knew what a dog was at all. There were no dogs on the *Hope*. Pratt had no memories of dogs. All the same, Pratt shared the cabin with Dotty, and Dotty, although she possessed the most affectionate of characters, also possessed the most incontinent of bladders. She had been sitting on the lower bunk watching the clowns' display and in the excitement a spray of piss jetted from her rear over the bedclothes. Dotty took one look behind her, crawled off the bed and slithered underneath, from where she poked out her nose and two mournful eyes.

'Don't worry, Dotty,' said Pratt. 'I'll wash it in the basin, using some of Mr Sellar's soap powder.'

As soon as his name was mentioned Mr Sellar popped out from behind the table. He wore a grey suit, grey shirt, grey tie, grey shoes and a hat (black), and he was clutching a great big box of Sudso washing powder. He sang a jingle:

> 'Sudso, oh Sudso
> It'll clean off your mud so
> It'll clear up that blood so
> It'll sort out that piss so
> So get Sudso
> If you know-ow
> That stains are no-go'.

'Sudso!' he cried. 'The newest, the latest, the bestest of all the new, late, best cleaning cleaner washing powders ever invented! It makes blacks grey and greys white and whites black. You won't know who you are! You won't know why you are! You won't know what you are! No mess, no fuss, no bother, no lather . . . Sudso!' Then he sang the jingle again so that no one could forget it or forget the name Sudso, and ducked back under the table.

Pratt stared agog at the space in the air that had just held Mr Sellar. Pratt had no great fondness for Mr Sellar because friends should never sell to or steal from one another and Mr Sellar seemed to be doing both, but Pratt also knew it was uncharitable to dwell on a friend's shortcomings. Friendship was about forgiving friends' failings and loving their virtues.

Pratt was proud of Pratt's friends. Pratt had chosen them from all the thousands of possible friends on the *Hope* and their company made each passing day passable, made living livable, from the moment when Pratt came down from the bunk in the morning, stretching and yawning (as Pratt had done barely quarter of an hour ago), to the time in the evening when Pratt would glide wearily back to bed wearing pink bedsocks, nightshirt and nightcap (as Pratt was wearing now). Not all the friends were friendly – Mr Sellar, for example, or Mrs Shame – but it would be pointless to have friends who agreed with you all the time.

Before Pratt had a chance to see to the soiled sheets, Pratt felt Pratt's belly grumbling and an urge coming on, so Pratt took out the slop-bucket from the cupboard. The bucket was nearly full to the brim. Doris the cleaning-lady (and friend) would have to empty it out soon. Pratt hitched up Pratt's nightshirt and squatted over the bucket. Pratt always squatted. If Pratt either stood or squatted purely for the purpose of urinating, it would be making a statement of sex, so as a rule Pratt had to wait until Pratt's bowels caught up with Pratt's bladder and then deal with both urges at the same time, as did men and women alike.

While Pratt was squatting there, up popped Mr Sellar again. This time he was advertising toilet paper. He hustled around on all fours for a minute in a passable impression of a puppy-dog (or was it a kitten?). Then he sang:

'Boggo, try Boggo
When you drop a loggo
It will oil the coggo
That's Boggo, oh Boggo, oh Boggo!'

'Boggo! Quick, clean, fast, efficient, better than any other product *ever*, neater, smarter, clever, farter, the best toilet roll since the last one, silent, keen, peaches, cream, you've never felt a softer paper up against your bum.' With that, Mr Sellar vanished in a puff of white feathers, leaving behind eight neatly folded sheets of Boggo in a special sample freebie presentation pack.

Pratt's concentration had been distracted completely by these antics and Pratt had to start all over again, thinking hard about bowels and bladder until the desired effect was achieved. Relieved, Pratt inspected the consequences of the urges, although it was not that easy distinguishing them from earlier urges. They seemed healthy enough. Pratt used Mr Sellar's freebie offering gratefully and then put away the bucket, tying a mental knot in a mental handkerchief to remember to ask Doris to throw it out.

Pratt drifted about the cabin for a while, curling a strand of fine hair around an index finger, having forgotten totally about Dotty's miscalculation. Pratt walked by the packet of Sudso several times and was not reminded. Pratt's cabin was hushed and darkened like a cinema, curtains drawn to create a twilight lasting all day. In the real cinema, before they closed it down, the pictures used to be invisible if the light was bright. The same was true of Pratt's cabin. In broad daylight the friends did not exist or at least, if they existed, they were invisible. They might still be heard but only as whispers melted into the rumbled mutterings of the *Hope*. Here and there Pratt might be able to snatch out a phrase or two, but without the lights off it was generally incoherent babble. In the perpetual twilight and especially in the half-sleep minutes before sleeping and before waking, the friends were visible and strong and as good as real.

Underneath the bunk Dotty whined. This meant someone was coming and Pratt suspected who.

Mr Panic and Mrs Shame wafted into the cabin and Pratt whined just as Dotty had done, but quietly so that the new arrivals would not hear. It was a mystery to Pratt why Panic and Shame could never get on. They were a peculiar couple and symptomatic of the great problem with having a sex: Having To Get On With The Opposite Sex. If you could not hope to understand each other by virtue of the spectacular physical and mental differences between you, what was the point in attempting to spend the rest of your lives together? Superficially, Panic and Shame were not dissimilar. They were both fattish and tan-skinned and dark-haired. But apart from these features, they had nothing in common. Where had the *Hope* got them from?

'Shocking!' cried Shame. 'Look at the state of this place. And that smell. Appalling!'

'I don't think it's that bad, darling,' replied Panic.

'And you, Pratt, you snivelling, skinny, wretched, moronic thing . . . ' Naturally Pratt did not enjoy being called insulting names, but you did not argue with her when she was in this kind of mood. It merely brought Shame down on your head. 'What have *you* done this fine day?'

'Well, I've only just got up,' explained Pratt meekly.

'Liar! You've been up sixteen minutes.'

'Pratt's only just got up, darling,' echoed Panic.

'I heard Pratt perfectly well the first time! Do you think my ears don't work? And if they didn't work, do you think I wouldn't have learnt to lip-read? Honestly! You take me for an idiot but it's me that has to treat *you* like a simpleton—'

'Darling—'

'Me that has to tell you what to eat and what to wear—'

'Darling—'

'Me that has to blow your nose and clean your bottom and wipe up after your—'

'*Darling!* These are matters between ourselves. Pratt does not need to know.'

'But I like to know,' Pratt piped up, 'because friends know everything about each other.' There was an itch at the back of Pratt's head and Pratt scratched it.

'Do you think we're your friends, miserable creature?'

'The *Hope* sent you, so you must be.'

'And where are these other friends that you pretend to have?'

'Some are here and some aren't. The Rain Man was my friend, but he ran away to seek his fame and fortune in the wide world. So did Lonely the Rat. I was sad when they ran away. The Rain Man was a good friend and poor Lonely was just unhappy. He thought he knew so much, thought he had the solutions to all the problems.'

'Ha!' exclaimed Shame as if she had discovered an important scientific theorem. 'Ha!' she repeated.

'Ha,' echoed Panic quietly.

A turtle scuttled across the cabin floor, too fast for anyone but Pratt to notice. Pratt decided to call it Wilbur.

'Moreover,' announced Shame, 'what gives you the temerity to think that the *Hope* is your friend?'

'What's "temerity"?' Pratt asked.

'Don't avoid the question. Pratt's avoiding the question, Panic.'

'Perhaps not, darling. Perhaps Pratt really doesn't understand the meaning of the word "temerity". You do use some awfully complicated words, light of my life. Sometimes even I find it hard to understand you. For my benefit, then, unbearable being of lightness, tell us, what does "temerity" mean?'

Shame drew breath. 'There is no reason why I should tell you – either of you pathetic individuals.'

'Probably doesn't know,' muttered Panic under his breath.

'What? What did you say?'

'Nothing, dear.'

'You said something. There's nothing worse than when someone says something and pretends they said nothing. And anyway, I heard what you said.'

'What did I say, lamp of love?'

'You know perfectly well. You said, "Profit is driven snow." I heard! I heard!'

'What does "Profit is driven snow" mean exactly?' asked Pratt.

'You mean you don't know?' rejoined Shame. 'Tsk! Idiot!

Fool! It's a very famous old proverb, like "Never look at a gift-horse," or "Too many cooks spoil the fish." '

'Oh,' said Pratt, very little enlightened, and itched again at the itch, which would not go away.

Wilbur the Turtle clambered on to the table-top, girded up his loins (proverbially, of course) and took a flying leap off the edge. He withdrew his head and limbs as he fell, and landed on his shell with a crunch, unharmed. The shell rocked on the floor for a moment. Then Wilbur put out his leathery head, smiled, bowed, flipped himself over, stuck out his limbs and raced off through the wall. Pratt wanted to applaud but Shame would almost definitely criticise, so Pratt refrained.

'Are you ever going to have this place cleaned up?' said Shame, returning to her first plan of attack.

'Doris, my friend—' Pratt laid great stress on the last word – 'is coming in soon.'

'Good. There is nothing worse than filth.'

'Or rubbish,' chimed in Panic.

'Filth,' pronounced Shame, 'is far, far worse than rubbish.'

'But there's a lot more rubbish on the *Hope*. Too much. The ship's filling up with rubbish.'

'She's filling up with more filth than rubbish.'

'She? Do you think the *Hope* is a she?' said Pratt incredulously.

'Of course she's a she. All ships are shes. It's common knowledge.'

Dotty whined. Pratt spoke as loudly as possible to cover up her whining: 'But the *Hope*'s a he. He's big and strong as iron and powerful as steel. A she wouldn't let men run her life the way the Captain and the crew run the *Hope*, would she, Mrs Shame? A she wouldn't let men take all the credit. Listen. He has a he voice.' They all three listened to the familiar bass rumble of the turbines.

'I don't hear anything,' said Shame.

'But you did say you weren't deaf, dear,' said Panic with as much glee as he dared.

'Well, what am I supposed to hear?'

'The voice of the engines,' Pratt said, letting impatience fracture the phrase a tiny bit.

'It is a low voice,' admitted Panic.

'Nonsense!' said Shame. 'It's a low high voice. It's not unusual for women to have low voices. Actually, some men find it very attractive. Women can have beards too, you know.'

Clearly this argument had clinched it for Shame because she folded her arms and looked at the ceiling. Pratt had not been aware women could have beards but was glad to learn the fact. It reinforced Pratt's case against having a sex. Pratt scratched Pratt's head and tried to re-open the conversation as tactfully as possible.

'I still think the *Hope* is a he.'

'She's a she,' insisted Shame.

'He.'

'She.'

'He!'

'She!'

'He!'

'She!'

'Heeeee!' Annoying, aggravating itch. Pratt scraped at the nape of Pratt's neck.

Shame sat upright and stuck out her not inconsiderable chest. 'I can see this is getting neither of us anywhere. Panic, we are leaving.'

'We only just got here, sweetness and saccharin.'

'And that is why we are leaving.'

'Very well . . . '

The instant Mr Panic and Mrs Shame had gone, Mr Sellar dropped down from the ceiling and held up a card. The card read:

EDWARD, WALLACE, SIMPSON
Marriage Guidance Counsellors

'We at EWS,' said Mr Sellar, 'believe that the only good marriage is a dead marriage. We aim to promote honesty between lifelong partners. Honesty is our policy. Had an affair? Spending too much time at the office? Closet homosexual? Drink problem? Tell us your secrets and we will tell your partner. That way, you'll never quarrel, you'll never suspect, you'll never doubt. Deadliness is next to goodliness is next to Loch Ness.'

Mr Sellar stepped closer and seemed to be confiding in Pratt.

'For you, sir or madam, we can offer a special discount rate. Two sessions for the price of one. You'll never be in two minds about anything!'

Then came the jingle:

> 'EWS
> Are really the best
> If your marriage is down the drain
> If it hasn't been the same
> Since your wedding day
> Don't despair, no need to pray
> If your partnership's depressed
> Come to good old E . . . W . . . S.'

'Mr Sellar?' said Pratt.

'Yes, sir or madam?'

'Is the *Hope* my friend?'

'A friend a day keeps the psychiatrist away.'

'Can I trust him?'

'Who?'

'The *Hope*.'

'Oh, her. Trust always turns to rust.'

'So how can I know for certain?'

'Can I interest you in some of my special sleeping-tablets? Take the bottle, all of it, and your problem's solved. Special bargain, for this week only. Buy one, get one free.' Mr Sellar took out from his unending pockets a special sample freebie presentation pack of two Nod-Offs, placed it on the tabletop and sank into the floor, leaving behind his black hat. A second later his hand reappeared, grabbed the hat, tipped it to Pratt, and pulled it under.

Take a whole bottle of sleeping-tablets? But that would be . . .

Anyway, Pratt could not afford to buy a whole bottle.

One of the clowns did a somersault into Pratt's line of vision. He had on a sad face, two bright green tears dripping from the corner of one eye and the smile turned down. He held a red rose in his hand. He held the red rose up to his red nose, sniffed hard and held it away again in a red masque of despair. He raised his eyes to the heavens, regretting the injustices of love and the torturous games played in love's name, and spoke with passion infusing every syllable:

'This bud of love, by summer's ripening breath,
May prove a beauteous flower when next we meet.'

The rose in his hand began to shrivel, to brown, to wilt, to droop, to die.

Pratt found it hard not to cry at this touching scene and sniffed back the tears hard.

'Ta-daa!' went the clown and all of a sudden his face was back to grinning normal. He bowed and applauded his audience appreciatively. Pratt, however, was still crying. These were good friends, such good friends. Pratt loved them all, as you could not help loving your flesh and blood, your pets, your playthings, and Pratt's kind of love was like a pure, clear stream, unmuddied by liaisons and confusions and infidelities and infelicities, its surface smooth with flowing content. Not to love was to dry up and wither, cutting off the springs from your heart, damming up your soul. Pratt tasted Pratt's tears and they tasted of salt and soil, moss and loam, chalk and lime. The clown carried on applauding Pratt's performance.

'You are teared,' he told Pratt, although Pratt thought he said 'tired' and Pratt *was* feeling tired. A yawn welled up inside Pratt and was let out. Pratt's eyelids would not stay up where they belonged.

But I have only just got out of bed, thought Pratt. Am I ill?

It was a silly question, because Pratt had never been ill. Pratt had always been healthy and regular, another advantage of renouncing the wearying, ageing conflicts of being a man or being a woman. But there was always the possibility Pratt was lovesick for Pratt's friends.

The clown kept up his clapping and Dotty started yapping and the itching was now a tapping coming from inside Pratt's skull, a dream aching to be released. Pratt's dreams were like that, like caged creatures scratching and pawing for freedom, and if they weren't freed quickly they became violent and scrabbled against the bars until their paws bled and the blood came out from Pratt's ears and nose. Pratt had to sleep if the dream was to be released before it harmed itself. Pratt had to let it fly and fade, to go wherever dreams went, into nothingness presumably. Pratt pressed the pair of Nod-Offs out of their foil presentation pack, swallowed them, crawled up to the top bunk and snuggled under the covers, too tired to feel the clammy spot where Dotty had pissed. The clown bowed one last time and made a polite but hasty exit.

'Night night, Dotty,' said Pratt.

Dotty barked a reply that could well have been saying, 'Good morning.'

Sleep came easily. It was a haven for the storm-tossed soul. It was a nest for the frightened fledgling. It was a womb for the growing foetus. It was . . .

Zzzzzzzzzzzz.

Pratt lifted away from Pratt's body, shrugging off clumsy folds of flesh like last year's fashions. Pratt's spirit unfolded its wet wings and held them open to the sunlight, pumping them up with blood until Pratt felt – Pratt *knew* – that Pratt could soar. Pratt floated up from the bed and through the cabin, careful not to wake the friends. Dotty wheezed and whined in her sleep at the passing of Pratt's soul, but did not stir. Mr Sellar was nowhere to be seen, no doubt plotting some dynamic new campaign over a lengthy brainstorming breakfast. Wilbur had come out to snooze in his shell in the middle of the floor. Pratt dreamed the dream of flying and Pratt had never had a dream like this one before. It was special, the sort of dream you worked and died for, you never wanted to wake up from. Pratt floated out through the door and along the walkway. Morning mist in drowsy curls shifted in Pratt's wake but the solitary passengers who wandered in the fresh daylight remained undisturbed. Pratt drifted by them, a breath in the shape of a Pratt.

Pratt rose up through the battened layers of the *Hope*. A dozing stopper twitched in his sleep, perhaps seeing

Pratt with his mind's eye and leaping to his dream feet in surprise. Gangplanks' railings gleamed in the sun, hung with fine arrays of droplets like wealthy widows' pearls. Pratt passed through them and the jewels twinkled.

Pratt reached the upper decks, the playgrounds of the bored unfortunates with fortunes. Swimming-pools glittered, their surfaces uncomplicated by bathers. An early game of quoits was under way, the players dressed in their best whites and agreeably subdued by the time of day. A flash of light caught Pratt's attention. A greenhouse, already perspiring and fogging up its panes, winked to its old friend the sun. Through the panes Pratt could make out the lime-greens and darker tropical shades of growing things. Better still, Pratt could hear the crackling of new leaves as they twisted to the sunlight and shoots stretching their aching joints into the soil and tomatoes murmuring with the blush of life and potatoes giving a solid, reliable, earthy reply.

Seagulls whirred around Pratt's spirit, squawking in bemusement at the strange man-shaped, woman-shaped creature of no substance that dared intrude on their airspace. Their vast wings beat fluttering tattoos in Pratt's intangible ears.

The funnels! Six cylindrical titans churning out black air, the witnesses to the *Hope*'s mighty efforts of moving. Pratt slalomed in and out of the gouts of smoke, singing in delight a hymn to the thunderous power of the ship.

And the ship below Pratt: five miles of blackened steel furrowing through the waves. The *Hope*'s trail spread out behind in a vast V of white water that only ended when it touched the horizon. The ocean seemed to buckle under the immense bulk of the ship, Nature tested to the breaking-point.

Pratt took in all the wonders, man-made and God-made, and Pratt's spirit glowed bright. Below Pratt a million waking lives were beginning another day. They crawled down from bunks, they washed their faces, they answered their urges, they kissed their loved ones, they cursed their enemies, they pulled back the curtains to inhale the sunlit air, they said their first words of the day, they rejoiced in the simple struggle of being.

– Little soul!

Pratt's spirit nearly exploded with the ponderous majesty of the voice. It welled up around Pratt's spirit and it rang like a bell forged from a billion tonnes of metal.

– Little soul!

It was calling to Pratt!

– Yes? Pratt answered, faint with awe.

– What are you?

– I'm Pratt. How do you do?

– I live. That is all I can say. That is all I can do.

– Who or what, may I ask, are you?

– I am the *Hope*.

Pratt's head spun. The *Hope*! Pratt was conversing with the *Hope*! Moreover, as Pratt had always believed, the *Hope* was a he.

– Pleased to meet you, Mr *Hope*. Thank you for my friends.

Pratt felt it was best to get off on a good footing.

– Not at all. What friends?

– The ones you sent me. The clowns, Dotty, Doris, Wilbur, Mr Sellar, Mr Panic and Mrs Shame . . .

– I sent you no friends.

– Well, if it wasn't you, who was it?

– I do not know.

– Don't you know everything?

There was a sonorous pause before the *Hope* replied.

– I know little and I was born to know nothing. I am only the *Hope*.

– You are a great and mighty ship, O *Hope*, said Pratt with all the reverence Pratt could muster. Pratt thought the *Hope* sounded in need of a little flattery.

– I am not. I am merely a toy.

– Toys are not made as large as you. Toys are only made little and weak to be played with by ungrateful children until they get broken.

– I am broken.

– You can't be! You're meant to get us all safely to the other side of the unending ocean. That is the way of the *Hope*.

– I am broken and I cannot be mended.

– Nonsense! Sorry, I didn't mean to sound so rude, but really, you're talking like a spoilt child.

– Am I? I did not intend to.

– No, I'm sure you didn't.

But the silence that followed alarmed Pratt. Had Pratt made some frightful blunder?

– Friendships can be broken too, said the *Hope* at last.

– Yes. Like when the Rain Man and Lonely ran away.

– The Rain Man is still your friend, I think.

– Where is he, then? Can I see him?

– He is in me and everywhere. He is above and below. He belongs and is content. He does no harm.

– How marvellous, marvelled Pratt.

– And Lonely is very special to me.

– He was to me too, for all his faults.

– I talk with him. I tell him what I feel and what I know. He is healing and helping me. But I forget things when it is so hard to remember. I – How far have I gone?

– I've no idea. I thought you'd be more likely to know that sort of thing than me.

– I am the *Hope*. Who are you?

– I told you, I'm Pratt.

– It is so difficult. I know so little. I wish I knew more. I think and I think until it hurts to think and I feel that I am ready to die. And all this time I have been kept in the dark.

– I'm kept in the dark too. In fact, I like to keep myself in the dark. That's where the friends are.

– Yes?

– You're not sounding very well, Pratt ventured. Are you all right? Are you healthy and regular?

– I do not understand. I am the *Hope*. I am not well. Something turns within me, breeds like bacteria, infects my insides. A foul taste. I wish to spit it out but I do not know how.

– Is it evil?

– No, not evil. Nor innocent. Ignorant. It knows as little as I do. It knows less, perhaps. Less than nothing. But it breeds and uncoils itself and its ignorance is its teeth.

– What is it?

– I do not know. I know only that it must be cured. I know only that I hurt.

– Is there anything I can do to help? I know I'm only little but I have lots of friends.

– You are little but your mind is great. I would like you to help me, yes. I would like you to take the suffering away. I would like you to heal me of this illness, as Lonely is healing me.

Pratt did a small spiritual jump for joy. Pratt, the *Hope*'s helper!

– How can I do it?

– What have you to offer?

– Nothing but myself and all my friends.

– Ah, your friends, then. You must make more friends.

– But I can't. You send the friends to me, I don't make them. I have no choice in the matter.

– You have all the choice. Your friends are of your own choosing. They are parts of you, the parts you cannot understand, the parts that sometimes frighten you.

– For someone who says he knows nothing, you know a great deal, Mr *Hope*.

– I know nothing. I am kept in the dark. Who are you?

This line of reasoning seemed to stick the *Hope* in a groove. Pratt floated around for a while, trying to be as casual as a spirit could, although it was hard to whistle without a proper mouth. Eventually Pratt guessed the conversation was officially terminated and said.

– I suppose I must be going. All right? Any last requests?

– Make friends.

– Is that it?

No reply. Pratt started to descend. The funnels' smoke was acrid and stinging, so that Pratt avoided it as much as possible. The seagulls were enraged now that this sexless being should invade twice in one morning and set off a volley of vicious caws. Pratt chose to ignore them.

Reaching the upper decks Pratt saw that the game of quoits had been abandoned after one of the players cheated. The pools were awash with swimmers who believed that a few lazy lengths was the means to peak condition and un-paralleled beauty. Passengers in rich clothing ambled about with hidden eyes. They were undeniably elegant, but in a louche, uncaring way.

In the greenhouses roses cried at the bites of the aphids that swarmed their stems looking like miniature warts grown from the flowers' flesh, and the roses were demanding to know why they deserved such disfiguration. A caterpillar squirmed in the heart of a cauliflower, rejoicing, the first of many. Brown-edged leaves sucked greedily at the foetid air.

The upper decks were crammed down on to the lower decks in awkward and untidy pyramids. Pratt had an inkling of the pressure this created, how it compacted in the belly of the *Hope* like bad food. There, in the belly, children strode about in parodies of adulthood, mimicking all the wrong aspects of adults: the fighting, the cynicism, the pessimism. They planned wars, tiny, insignificant, ugly wars. Pratt saw too that there were stoppers everywhere, meandering through life, sitting, stopping, wishing they were part of the ship and not merely the ship's filth and rubbish.

And finally Pratt's cabin: a dismal cell of greying light where the smell of urine hung dense and potent. Dotty's sleep was agitated. Her paws scratched and her claws clicked against the wall. Pratt saw Pratt's body. It was a clumsy slice of flesh and bone. Pratt's spirit swallowed its metaphysical pride and gingerly lowered itself back in. It was like drowning in oil. The flesh clutched desperately to the spirit once more and the heart spurred itself to beat again and the bowels resumed their sluggish contractions.

Pratt's eyes flipped open. Pratt yawned a great yawn. Pratt's nightcap had fallen off on to the floor.

But Pratt was not the same as before. Pratt was the *Hope*'s helper now and it was an important position to hold. As the *Hope*'s helper, Pratt could not wait to carry out the *Hope*'s instruction.

Make friends.

How? Go out and introduce Pratt to the people outdoors? Unthinkable. Those people did not understand Pratt. They treated Pratt as a freak, a monster even.

Pratt sat at the table and thought carefully. How could Pratt hope to make friends if the *Hope* didn't send them?

In came Mr Sellar:

> 'Friends?
> That depends?
> Can you make them?
> Can you break them?
> If friends are what you need
> If friends are what's decreed
> There's one thing you can do
> (That's one – not three or two)
> It's cheap and neat and clean
> And it's called the Friend Machine.'

'But what is it?' complained Pratt.

'Here, sir or madam,' said Mr Sellar, taking out the product, 'is the Friend Machine. Send no money now! Just clip out the coupon and we will send you the Friend Machine on approval for ten days. If you are not delighted, you are under no obligation to buy. Simply return the Friend Machine to us and we will refund your postage. If you wish to keep the Friend Machine, send us the money and it's yours – absolutely free!'

Mr Sellar held up the Friend Machine for Pratt to get a closer look.

The Friend Machine was a mirror.

'I'll give it the trial ten days,' said Pratt with swelling excitement. Mr Sellar smiled on approval, raised his black hat and vanished. Pratt stared at Pratt in the mirror for several minutes, at Pratt's sensuous lips and starry eyelashes and thin golden hair. Finally, after several minutes of acknowledging the undeniable beauty of Pratt, Pratt realised what the Friend Machine was.

Pratt voided Pratt's mind and concentrated hard on squirrels. Pratt liked squirrels. Pratt had read a book once about a squirrel which had an argument with an owl, so Pratt knew what squirrels were like. The wild dream in Pratt's head growled and began running up and down its cage. Pratt thought of squirrel-type things: bushy tail, beady eyes, hoarding hazelnuts and acorns, leapings from tree to tree. The dream howled and wrenched at the bars and the ache got worse and worse and it hurt and it hurt and then it was *free*!

Cedric the Squirrel, still steaming-wet with afterbirth, lay on the table and panted. Pratt reached out and touched Cedric's chest, which throbbed with life beneath Pratt's fingers. Cedric opened his eyes and chirruped blearily.

Pratt felt an ecstasy of the soul and the pain in Pratt's head was an emptied but happy pain, eased by the warmth of Pratt's achievement. All along, it had not been the *Hope* sending the friends. Pratt, unaware, had been making them on Pratt's own, with Pratt's mind.

Cedric started up and began squirrelling around the cabin, jumping from surface to surface, wall to curtain, hanging from the bunk and catapulting himself to the floor. Pratt chuckled. Already the birth-pangs were fading from Pratt's head and the uncaged dream was a ghostly memory, an outline in the shape of a wild beast. It had companions, that dream-animal. So many thousands of caged brothers and sisters yearning to be freed. The potential. The possibilities.

Pratt deliberated as to what friends Pratt would make next. Pratt was already thinking of the Rain Man, Pratt's good friend of old, a creature of the whim of the tides and the skies, the moon and the sun, never truly happy but never sad, content to be the slave of gentle masters. Perhaps Pratt should consider another Rain Man. Pratt knew how to make one. Perhaps dozens . . .

Big

General

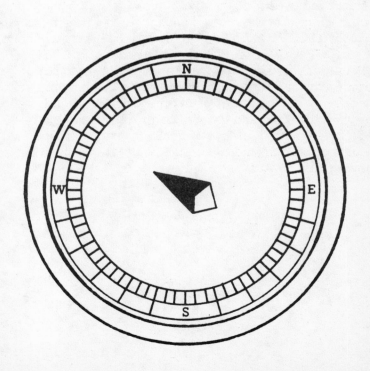

'Where's Eddy?'

'Hasn't been around for days. Stopped turning up at the bar. I think it's that woman he's been seeing. Pussy-whipped.'

'Ssh. Don't let Delia hear you.'

'Well, that's fucking great. Our best man down. And he was looking forward to this, the dumb fuck.'

'Chicken!'

'Anyone see Lock yet?'

'Probably chicken too.'

'Yeah. Running scared.'

The hard men stood at the poolside, their noses filled thickly with the smell of stale, rancid chemicals, old chlorine swollen with old sweat and old urine, their feet ruining still puddles of stagnant water. The smell was the pool's breath and the pool was a hungry sky-blue mouth, its teeth white-tile enamel stained yellow and brown in places like a chain-smoker's. Endless streams of water trickled down from the ceiling but failed to raise the water-level above an inch or so in the deep end. Liquid sparks sprayed up where the streams fell and the wet tiles writhed with the effort. Along the bottom ran black parallel lines. If you looked closely you could see they were elongated H-shapes, but their purpose was anybody's guess. There were useless, meaningless signs at intervals along the walls, faded but just legible: NO RUNNING, NO DIVING, NO DUCKING, NO SPLASHING.

You might as well add NO SWIMMING, thought Small.

There had not been any swimming here for as long as he could remember. The idea of a pool full of water was almost as incomprehensible as a sky clear of smoke or a belly full of food. This pool was not for swimming, he knew. It was one of those places you didn't go unless you were going there for the correct purpose. The pool was for fighting.

'And where the buggery fuck is Paolo?'

'Dunno. He took off earlier, just like that, no reason. Saw Longpole talking to him and then they both ran off, never came back.'

'Where the hell are these people going? What the hell is happening? This is a scrap, isn't it? Tell me I'm right.'

'Yeeesss.'

'Good. Thank you. For a moment I thought I was in the wrong place. For a moment I thought I was at an upstairs tea-fucking-party.' Riot stalked backwards and forwards along the lip of the pool, flicking his knife open and clasping it shut repeatedly to show his agitation to the rest of them. He had his name tattooed in tiny letters on his right cheek but in mirror-writing so that he could be the only one to read it properly. His short back and sides was evidently self-inflicted to judge by the razor-cuts above his ears and on the back of his neck. It was certainly one of the shortest back and sides Small had ever seen. There were patches where it looked more like 17.00 shadow.

Riot's scared, thought Small, only he doesn't show it because he's too cool. Small wished he could do that too, not show that he was scared, but Riot was a hard man and the leader while Small, he of the famous 'Small is beautiful' graffiti campaign, was nothing but a snotnose kid.

Wild Billy was there, scraping underneath his fingernails with his blade like he was waiting for a friend to turn up so they could both go and get pissed, not waiting for Lock and his shitheads to come along for a bit of serious mutual damage. Billy had this stupid hat on, a sailor's hat, which he said he wore as a joke, only Small thought the joke was on Billy. Actually, Billy wasn't a bad guy. He had confided in Small the other day, 'because you're a little tosser so it doesn't matter what I tell you,' though Small knew really Billy liked him a little bit and valued him as an audience. No one didn't like Small but it wasn't cool to say you did since Small was so small and only a kid.

Billy had said: 'You know, I'm lucky to be alive. I've seen some weird stuff this week, stuff that would make your teeth sweat and your nipples shrivel and turn your dick green. I don't think I'm going to live much longer, Small. I thought you should know that.'

Small had tried to cheer him up, but it had been useless. Billy had been enjoying himself too much.

'Yeah, I'm going to die, and it may be in a scrap and it may not. I could die just falling off a walkway tomorrow. Or some arsehole could stick me with a blade. Whatever it is, it's going to be soon. This ship's going to hell in a handbasket, Small. We're all fucked, all of us, and we're all going to die soon.'

Of course it was crap. Billy had been well tanked and Small knew that all the hard men talked stupid like that every so often when they got tanked and didn't have a woman to talk to. Besides, Billy was wrong. The only people who were going to die soon were old people. Everyone kept telling Small how lucky he was to be small and young because he had a long time to live and might well live to see what was on the other side of the unending ocean. That made Small feel big and sort of special.

Riot stamped his foot.

'Damn it! Where are those knobheads?'

'Maybe they surrendered and decided not to tell us,' Acid Cas proposed. There were a number of things Small didn't like about Acid Cas and his sense of humour was near the top of the list. It was rumoured that Cas had lost the use of three-quarters of available brain and Small wished he had lost the use of the part that kept saying crass, dumb fuck things, had maybe swapped it in exchange for the bit that contained common sense. Sometimes, when Cas's hands started shaking and the whites of his eyes started showing, Small preferred not to be around. In scraps Cas just went crazy and stuck everything that moved. He was a bad man to have against you in a fight. Then again, he was a bad man to have on your side.

There were about thirty of them all told. Riot and Eddy had done a good job whipping up a frenzy against Lock and rounding up the resident fighting talent. The charges against

Lock were many: that he and his gang had raided the cellars of the Trident and stolen half the booze; that they had raped three girls from the area (nothing enraged the hard men more than the idea of their women being raped – all of a sudden, it brought the chivalry out in them); that they had damaged property; that they had killed Popeye and Jones a couple of days ago when they were out with Billy on a scavenging trip (Billy said there were at least ten of the enemy but he had done for every one of them single-handed); and the list of crimes went on and on. By the end of Riot's exhortation, which was just over an hour ago, there was bloodlust and fury worked into the crowd that left the Trident and headed for the pool, and the air rang with threats and boasts and the promise of violence.

'Hey, Riot!' A sneering voice sang echoing clear across the empty pool. Lock. 'I didn't realise it was a poofs' evening. I'd have brought my boyfriend!'

'Which one?' Riot yelled back.

Both remarks achieved the desired laughs from each of the opposing camps. Small didn't like that kind of laughing but it was something you had to do as a hard man, make a laugh an insult. He couldn't quite manage it yet.

'I don't see Eddy,' said Lock.

'He didn't think it was worth his while coming.'

'Oh, dear. We'll have to prove him wrong, won't we, lads?' This was a cue for a roar of approval from Lock's men. Lock was wearing khaki and green, his shirt rolled up at the sleeves and open at the front. Big General. He was tall and Small thought his muscles were vast, like barrels strapped to his arms and chest under liquorice skin. He had never seen Lock before, although stories about him, apparently exaggerated, had been rife these past few days. However, the truth lived up to the fiction. The guy was a giant. Compared with him Riot didn't look as impressive as usual, just an ordinary white guy in a patched and tattered jacket. But Riot was ace with a blade, Small knew. Riot knew it too.

Small remembered when he had asked Riot if he could come along to the scrap. They had been in Riot's cabin. Every inch of wall space was covered in dog-eared posters of old movies, Small couldn't tell which ones because he couldn't read. Nor had he ever been to see a movie. The ship's cinema had closed down a few years after the voyage began, long before Small was born. People had got tired of seeing the same old movies again and again, even one called *The Sound of Music*. Riot said the movies were cool, especially the ones with actors called Marlon Brando and James Dean and Harry Dean Stanton and Robert de Niro in, and he could have watched those again and again without ever getting bored. He said the cinema had been closed down because 'they' didn't like kids seeing those kind of movies, the ones with the cool actors in. 'They' thought they were a bad influence.

Small had just popped the question.

'Yeah, OK, you can come along,' said Riot. 'But you stay at the side and you watch. You watch. You don't join in. You'll be safe if you don't get into the pool because everywhere outside of the pool is neutral territory. Got that? You might even learn something by watching. You're a good kid, maybe a good fighter, who knows? Maybe one day you'll take over from me.'

'No, I want to survive to see the other side.'

'You cheeky bugger!' laughed Riot. 'I'm going to live that long too. I'm the best with a blade.'

'What about Eddy?'

'I'll tell you about Eddy. We had a scrap a few years back, I think over some girl. Either I was screwing her and he wanted a bit or the other way round, it doesn't matter. So we got down into the pool with everybody watching and got out our blades and we danced around for a bit, testing the water, so to speak, and it was like poetry, Small. The best knife-men on the whole fucking *Hope*, playing to the crowd. He gave me this.' Riot showed him a white line down his arm, red and pinched at the edges where it had not healed properly. 'And me, I sliced him from neck to dick, right down his front, here. And that was it. We'd both drawn blood, end of scrap. I'd drawn more, so the girl was mine. Now you tell me, isn't that much easier than going to the Captain and asking him to decide for you like law-abiding people do? I mean, our sort wouldn't even get in to *see* the cocksucker! So how are we supposed to get anything done unless we do it ourselves? It's common sense, isn't it?'

Small had felt a strange emotion listening to Riot talk like this, a charge of static electricity in his heart that he would have been hard pushed to name, but it was like standing at the outer rim and staring down at the ocean until your head went woozy and wondering how it would be to jump and what you would think about on the way down. He had this idea he would think about doors, a whole corridor of them, one opening on to the next and closing behind you, never to open again. At the end of this corridor something waited, something like a knife, only sharper and deadlier, and it was crouching. Small didn't know where the idea had come from. It just happened into his head, accompanying the idea of falling over the side of the *Hope*. Was that dying? A corridor of doors?

But that emotion was nothing compared to the surge of pleasure he felt when Riot said: 'If I die, you can have my blade, Small. But wait until I'm dead, all right?'

With that, he took the knife out to show Small. It had a mother-of-pearl handle, which gleamed with rainbow flecks of colour against cool ivory white. Small turned it over in his hands, ran his thumb over the fake-silver stud.

'Hey, careful. This is how you do it.'

Riot pressed the stud and the blade flicked out.

'You've got to keep it sharp,' Riot continued, 'or it won't cut shit. This is sharp.' He took a pencil and laid the cutting-edge over it. Exerting the slightest pressure, he sliced the pencil in half. Small gasped.

You see, Riot wasn't a bad guy either, if you got to know him.

Small seemed to know all the hard men better than they knew each other. He learned how they feared each other and threatened each other. It wasn't much of a way to live but Small wished he also could threaten and fear his friends. You might never sleep easily in your bunk and you might have to keep looking over your shoulder, but it meant you were a hard man.

Riot and Lock were lowering themselves over either side of the pool. Droplets pattered into their hair and on to their shoulders, falling from fine-line cracks and the joints of the pipes that criss-crossed the high ceiling. The ceiling was painted with clouds like thought-bubbles on a glaring blue background, one cloud with a bold sun staring out from behind. Four out of the six overhead lamps had shorted out and the last two were swinging steadily, pendulums hung with weights of feeble light. More light, steam-grey and uninspired, came in from the portholes along one wall.

The leaders of men faced each other wordless with the ringing chatter of falling water all around them. Lock spoke first.

'I've been hearing some lies about me, Riot. And I hear you've been spreading them.'

'I don't spread lies. The truth, however—'

'Truth, my arse! You wouldn't know the truth if it came up and fucked you.'

'Well, at least it would have the good taste to want to fuck me. It wouldn't even give you a blowjob.'

The insults were a litany, the breaking of bread and the pouring of wine before the communion of battle. The rest of the combatants stood or sat beside the pool and radiated nonchalance, ignoring the leaders and their sabre-rattling business, which was nothing to do with them, just prolonged the time before the violence began in earnest. Billy yawned. Cas picked his nose. Delia was there, the token woman, also known as the Chorus Girl because she was supposed to turn her opponents into choirboys. And Joe Portside. And Bateman. And many others Small couldn't put a name to. Riot's men looked exactly the same as Lock's men: ragged, mean, careless, here because they couldn't find anything better to do. Lock's men, he assumed, had fears and secrets too. They couldn't just be the crazy killing-machines Riot had said they were.

'Are the doors shut?' asked Lock. 'Don't want any inter-ruptions. Don't want anywhere for your wounded to go.'

Cas, giggling inanely, clamped shut the emergency bar of the main doors, on which a sign said FIRE EXIT, and his counterpart on Lock's side did the same to the entrance to the changing-room through which Lock's men had come. Cas stopped giggling and turned round with this spooky, serious look on his face.

'We're trapped.'

Then he burst into giggles again.

'Get me some of that stuff he's on!' declared Lock.

'Hey, dickhead, are you ready to fight or are you going to stand there with your thumb up your bum until I stick you?'

'I'm ready, Riot,' said Lock and his blade snicked open. It was about six inches long.

There were intricate rules to these scraps (as opposed to single combat such as the fight between Riot and Eddy). No one could get into the pool until first blood had been drawn by either leader. After that, it was a free-for-all. And those were the intricate rules.

Riot and Lock circled round each other, blades held forward pointing at each other in perfect symmetry. Their eyes, like lovers' eyes, never left each other. They circled around these two axes, blades and eyes, and the two of them were private worlds, deadly suns, oblivious to the slope of the pool and the water running treacherously slippery beneath their feet. They chose their steps with casual precision, laying toe then heel softly, foot by foot, steadying their bodies to keep their balance. Small decided that this way of moving was instinctive because their minds were elsewhere, looking for weak spots, a second's indecision, a blink in the enemy's eye. He longed to be able to do that, to move with such lethal grace. Riot had said one day he'd make a good fighter. He couldn't wait.

Riot lunged, testing the water. Lock snapped back his arm and returned the lunge. Riot leapt back a yard, crouching, water splashing over the hand he put down to steady himself.

'How's your mother, Lock?'

'I don't have a mother.'

'Funny, that's not what she told me last night.'

'That was your own mother you were sleeping with.'

'Damn it! I knew she was too good a lay to be yours.'

'You don't just want to be close to my mother, Riot, you want to *be* my mother, because you want me to suck your tit.'

'You want to look like my mother.'

'You *will* look like my mother when I've cut your face open.'

'You already look like my mother and she's been dead ten years.'

'So that's why you were in bed with her last night!'

Lock sprang at Riot and his blade was a sliver of blurred silver at the end of his arm. Riot raised his arm to ward off the blow and Lock's blade snagged the sleeve of his patched jacket.

On both sides the combatants clustered forward. Was there blood? Was that a scent of . . . ?

Lock stepped back, a courtesy to allow Riot to inspect the damage.

'Nice try, arsehole. No good.'

Riot ducked low and came at Lock around waist-height. To his credit Lock managed to twist himself half out of the way, but the attack was swift and Riot's aim was perfect. He scored a line down Lock's thigh and a second later the khaki began blooming with dark spots.

A cry went up, assaulting the whole room with hollow echoes, as the cries of children playing and adults horse-playing must have done when the pool was a place of pleasure. There was pleasure in this cry, but then there is pleasure in the howling of a pack of hounds as they descend on the fox. Figures jumped down over the sides. Suddenly, the pool was crowded. Riot and Lock were soon lost in the mêlée, and maybe they were carrying on their private fight and maybe they weren't, Small couldn't tell for sure. He was only watching and he was pressing himself against the wall to make himself as small as possible and covering his ears against the cry of dozens of hard men (and one hard woman) as they tore into each other under the pelting indoor rain of the *Hope*.

He had to watch. He might learn something by watching, that's what Riot had said. But what was there to watch? Acid Cas coming up behind one of the enemy and clapping his ears. The guy's eardrums bursting and trickles of blood seeping out. Delia shouting, 'Come and get me! Try and stab me, you pricks!' Bateman gargling blood and groping for the slash in his neck as if that was going to staunch the flow. Billy, eyes narrowed, pushing his blade again and again into some guy's guts, holding his shoulder all the while as if they were best of mates, and with every push and pull of the blade a little more of the guy's insides turning out. When you stood outside of it all and watched, you couldn't distinguish between one side and the other. The fighters only knew to stab someone if they didn't recognise him. To the observer it was simply random slaughter and you felt about as much sympathy for the victims as you did for your fish lunch.

Finally Small tried shutting his eyes but he wasn't able to keep out the screams, the yells, the swishing of water . . .

Don't let me piss myself, he thought. Jesus! I'm scared, I'm scared.

He realised his clothes were soaked and clung coldly to his skin. It was possible he had been sweating too much but when he opened his eyes his vision seemed hazy, the scrap in the pool somehow distant, and he knew it wasn't sweat. It was raining, a monsoon from the ceiling. The puddles at his feet were growing and flowing into each other. The fighters in the deepest part of the pool were already wading knee-high. A corpse was covered, its eye-sockets drowned, its hands floating clumsily on the surface as if it was fumbling in the dark. The water was streaming, wheeling, sheeting down, gathering speed, gathering weight. The pipes and cracks in the ceiling gushed water. Water poured down over the lip of the pool in glossy, glassy, shimmering waves.

And Small was more scared than he'd ever been. He seemed to be the only person to have noticed what was going on. For the others, there were only notions of blood and battle occupying their heads. The water fell in cataracts.

Jesus, it hurts! he thought. It hurts my head and it hurts my eyes.

He made a blundering dash for the door and slipped and fell and found himself slithering towards the pool. He didn't want to go in, he didn't want to go in there! But his clutching fingers raked ineffectually across the slimy-wet poolside tiles and his kicking legs got him nowhere, and then they were kicking over space and he felt the rim beneath his groin. Water – the enemy – tugged at his trousers playfully, teasing him into the pool: 'Come on in! I'm fine, really, once you get used to me.' Small made a last, desperate grab for the side, knowing there was nothing really to hold on to, and then finally resigned himself to going over. He could get out. He could get out again, easy-peasy. Let's fall, then.

Hands grabbed his waist and he was being pushed back. He managed to turn his head as he floundered onto the poolside and he glimpsed Billy's sailor's hat and Billy with his blade clasped shut in his shirt pocket laughing and saying: 'Back you go, shrimp. I always throw the little ones back.'

There was someone behind Billy – another helper?

Small tried to scream: No! Leave me, Billy! Get your blade out!

Billy was laughing.

'Don't . . . !' cried Small. Billy was laughing.

Billy was still laughing as the guy behind him grasped his face with one hand and drew a red grin across his throat with a knife. The image of Billy's two laughing mouths scored itself into Small's mind. The joke was on Billy.

Billy's eyes weren't twinkling any more and his real smile had gone all sad.

'Run,' said Billy, and fell backwards to the bottom of the pool.

Small did not want to run. He only wanted the last ten seconds over again, so that he could warn Billy properly and save him. He wanted to see Billy laugh once more and say, 'I always throw the little ones back.'

The water had risen to belt-height in the deep end and it was beginning to filter through to the fighters that another enemy had wandered into the scrap and joined in, even though it was against the rules. They carried on trying to stab one another but this was getting harder to do properly. They kept falling over, their legs splashing heavy.

Small crawled on all fours towards where he thought the doors were. He could only see the slick tiles on the floor. The rest was fluid blur.

The pool was filling quickly now, water boiling up from its filters and drains and deluging down from the ceiling. People staggered bowed under their soaking clothing and groped for the sides and fell and tried to get up again. Their panic had a gaping mouth and a screaming tongue and streaming eyes. It was hard to tell which were swimmers and which were corpses.

Small found the doors and clung to the bar as water drenched down on him, trying to wash him away back into the jaws of the pool. He pulled at the bar, which was slippery in his hands and would not budge.

The pool was pink with blood and clogged with corpses and the water was up to its rim.

Small beat at the doors. Because he was still a kid, a snotnose kid, his fear became pure fury and he battered and battered until his fists ached.

The water welled up over the rim and spilled out. The living thrashed amongst the dead, old animosities thrown aside. Enemies gripped on to each other to survive. Acid Cas floated on his back, going, 'Oh God, oh God.' He thought he was a corpse already.

The doors stood resolutely shut.

The water gulped at Small's feet, engulfed his knees, swallowed his lower body.

Small thought: I am going to die after all, although I'm only small and young and a little tosser and a cheeky bugger and a snotnose kid.

The roar of the pool was punctuated with the screams of the drowning. Small was forced to let go of the bar and found he had to tread water to stay above the surface. It was rising so fast now that he was pulled this way and that by powerful currents. He swallowed water and sputtered and choked.

Was this dying?

He was sucked under in a gush of bubbles and could see the bright patterns of the surface.

Was it really so bad?

He wished he could speak, empty his lungs and tell the whole ship: 'My real name is Thomas but I am Small and I am beautiful.'

But the *Hope* knew anyway and didn't much care.

Small felt the current take his legs and guide him downwards in a rush that made his head whirl so much he had to shut his eyes. His chest ached with the words he had to keep inside himself but it would not be long before he screamed them out loud – such release! The current dragged him along with it, faster and deeper, and there was a rushing sound in his ears like a howling gale on a stormy sea.

Small wanted only to drift and flow, ebb and rise, but the water was rushing him along.

There's plenty of time, he thought. No hurry.

But he was racing and rushing and the roar was increasing.

Air!

Small exhaled and sucked in. It was clean on his face and sweet in his lungs. This must be the afterlife. He had gone to heaven, as all kids did (snotnoses and cheeky buggers and little tossers alike). He was gliding, sliding, flying on a wave.

No, it wasn't heaven, but the corridor that led to the pool. Flotsam, pieces of door and clothing and rubbish, rushed along with him, some fetching up against the walls and some rolling over and over. Small rolled over and over and fetched up with a bang against a bulkhead, which he grabbed and held fast while the wave carried on down the corridor to splash into the doors at the end and lap back, spent.

He clung there for a long time, breathing deeply and shivering.

The flood that had been trying to drown him had in the end proved his salvation. Its sheer weight had burst open the doors and sent him hurtling out. His legs and back were a tender mass of bruises and one arm didn't like moving very much where he had banged it against the bulkhead, but this wasn't heaven. No, sir. This was life.

Small got unsteadily to his feet, leaning against the wall for support, and shook sodden hair out of his face. The water had receded, leaving only a glaze on the tiles of the floor, and this was already drying in patches.

He heard voices coming from the pool. He wasn't the only survivor. His shoes squelched as he approached the hole where the doors had been – jagged hinges peeling out from the frame to mark their passing – and then he could hear what was being said: '—gone like they weren't ever here.'

'Shit! All those corpses don't just disappear! Shit! Thank God we got out when we did.'

'Where the buggery fuck are they then?'

'I don't know. Maybe they got washed away somewhere.'

'Like down that drain, eh? Grow a brain, Lock!'

Small hovered in the doorway. He could not believe anything he saw. Where were all the dead people? Where was Billy's body? The pool was empty, its sides dripping and its tiles wet, and it no longer seemed like a hungry mouth. Not hungry. And there were Riot and Lock, standing at the poolside talking like mates. Riot was saying: 'It's a bit more drastic than planned but it's done the trick. No one to challenge us. Christ only knows how it happened.'

'Leak, probably.'

'Yeah, big leak. I mean, look at that plumbing up there. Primitive, that's what it is. We'll tell them to seal this place off for safety's sake. We don't want the same thing happening to kids playing here.'

'Right. How's your arm?'

'Fine, dickhead. You only cut my jacket.'

'My leg hurts like fuck. Couldn't you have been a bit more careful?'

'It had to look good. I am the best knife-man around, you know.'

'Second best.'

'After Eddy?'

'After me.'

'Piss off! You couldn't cut a pilchard with that thing.'

'Want a fight about it?'

'What's the point? We've got rid of all the competition.'

'Riot . . .' It was barely a whisper. Riot and Lock swung round in surprise. Riot's jaw fell.

'Who is it?' asked Lock.

'Small. You're alive,' said Riot, deadpan.

'Riot,' said Small, coming forward, 'give me your blade.'

'Eh?'

'Your blade. You said I could have it.'

212

'I said you could have it when I was dead. As far as I can tell, I'm not dead yet.'

'Brain-dead,' muttered Lock.

'Yes, you are. You're dead, like all of them, only they've gone to heaven, that's why they're not here any more and you are.'

'I don't know where the fuck they've gone but it's not heaven, I can tell you that for nothing. More likely to the bottom of the ocean.'

'No,' said Small with conviction.

'Look, sonny,' said Lock with a contemptuous leer, 'this is none of your business, so sod off.'

'The blade, Riot.'

'Come and get it, Small,' jeered Riot, making Small's beautiful name sound like an insult, and Lock laughed heartily like the little dog to see such fun.

Small ran at Riot, head down, fists out, and slammed into him. Startled, Riot lost his footing and fell backwards. He grunted as his back connected with the rim of the pool and then Small was upon him, howling in fury.

'You killed them! You killed them all! You killed Billy!'

Riot pretended that they were just playing a game, a boys' rough-and-tumble type of game, and was laughing.

'No, we didn't. We wanted to, but the pool did it for us. The final solution, ha ha.'

'You fucker!' squealed Small, astride Riot's chest, his fists impotent in Riot's hands. 'You fucker, you fucker, you fucker!'

'Can't you handle him, wimp?' said Lock.

'He's gone apeshit! Fucking apeshit!'

'You killed them! You killed them!' Small wrenched his hands free and tried to pummel Riot's face. Riot was considerably more anxious now and raised his arms to protect himself. Small reached down between Riot's legs.

'Jesus, Small, don't . . . '

Riot jerked as if he had been given an electric shock and he screamed and Small rolled off him and Riot tumbled head first into the pool. The scream was cut off. Lock clutched his face in horror. Small rocked back on to his hindquarters at the rim of the pool, looking down at the acute angles of Riot's body and the upturned eyes and the single droplet of phlegm oozing out of the nose. Riot's scream still hung about the pool. Small crawled over, lowered himself carefully over the edge and rummaged around in Riot's pockets until he found the blade. It was cool and sharp, crouched in its mother-of-pearl casing. He hauled himself on to the side again. Lock, for all his muscle, backed off a few steps, turned and fled.

Small flicked the blade out, the hard man, leader of men, Big General.

Lonely

the

Rat

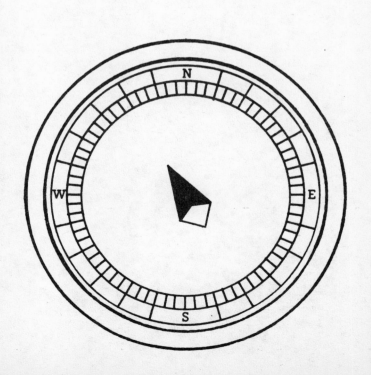

Paolo had seen dead people before, millions of times. Killed four himself in scraps. Easy. It wasn't Paolo killing them at all, it was the blade. Slip it in, twist, pull it out. Easy. The victim maybe chokes a bit and there's always blood, but it's no big deal. Death? Piece of piss. But when Longpole ran into the Trident and asked him if he wanted to come and see some 'corpuses', some real 'corpuses', Paolo jumped at the chance. Longpole was a bit dumb (that's why he couldn't say corpses) but he'd been hopping about like his bladder was ready to explode because these corpuses weren't freshly dead corpuses – they were nearly a week old and beginning to rot. Paolo slammed his glass down and agreed to go with Longpole immediately. Although he was used to dead, this was *real* dead. When you killed someone in a scrap, they didn't really look dead, they just looked . . . not very well, like they'd disagreed with something they ate. Usually their hands were clutched around their stomachs, which was Paolo's favourite place to stab because it took them longer to die, and this added to the impression of illness. So that kind of dead wasn't very interesting at all.

The corpuses, according to Longpole, had just sat in their cabin all this time waiting to be found. He wasn't going to describe them to Paolo because it was more fun if he saw for himself. He didn't want to ruin anything.

The two of them raced out of the Trident even though they were due for a council of war in an hour. Longpole had said it wouldn't take long to get to the corpuses and they could make it back in time for the meeting, although everyone knew that it wasn't a meeting as such, more of an excuse for Riot to make a speech and flick his knife a few times before they all marched off to the pool without anyone being asked if they had a better idea. Not that anyone would have. But Longpole said if they didn't go now, they'd never get another chance like it. Someone was bound to take the corpuses away and do something crass like give them a burial.

And so Paolo, who had seen dead bodies millions of times and thought that death was a piece of piss, stood beside Longpole at the door to some unidentified cabin way, way downstairs and let Longpole swing the door open theatrically and looked in at the four corpuses and was afraid.

It was dark in the cabin and only a bit brighter outside. The bodies were not much more than human-shaped outlines until Paolo's eyes grew accustomed to the darkness and then he could see them sitting or lying in there like bored people expecting something to happen. Death seemed to have been quite a surprise. One moment everything hunky dory, the next – Oops! Look, Ma, we're all dead. Three of them were little kids. The adult was still cradling one of the kids on its lap, bony arms locked around bony body. There was a defunct candle on the table in front of them. The other two were in bed and the only thing that told you they weren't actually asleep was the stain on the bed-linen which spread where it touched their skin. The heads of the two seated corpuses were lolled back, as if they had been staring up waiting for death to descend and had been staring for so long that their eyes had misted over. The skin of their cheeks was pinched and rilled, pale as dust and flaking off in patches. The bodies were stick-thin. This gave Paolo the freaky idea that all the good bits had been emptied out into a bin or something and taken elsewhere.

The worst thing was the stench of the place, like all the most awful smells you could think of all rolled into a nose-curdling, bowel-churning one. You noticed the stench before you got near the cabin. It came up on you as you were trotting along the walkway, tapped you on the shoulder, said, 'Hello, you don't know me, but I'm sure once you've met me properly and got to know me, you'll never forget me. And one day we'll become good, good friends.' And like all nodding acquaintances, it proved to be eager and irritatingly persistent.

Paolo peering through the doorway at the four corpuses (as surprised to see him as he was to see them) pulled his T-shirt up over his face. It was just an ordinary cabin, he told himself, but he couldn't get over the feeling that it was a tomb. Longpole hopped from foot to foot beside him.

'Isn't it great? Real corpuses, straight up, no shit. Soon as word got around, I came down here to have a look. Knew you'd be interested.'

'I am,' said Paolo through the cotton. 'But I've seen worse. Who found 'em?'

'Lil. Said she was paying a social call and the door wasn't locked, so she went in and there they were. Yeuch! Can you imagine it? I mean, they were friends of hers. Yeuch!'

'Lil doesn't pay social calls,' said Paolo. 'Bet she wanted something. Bet it was one of her customers.'

'Naah, it's a woman, can't you see? Look, she got tits.' Longpole scampered into the cabin and went right up to the adult corpse. He put out a finger to prod the corpse's chest but poked so hard that his finger went through the fabric of the dress and sank two joints deep into the flesh. He screeched and pulled his finger out, which made a sucking noise Paolo would have preferred never to have heard, and then Longpole was wiping his hand in a frenzy on the nearest available set of bedclothes.

'Eurgh, eurrrrr ... ! Oh, Christ! Shitshitshitshitshit!'

Paolo was trying to smother his laughter under his face-mask but Longpole could see the creases around his eyes.

'Shut up, you fucker! It's not funny.'

The adult corpse now had a gimlet-hole in its left breast, edged with an ooze of gore. That looked pretty funny, too. But Paolo was still scared even as he laughed at Longpole. That corpse, dead for days, seemed as if it could turn its head right now and raise its mildewed finger to point at him, stare with blanked eyes, open its mouth until the hinges cracked under the strain and the jaw fell away in a soundless scream of condemnation framed by yellow rotted teeth.

'OK, joke's over,' said Paolo. 'Let's go back.'

'Why?' asked Longpole coming back out into the daylight, wiping his finger on his shirt as if he was determined to remove every last scrap of his own skin. 'Scared? Don't you want to go in and have a closer look? You chicken?'

'No, just don't think we should be late, that's all.'

'They're, well, nasty, aren't they?'

'Why hasn't someone come to take them away yet?'

'Would you want to?'

'No, but hasn't someone reported it to the Captain or something?'

'Probably. Who cares? People die all the time.'

'Hey you! You kids!' It was Lil hurrying towards them along the walkway, accompanied by three men. 'Get away from there!'

'Only having a quick look,' said Longpole with a shrug. 'No harm in that.'

'Leave poor Mary alone! She had a hard enough life without little brats like you making it hard for her when she's dead.'

'Friend of yours, then?' jeered Longpole. Paolo kept a tactful silence.

Lil reached them with her entourage in tow and made to clip Longpole around the side of the head, but he was too quick for her bulbous, flabby arm and ducked out of the way.

'Come on, Paolo, let's get out of here.'

'Little brats!' screamed Lil after them as they showed her their heels. 'No respect for the dead.'

'Want us to get them, willow blossom?' asked one of the entourage.

'No, love, you and your mates just deal with the bodies like I asked you.' Covering her nose with her hand Lil strode into the cabin and took a quick but thorough mental inventory. It wasn't a bad place. Bit of cleaning, bit of decoration, and it could be quite nice. At last the useless bitch had proved useful for something.

Paolo and Longpole ran and giggled as they ran. Somehow, close scrapes with adults were ten times more exciting than scraps with other kids or even close encounters with week-old corpses. Paolo followed Longpole, who was as lanky as his name suggested and had a strange way of running like a speeded-up impression of a long-legged stalking bird, a method that kept him well ahead of his companion. When he turned corners, he leaned into them and his legs shot out centrifugally. Every so often he would look over his shoulder at Paolo and give a manic leer and pour on the speed.

'Look out, you daft bugger!' panted Paolo. 'You'll run into somebody!'

'My arse!' replied Longpole, looking round, and a few seconds later ran into somebody. He turned round to launch a volley of insults at the dumb fuck dickhead who had been deadhead enough to get in his way, and the insults died unformed in his throat. Paolo skidded to a halt behind Longpole. He couldn't see the other guy at all because it had got dark all of a sudden – maybe the smoke from the funnels had thickened or a cloud had passed over the sun. Then he heard the other guy speak in a voice that was the last gasp of a victim on the rack: 'Do you know?'

And he heard Longpole say, 'Holy Jesus, shit!' Longpole turned his head round to look at Paolo and he wasn't grinning any more. He turned his head a bit further. Paolo thought that wasn't natural, you couldn't twist your neck that far, before he saw a pair of hands either side of Longpole's face and there came a sound from Longpole's neck that reminded him of the sound ivory dice make when they're thrown down. Longpole was looking over his other shoulder now, Longpole's tongue was pushing itself out between his lips, Longpole's pupils were drifting upwards into his head, Longpole's neck was a twisted rope, Longpole's long legs were kicking at the walkway. Paolo spurted urine into the front of his jeans. Tnen Longpole was dropped to the deck like a full sack and his killer, hands held forward, had this look on his face that wasn't mad but sad.

'Sorry,' he said, but Paolo wasn't listening because he was trying to figure out what those patterns were on the man's chest and stomach. The man was naked from the waist up and so emaciated that his veins were like lengths of string wrapped around his skeleton and his muscles no more than tumorous swellings trying to scratch a living from their owner. The corners of his mouth were tilted downwards.

He said, 'Do you know?' His scars were a wide, imperfect circle crossed half-a-dozen times diametrically to form the spokes of a crude wheel. The lines were shaded with angry red inflammation, and here and there black scabs hung grimly on. Who the hell had done that to him?

Paolo clawed for his back pocket and found it and slipped his hand in and drew out his blade. The thin man took a step forward over Longpole.

'Do you know?'

Paolo groped for his voice and found that too: 'I know you're in big trouble if you come an inch closer.' He slid his thumb up the knife-handle to find the stud. He wished there was someone else around, even a stopper. Where had everybody gone? The lower decks were usually crowded at this time of day. But Paolo was alone with Longpole bent and dead and a madman coming towards him. His thumb tried to press the stud but didn't really want to, had changed its mind about this fighting business, you can look after yourself, Paolo, me old mucker.

No, I can't, thought Paolo, and wished his father, the great *signor*, had never thrown him out into this cruel nightmare to make his own way and fend for himself. He didn't want to end up like those corpses, loathsome and rotten and perpetually startled by what the *Hope* had held in store for them, the big surprise that had been kept until last, crouching to spring when you least wanted it or expected it.

'Do you know?'

Paolo knew death, knew what dead was, knew he was looking at death's little helper right now, coming at him, hands reaching out in a pitying embrace.

'Yes, I know all right,' he said. The thin man stopped a yard in front of him, perplexed. The hands that had twisted Longpole's head round as easy as a bottle-top faltered and fell. Paolo's thumb at last did a nervous spasm on the knife-handle and the knife responded with a familiar click and jerk in his fingers. Without pausing Paolo's blade flashed out to the thin man's mutilated chest, not stopping when it met the weak resistance of skin or flesh, glancing upwards inside the thin man's chest as it grated off a rib. The thin man coughed politely and an apologetic dribble of blood abseiled down his front, making diversions around scar tissue, with two more dribbles in hot pursuit.

'Sorry,' said Paolo, working the blade free, drawing back his arm and plunging it in again.

'Sorry,' said the thin man, as he lumbered into Paolo, dying arms groping for a last, lethal embrace with someone who didn't know.

'No, I'm sorry,' hissed Paolo as he caught the thin man's insubstantial weight and fended it off with a few more thrusts of the blade. 'I'm just so fucking sorry, you wouldn't believe it.' The thin man's blood was spraying from several apertures and patterning Paolo's shirt and joining the other stains already there on his trousers. The arms were shuddering at Paolo's shoulders, still going for his neck even though the brain was sending messages that the body was dead, no use, mission aborted.

Paolo dropped back against the walkway railing and let the thin body tumble at his feet. He breathed out hard and breathed in and steadied himself as the outstretched hands gave a final valiant twitch and lay still. The two of them, the quick and the dead, remained in that position until the quick's heart-rate slowed down to something approaching normal and his breathing was no longer an urgent rasp.

Paolo felt the cool wetness of his jeans against his skin and wondered how and when that had happened. He saw the blade in his hand smeared with the thin man's blood and he could not count how many times he had stabbed him. He knelt down and wiped the blade against the back of the thin man's trousers, and as he did so he noticed a notebook poking out of the back pocket. It had a red cover, grainy like calfskin, with tattered corners and a couple of fingerprints. He did not want to touch it because it would be like touching the dead man's skin, taking a part of the body. Paolo remembered Longpole's finger going through that corpse's dress and skin. Longpole was a corpse too, you know, and it was as if they all had a contagious disease like the plagues that hit deck areas now and then. Longpole had touched the woman's corpse, the thin man had touched Longpole, that's how it spread. Paolo was unwilling to follow suit and catch it in turn. But the notebook was fascinating. Why did he carry it? What did he have to take notes about?

Tentatively Paolo took hold of one corner of the cover and extracted the notebook. There was a square of white on the cover which had been hidden in the thin man's pocket. On this square were two lines ruled in anticipation of a title, and there was the title in tortuous pencilled letters:

Lonely
the Rat

Paolo didn't think much of the title. He hoped the story would be better.

He got to his feet and, barely glancing at Longpole, who was only dead, after all, he walked off with *Lonely the Rat* in his hand. There was dead and there was dead, he decided. Riot had once said that death made everybody equal. When an upper deck guy died and rotted, you wouldn't be able to tell him from a lower deck guy who had died and rotted. Both ended up as fish-food in the ocean and the fishes weren't fussy. Paolo didn't think this was true now. There was a world of difference between the corpuses in the cabin and the two broken bodies lying across the walkway. Longpole and the thin man, well, that had been a scrap really, hadn't it? Death had been sudden but expected and evenly shared out. You didn't go into a scrap at the pool without thinking there was an odds-on chance you'd get stuck by someone, although you hoped you wouldn't and if you were a good enough fighter you probably didn't. But that family in that cabin – they hadn't stood a chance. For whatever reason they'd died (that was something Paolo could not figure out), it was an all-round shitter. They hadn't got anything, not a blade, nothing, to defend themselves with.

If I'm lucky, thought Paolo, I could get to the pool in time for the scrap with Lock. But first things first. New shirt and trousers. Wouldn't do to turn up looking like you'd already finished.

Paolo shared a cabin with three other guys, although

it was rare if more than two of them were there at any given time. People like them had better things to do than fart around all day inside and if they came back at all, they came back to sleep. One was an engineer who worked long shifts and always came in pissed to crash out in his bunk at about 23.00. Nice enough bloke, but Paolo had never caught his name, which gave a fair indication of how well he knew his cell-mates.

Everyone was out. Paolo sat on his bunk and pulled off his clothes. The stains had dried but were starting to smell. He grabbed a fresh pair of jeans and someone else's shirt and put them on. While doing so, he saw *Lonely the Rat* had fallen out of his pocket on to the floor. He picked it up, sat down, turned back the cover and started to read. The handwriting wasn't much better than a scribble but Paolo soon worked out how to decipher it. As he read, thoughts of scraps with Lock vanished from his head.

Lonely the Rat
A true story

I am a dream. I was not born in a woman's tummy. I was born in a head, like all dreams. I began. I licked off the wet bits of my birth. I took my first breath. I lived. I live. I live in *Hope*. My name is Lonely because I am alone. I am the only one, the only rat. When I was born I knew many things. I knew how to walk. I knew how to talk. I knew how to read. I knew how to write. I knew how to eat. I knew how to shit. I knew my name and my place and my purpose. This is very important, that I knew my purpose, for I know that many people do not know their purpose and they waste their lives. If you only have one life, it is a good thing to know your purpose, otherwise you will waste your one chance at life. A rat's (I am a rat) purpose is very simple. I deal with the rubbish. I sort out the rubbish. There is too much rubbish here and it is my purpose to do something about it. If the rubbish was left to keep piling up then there would not be enough space, which would be silly, so I sort it all out. Is anyone else's purpose so good? I don't think so. In the first few days of my life I simply lived and thought about my purpose because I wasn't sure of myself enough yet, though I am now. Then I just hid and lived and ate and shitted, but I was not wasting time. It was a time to think. I had lots of talks with the *Hope* in that time and the *Hope* told me many different things about my purpose. The *Hope* was launched to travel across the ocean to the other side, everybody knows that. The *Hope* is a big ship with lots of people on board, everybody knows that. All the people are here because they are here. Many cannot remember why they were here in the first place and that is why they have no purpose, because they can't remember. When they get up in the morning, they can't remember so they just go through the day expecting all of a sudden to remember everything. Those are the older people.

The younger people have no memory of anything at all. They have not been told their purpose and they don't care about it and would rather make lots of noise and fight. They make my purpose easier by fighting. Younger people are rubbish from the moment they are born. Older people are mostly rubbish too, or if they weren't rubbish before they came on board they are now. They are empty tins and old cartons and bottles. All the good bits have been used up and there is only rubbish left, which has no purpose. They do not think they are rubbish, they think they are really good because they have been used up, which they think is living. They are silly. They are rubbish. I sort them out and clean them up and tidy them away. I am a rat. I have a purpose. While I was hiding in the first days of my life and thinking, the *Hope* came and told me about the launching which was all black smoke and black paper. It was meant to be a happy occasion and all the people were smiling as if it was a happy occasion, but it wasn't because the man whose purpose it was to make the *Hope* was dead. He was sensible because he threw himself away and didn't wait to be thrown away by someone else, which is more wasteful. That was the launching. The *Hope* set out straight, pointed in the right direction, and sailed for days and then for weeks and then for months and then for years, and this is a long time because I have not lived for that long. The *Hope* did as the people said. The *Hope* sailed on and on and on. The *Hope* got bored. It didn't like the people very much. They thought they knew everything. They thought they were better than the *Hope*. They thought they could order the *Hope* around like they ordered each other around, but it wasn't as simple as that. After all, people thought they could order around the wind and the sun and the moon and the sea and the land, but they were wrong. The wind and the sun and the moon and the sea and the land just let people do what they wanted because they didn't care really, they were so much better and bigger than the people. Sometimes the wind would get angry and the land would shake and the sea would clap its hands, but this only kept the people quiet for a little while. When they had got over being scared, they would go back to thinking they were the best things ever. But they weren't! Because people got used up and died while wind and sun and moon and sea and land just went on for ever and for ever and never got used up and never became rubbish.

The *Hope* wasn't quite like that because the *Hope* was made by the people. The *Hope* found that it couldn't ignore the people so easily because the people annoyed the *Hope* and were like a sickness, filling the *Hope* with themselves and their shit and rubbish, making the *Hope* not feel very well. That was not nice. The *Hope* decided on a way to get rid of the people, first with rats and then with things that were like rats only much much worse. These didn't work. I don't know why they didn't work (I don't know everything, do I?) but I know they didn't work. Perhaps they weren't good enough. Perhaps people could beat them at their own game. Whatever the reason, the *Hope* admitted it had lost this time. But this was early on in the journey, so there was plenty of time for the *Hope* to think up another plan. So the *Hope* thought and thought and thought so hard you could hear brains turning and rumbling and roaring as they thought. People got scared by the noise but they couldn't understand why they got scared, but it should have been obvious why the noise was scary if they had any sense of purpose which they didn't. There were lots of times when people killed themselves off, which was a good thing for the *Hope*, getting someone else to put out the rubbish. When people live together, because they are so horrible they get diseases of their own, diseases like themselves that kill themselves. Sometimes the diseases hurt their bodies and made parts of them suffer and bleed, sometimes the diseases hurt their minds and made them make others suffer and bleed. It didn't matter to the *Hope* which it was, because people died. Which was a good thing. But still they were not dying quickly enough and so the *Hope* kept on thinking, but it was always a struggle to think because the *Hope* had been made by people and people didn't want their creations to think. Often the *Hope* felt that thinking was too difficult, like trying to see in the dark, but it found after a while that thinking got easier and easier, just as it gets easier and easier to see in the dark as time goes on, although there are always darker bits where you cannot see a thing.

Then the *Hope* made a friend of one of the people who was not like the other people. Neither this person nor the *Hope* knows they have made friends, as far as I know. Perhaps they will. They didn't have much in common. After all, one was a little human and the other was a big ship. But they did have one thing in common, which was that both of them wasn't a man or a woman. This was what brought them together and made them make friends even though they didn't know they had made friends. Sometimes one was a man and the other was a woman, other times one was a woman and the other was a man, it didn't matter which. When they met and made friends without knowing it, they made dreams and the dreams were born. The first dream was a dream of water. Water goes around in a big circle, from sea to sky to land to sea and back to sky again. Water can be diseased for a while, but it will always become pure again. The *Hope* had a dream of people of water, pure, cured, living for ever, hurting nothing. The dream came to life. It will be one of many. Like it, I am a dream. I was born. I live. I am a rat. I have a purpose. Some dreams are nice and some dreams are nasty. Nobody can say what dreams they are going to have, they can only go to sleep hoping that it is going to be a good one to make up for the way that life is so horrid and rubbishy for them. Dreams really belong to the bits of life outside, like the wind and all the rest, the bits that don't really care about people and can be beautiful and angry in equal amounts. I was born perfect with my purpose and alone. I ran away almost straight after I was born, because I did not need to learn anything from the things that had given birth to me, the *Hope* and the person. I was born knowing my purpose so nobody could tell it to me, although in the first days of my life the *Hope* did come and tell me lots of things about the *Hope* because that was all part of my purpose. It is no good sorting out rubbish if you aren't told what to do with it. So I listened to what the *Hope* had to tell me and I knew my purpose better and I knew what I had been born to do better. After all those years of thinking, the *Hope* had at last come up with the answer, the cure to the sickness. I was only part of the answer.

The *Hope* tries to cure itself in many different ways but the *Hope* cannot do it alone. I promised to help, knowing that it was my purpose. Agreeing to the promise, the *Hope* gave me a knife, which was old and had been thrown away and had been lying in wait for me. I took the knife and the *Hope* told me a shape and I cut that shape into myself to swear to the *Hope* that I would do my purpose. It hurt! It still hurts a bit, but that makes me keep the promise. The *Hope* called it a 'bond'. It would join us together. I would carry on me the answer to the *Hope*'s sickness. It is a circle. The *Hope* is travelling in a circle. The Captain does not know, the crew do not know, the passengers do not know, all the people do not know. The *Hope* lies to the Captain and the crew. They think their charts and their compasses are correct, but they know nothing. The *Hope* makes their charts and compasses lie to them. Their purpose never has been and never will be to steer the *Hope* because the *Hope* needs no steering. The *Hope* chases itself round and round in a circle that takes a year. It has been doing so for a long, long time. Nobody knows. I know nobody knows because I ask them. If they do not know, I kill them to cure the *Hope*. I do not always like doing this. I have never said my purpose is a nice purpose but it is a rat's purpose. Although it is my purpose, I feel sorry for them. In many ways they are like me, it's just that they don't have a purpose. I always tell them I am sorry. It makes me feel better. I make the *Hope* feel better. The *Hope* will keep going in circles until I have had time to cure it completely. The *Hope* is patient. The *Hope* needs time to think, because the darkness is still there in the *Hope*'s thoughts and it takes time to see. I will keep going too, with the bond on me as a promise. The *Hope* calls me the last and best rat. I am only one. I am Lonely the Rat. I have a purpose. I will save the *Hope*.

As Paolo finished this last page, he no longer wanted to hold the notebook. Death, which he had decided was a disease, infected that notebook on every smeary, scrawled page. Paolo put it down, went to the basin and washed his hands for five minutes. Then he splashed cold water over his face and rested his hands on the edge of the basin and let the water drip off his face. His eyes were closed.

Lonely the Rat was the story of a madman. There were plenty of madmen on board and no doubt plenty of alternative *Lonely the Rat*s. The thin man had been deranged, no more, no less. He was not a dream born to life. That was plain fantasy. He had no purpose other than to kill as many people as he liked. Paolo opened his eyes and took a look back at the notebook's red cover and childish handwriting. With that one look, he knew he was lying to himself. *Lonely the Rat* was, as its title had promised, a true story. Paolo knew that without knowing why. He sensed it. He had lived his whole life on board this floating shitheap. His ship-born instincts could not let him kid himself. Now that the thin man, Lonely, was dead . . . Now that Paolo had killed the thin man, Lonely . . .

No one else knew. Paolo Bellini was the only person on board who knew.

Wasn't that funny?

There was no other side. The ocean really was unending, it didn't just seem that way, it really fucking was! The *Hope* was chasing its tail like a mad dog driven crazy by fleas.

'Bullshit,' said Paolo out loud and the word was false from his tongue.

*

Paolo hung on to the railings. There were a handful of other people here, all minding their own business as he was minding his. The whole *Hope* was spread out behind him. Seagulls hovered around the ship in a speckled cloud. The wind came thickly salted off the sea and into his face, tugging at his hair the way a child pulls its parent's hair for attention, and the seagulls played games with the wind but cried as they played, their falling-down notes of dissent answered by distant cousins higher up, further away, grey specks of sound lost in a white-noise sky. Some of the gulls strutted close by Paolo and made loud interjections as the passengers inhaled the torpid air and chose to feel invigorated by it.

This was a popular spot, the pinnacle of the outer rim, the point of the *Hope*. It was a view of a wasteland expanse of ocean but you thought you were looking out the way the *Hope* was heading. One day you might even be lucky enough to glimpse land. There was a small sign commemorating the obvious:

Welcome to
The Bows

Paolo leant over the railings. An old couple cast a nervous glance in his direction, worried he was about to jump off although not prepared to do anything if he did. He didn't.

Instead he looked down a cliff-face of iron, pitted and bolted and riveted and streaked with rust. Near the level of the sea the rust became dominant, surrounding the ship with an orange skirt. There, at the bottom, the ship's sides met in a blunt apex. Paolo blinked out of his eyes the tears that the wind had put there. He focused hard.

Was it just visible? Was one bow-wave bigger than the other? Was it true?

Paolo leant back. Out from under his shirt he took a package, something small wrapped in an old T-shirt (one like Eddy's, with the same slogan). He checked *Lonely the Rat* was still safely inside, unwilling to touch the cover ever again.

He hesitated. Perhaps he should tell somebody. Perhaps he should inform the Captain. But he knew the Captain would never believe him. He'd say Paolo wrote the thing himself, just a kid trying to make a name for himself, playing a big joke on the passengers, don't be ridiculous, go home, son.

Paolo tried hard not to smile to himself.

Then, with the seagulls wheeling and wailing overhead, he drew back his arm to hurl the package overboard.

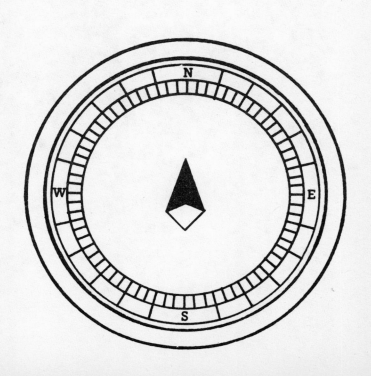